ANDERSON
ANDERS

Beautiful

Bounty

By
MJ Nightingale

Book 1 of The Bounty Hunters (The Marino Bros.)

Published: MJ Nightingale December, 2014:
authormjnightingale@gmail.com

Editing: Keriann McKenna

Cover Design © Melissa Gill at MG BookCovers

Formatting by: Brenda Wright

This book is intended for a mature audience of eighteen and older.

ISBN-13: 978-1505221756

ISBN-10: 1505221757

Dedication

To my readers. Your support means everything.

To MaryAnn. Your friendship is golden.

MJ

Table of Contents

Prologue

One year earlier . . .

Ronnie knew she was drunk because this was just feeling so good. She needed to stop him. But somehow she couldn't. He smelled so damn good. The cologne, the sea breeze, the wind, and his tongue trailing down her neck had her senses spiraling. That and the three glasses of champagne she had consumed. His lips and teeth nuzzled her neck, little nips that felt like tiny explosions. His hand slid up her rib cage. She felt the timeless exploration under her breast as he tested its weight. He gently squeezed, and then flicked her nipple beneath the thin material of the bridesmaid gown she wore. He pulled the cup down and a cool blast of night air hit her before his mouth descended on the tiny bud. His mouth was hot. Oh yes! His tongue divine as it titillated her even further. She was the opposite of senseless. She was on fire.

Nikko couldn't believe his luck. The blond beauty had given him the cold shoulder whenever their paths crossed. But, the little ice princess had warmed up to him. All it had taken was a few drinks, a few dances, and a few suggestions whispered in her ear. He murmured his appreciation around the mouthful of the most amazing breasts he had ever seen in his twenty six years. This little spitfire with the snapping brown eyes had continued to ignore him throughout the ceremony. But at the reception, she loosened up. Let her hair down so to speak. Once he got her on the dance floor, and showed her a few moves, she came undone and began to relax. He liked her like this. Very much.

"Oh God!" she whimpered as he circled her nipple with his tongue and then gently pulled on it with his teeth. She was tugging on his dark hair, pulling him closer, showing him her true nature. She wanted this, and he was more than happy to comply.

They met two weeks ago at the rehearsal dinner for his cousin's wedding. From that moment, he knew he wanted her, underneath him, on top, he didn't care. She was every man's wet dream even though it seemed like she didn't know it. And right now, she was making one of his fantasies come true, up against a palm tree on the beach in a relatively secluded alcove. She was pushing against him, craving the contact. There was no denying he relished it. And he thanked his lucky stars, because he wanted her, badly. His cock had been at attention all through their dances. Now, it was straining against his black dress pants needing its own gratification.

But, he meant to please her first. She was leaning against the coarse bark of a skinny palm, on the beach where hours earlier his cousin, Victor, wed his lovely bride, Monica. His free hand snaked up her thigh. It was shapely.

The girl's legs were defined, hard under the smooth surface. He could feel her muscles tremble under her silky skin as he slid his hand up the inside of her leg. He cupped her, and again she pushed into his touch. Not one to deny anyone their pleasure, least of all himself, he felt Ronnie part her legs and slid a finger inside. She was already aroused, and wet. He began to flick her clit as she squirmed in time to his ministrations.

"Oh God, Nikko . . .," she murmured, "that feels so . . ." Her words were lost as he left her breast to claim her sweet mouth. He explored and used his tongue to plunder it. She tasted sweet, and he liked it. He couldn't wait to explore her further. Ronnie continued to respond to him, grinding her tight little body closer and using her tongue to match him stroke for stroke.

"Have you seen Veronica?"

They both froze when the night sounds were suddenly broken by her mother's worried voice. Although they were in a clump of palm trees along one of the winding paths that ran along the beach, and it was full dark, the lights along the path could reveal them if she continued to come forward. He and Ronnie had come out for a breath of air, and wandered several hundred yards away from the tent that had been set up for the reception. The alcove was well out of the way of passersby or so they thought. Nikko was frustrated and so damn angry at himself for not taking her to his car, or going even further down this stretch of private secluded beach owned by the hotel that hosted the wedding.

"Your daughter?" another voice responded, a bit further away but getting closer.

"You've got to stop!" Ronnie whispered, pushing his hands away and pulling up the top of her dress, covering herself.

Great! Nikko fumed. Just perfect! He began to adjust his clothes quietly, yet inside he fumed.

"Yes, I saw her leave with Nikko about twenty minutes ago. They haven't returned," a nervous Louisa murmured, her voice carrying on the night air.

"I just came from the restrooms and I didn't see her over there," Brenda, Monica's sister's new mother-in-law, replied. "Shall we go look the other way? I'm sure they just went for some fresh air. They seemed to be getting quite a workout on the dance floor." Brenda's voice took on a positive note trying to ease Ronnie's anxious mother.

Yes, go look the other way, Nikko thought. His cock was still hard, and the beautiful blond before him with that crazy purple streak in her hair just might consider letting him finish what they had started. He began to push her back towards the tree. His hand found her breast once more and his lips found her mouth. He began to use his tongue to make magic again.

The two older women's voices began to fade.

Hearing her mom's voice echo in the darkness brought a moment of clarity to her fuzzy mind, but just a moment. Nikko was that good. He knew what he was doing and soon Ronnie found herself focusing only on the sensations he evoked in her.

Ronnie loved how this amazingly hot man made her feel, but a small part of her mind, the part that was coherent, knew her mother would be back. The paths did not go that far, and once her mom searched all the way down to the south beach, she would double back and go north. Reluctantly, Ronnie pushed Nikko away from her and broke the kiss.

"We can't. . ." she started to speak and then she saw the pained expression on his face.

He pulled back a few inches and looked at her to see if she was serious. She was. "You're kidding me, right," he fumed. Her expression remained firm. "Just wonderful," was his frustrated response. His hand whipped to his head, pushing back a stray lock of black hair.

She was about to say, we can't, not right now, but he had turned from her by then and she could hear the disappointment in his sighs as he began to once again readjust his clothing.

"I'm sorry Nikko, but I know my mom. She will come back," she muttered irritably. Didn't he realize she wanted this too? Selfish jerk, she thought. Just like a man to only think about himself.

Her annoyance dissipated like vapor the moment Nikko turned to her. His blue eyes, tanned face, and chiseled features took her breath away. Gone was his earlier look of irritation. No man should be that gorgeous. That was the problem she had with him from their first meeting. He was one of those guys who was unbelievably hot, and knew it. She watched him flirting with numerous girls prior to the wedding, batting those incredibly long eyelashes at several of Monica's friends. No man should have lashes like those.

"Sorry Ronnie," he grinned, and dimples appeared in his chiseled cheeks. Fucking dimples, too! What the hell kind of genes did this guy have in his genetic pool? His three older brothers were also drop dead gorgeous. "I'm just frustrated. Maybe . . ." he started to say as they got onto the path before being interrupted by a voice as rough as gravel.

"Veronica, holy shit, your mom is having a conniption fit. She's looking everywhere for you." The voice belonged to Jay, her mom's boyfriend, um, well fiancé now, apparently. He had proposed earlier. Her mom and her crazy friends had made Monica's wedding truly memorable with all their announcements and surprises this evening.

"Hey, Jay," Veronica, aka Ronnie, called out clearing her throat and giving Nikko one quick glance that was meant to silence him. Looking to Jay again, she gave him a smile, preparing her excuses as they approached. She liked him, and hated lying to him, but felt she had no choice. He was a hoot, made her mom laugh, and he loved her. She was thrilled that they had found each other. Her mom had finally gotten this relationship thing right. "Um, Nikko took me for a walk to help me clear my head. I had a bit too much to drink I think, and was feeling over heated."

Jay stared the younger couple down, a telling expression on his face. He used one of those grimaces that said, you little liars, but I'll go along with that story if you want me too. Then, he said just that. "You want to use that story, fine, but you'd better let her see you soon or she'll freak the fuck out. I know your twenty one now, but you know your mom," he told her contritely, winking at Nikko and shrugging his shoulders.

"Yes, I know my Mom," Ronnie sighed resignedly as she gave Nikko a sad look and shrugged her shoulders too, in apology.

Nikko had calmed down and knew this opportunity was lost, but hoped there would be another. He wasn't ready to let this one escape just yet. Smiling, he brokered, "Well, let's get back to the reception then." Nikko took Ronnie's hand. All three of them made their way back the last dozen or so yards.

As they slipped inside the white flap of the massive tent, Ronnie noticed that Nikko turned his charm back on rather quickly. He hid his frustration well. The sound of the music soon drowned out her other thoughts as they followed Jay to the rear of the tent where the wedding party was seated.

Nikko trailed behind, and seeing Louisa approaching, he gave her his most innocent of smiles. Ronnie's mother did not look pleased.

"Found her babe. Nikko walked her to the restroom." Jay winked at Nikko who smiled and nodded his appreciation. Nikko stayed long enough to make polite small talk with Ronnie's suspicious mother, and soon had her laughing and blushing as he pronounced her too beautiful and young to have a twenty-one year old daughter.

Ronnie took a sip of the water Jay thrust into her hand, and watched as Nikko worked her mom over. Damn, he was good. She couldn't help but smile though, when he grabbed her mother and pulled her onto the dance floor. Yes, the man was better than good.

When he returned minutes later, he hastily made his goodbyes to Jay and Louisa, saying he wanted to check in on his brothers and aunt; he kissed Ronnie on the cheek, and whispered a promise to return for another dance later. Yes, why not, she thought, the butterflies in her stomach swarming again at his closeness. You only live once.

***

One hour later that dance never happened. The reception winding down, Ronnie began her search for Nikko. She had seen neither hide nor hair of him since he left. About half of the guests had said their goodbyes and Monica and Victor were about to announce their departure for their honeymoon in Cancun.

Even Jay and Louisa were making preparations to leave, and she told them that Nikko had promised to give her a ride home. She'd braved her mom's cool look, and now she couldn't even find him. Where the heck was he? She wanted to finish what they started. She thought he did too.

Ronnie searched high and low. He wasn't in the reception. She signaled to her mom to go ahead and leave, that she would be fine, then ducked outside after she saw Lou nod her understanding.

She began to make her way around the tent. There were people outside, but not one of them was Nikko. She went to the restrooms, and he wasn't there either. She began the trek back to the tent, disappointed that her summer fling apparently was not to be. Even though the summer had just begun, she had been excited by the possibility of starting something new. Nikko had not taken the hint apparently. Resigned that tonight would not be the night, she began to walk back to the reception, in the hopes that her mother had not already left. She wasn't too concerned though. Many of the guests were friends of her mom and would be willing to give her a ride home. Maybe she could get his number from Victor when he and Monica returned from their honeymoon in a week, she thought glumly.

Just a few feet from the tent's entrance, she heard something. Nikko's laugh; she stopped short. Her heart leapt. The parking lot! She turned in that direction and saw his head just over the top of a black SUV. Yes! Score! Her plans were not ruined after all. She quickened her pace. His head disappeared from sight, but she could still hear him.

"Really?" His deep, sexy laugh floated across the lot. Her steps faltered when she heard a woman's voice.

"Yes." In Veronica's mind, that sound came out like a seductive purr.

Her pace remained slow, but she walked softly not wanting the sound of her heels on the pavement to give her away. She wanted to surprise the couple. Surely, she thought, he wouldn't. An hour later? She took those last few steps around the corner of the vehicle. Then she knew. He would!

All was silent for a moment and then the blood rushed into her ears like a tsunami. She lost it.

"You ass!" Ronnie hissed at Nikko and the scene she stormed upon.

Nikko's blue eyes widened in surprise and shock as Ronnie began to turn on her heel. He was at a momentary loss, but recovered quickly. "Wait!" Nikko tried to explain as he pushed the other woman's hand off of the fastening of his slacks again, but Ronnie had already fled. The red head, Nancy, was still trying to clutch his waist band with her greedy hands. She pulled him back to her with a strength he didn't know a woman could possess all the while laughing. By the time he wrestled Nancy's fingers off of him and freed himself from the drunken woman's clutches, it was too late. He wanted to give chase to the beautiful bounty he truly desired, but Ronnie wasn't anywhere to be seen.

Minutes later Ronnie saw him still searching for her, and fumed as she sat in the back of Francine and Tom's car. She was lucky she had seen them just pulling out. She bummed a ride home from them since her mom had already left. Nikko looked upset as his eyes scanned the parking lot, and she sunk lower into her seat to avoid him seeing her. Great, just ab-so-lute-ly great, Ronnie thought. That image of him and the red head with her raspy laugh would plague her all summer long! Even though it seemed he had left the willowy vixen to come in search of her, she was disappointed. Her earlier judgment of him had been correct all along. Nikko Marino was a dirty dog, slime-ball Casanova who chased anything with tits and a skirt. Although she wanted a summer fling, wanted to experience a bit more than her limited world, she didn't want to be just another notch on his bed post. Good riddance, she thought as the car slipped out of the parking lot along Pier Sixty. As mad as she was at herself for even considering him a possibility in the first place, albeit briefly, she couldn't help but turn and gaze one more time at the fine specimen of a man that was Nikko Marino.

Chapter One

Nightmare

"What a nightmare!" Veronica muttered and groaned under her breath as she rolled to a sitting position from the hard cot. Rubbing the grit from her eyes, she finished the maneuver and began to stretch the tightness from her shoulders and muscles from such cramped quarters. Waking up from a cat nap induced by stress and exhaustion in a prison cell was a whole new experience for her, one she didn't want to get used to. The clang of metal resounded as her breakfast tray slid against the bars onto the small table at the foot of her bed. She glanced unpleasantly at the congealed oatmeal, and toast, with the small packet of jam they had given her. Three days in a row. Yum, she thought, as her stomach growled and she scooted across the bed towards her repast.

Three days of this, and she already had the routine down. She reached for the milk and felt the moisture on the container. Again, she realized it wouldn't be very cold. The guards never seemed to be in a hurry to deliver meals. The hot stuff was cold, the cold stuff warm. Delish!

She opened the cardboard container and took a long swallow trying to choke it down. Her stomach needed something, and though not as active as she usually was she found her energy sapping. One more look at the oatmeal, and she knew she couldn't do it. The milk was already curdling in her stomach. She pushed it away, and reached for the toast and jam. Peeling off the cover on the small plastic packet, she stuck her finger into the gooey contents, and spread the strawberry jelly-like substance across the surface of the barely toasted bread. No knives in jail, not even plastic.

Her hearing was today, thank goodness. Then she'd be out of here. Out, and ready to fight to prove her innocence. The first day she had been in complete shock and denial. The second day, she'd been a mess, an emotional basket case. But after her visit with her mom, her gumption and fight returned and last night she began putting the pieces of the puzzle together. She was ready to fight.

Seeing her mom had helped. Tremendously. Her mom was a beacon of strength, had always been. She told her not to worry about bail and a lawyer. She was already on it.

How could she not worry about those things? Her mom didn't have that kind of money. But, she was glad for the reassurance anyway, and despite the tell-tale signs, her mom's red rimmed eyes, the twisting of her wedding band around her finger, Ronnie knew she was worried but trying not to show it.

Ronnie hated putting any kind of hurt and stress on her mother. Not just the worry, and the fear, but now the economic burden of trying to prove her daughter's innocence. She'd pay back every penny, she swore to her.

"Baby, you're my daughter. My heart. I would do anything for you, you know that." Her mom reached out putting her palm on the glass partition separating them. Ronnie touched the surface of the glass as well, hating that her hand shook as she placed her palm against the cool surface.

She had never been in this kind of predicament before, and disappointing her mother was the worst thing of all. Her mom had worked hard, put her dreams on hold, and lived only for Ronnie for twenty years. She was supposed to be making her mom proud that all her hard work had not been in vain.

Choking back the sob that threatened to come out of her throat, she asked, she had to, "Mom, you believe me, don't you?"

"Baby, Veronica, of course I believe you. I have more faith in you than in anything else in my life." Lou looked into her daughter's frightened eyes, and wanted more than anything to pull her daughter into her arms, rock her, and chase away the nightmare she was going through. But this wasn't one of her childhood nightmares that could so easily be chased away with soft soothing words. This was real, and she was terrified for her daughter.

"Thank-you Mom," Ronnie sniffed and pushed a blonde strand of hair out of her eyes. "I'll pay you back for the lawyer, for the bail, everything, some day,"

"Hey, none of that," Lou chastised, wanting to build up her daughter's courage. She knew she raised a strong girl, and she would need to be strong now. They both would.

After Veronica had described the public defenders response to her, Lou knew getting a lawyer, a good one, was absolutely essential. She also had a person in mind. Her dear friend Ana's brother-in-law. She had heard stories of his successes in the news. Surely, he would help her for a friend of the family, for his new sister-in-law. Not one to normally ask for favors, Lou would grovel for her daughter, on her knees, on broken glass or hot coals. Whatever it took. "I've got a great attorney in mind. Jay is working on the bail now. He went to talk to a bondsman this morning."

"Thank-you," Veronica muttered again, hanging her head in shame. She knew this was critical. The public defender she had been assigned was a total loser in her opinion. He hadn't asked if she was innocent, probably wouldn't have even believed her. He had been stiff and formal and quite detached in the brief meeting this morning. In fact, he'd seemed bored and hadn't even made eye contact.

A lawyer who believed her was critical. She swore that whatever it took, she would pay her mom back, every last cent, for the bail money too. She had no idea how much a thing like this would cost, but she was determined to do it.

Ronnie heard the clang of metal and it broke through her thoughts. She knew someone would be coming to pick up her tray soon, and perhaps take her to the showers. She popped the last bit of dry toast into her mouth. She was wrong about the shower. The guard who came to take her tray, left with a brief parting shot. "Hearing in ten minutes, someone will come get you."

***

Exactly ten minutes later, a new guard entered the corridor and approached her cell. "Veronica Louise Sears?" she asked, checking her paperwork in front of her.

"Yes," Ronnie confirmed, and the door slid open at the deputy's nod to the man on the other side of the corridor through the glass window.

"Turn," the female deputy commanded, and Ronnie automatically turned and put her hands behind her back. The woman placed cuffs on her, and holding them loosely steered her out of the cell. As she was led down the corridor, a few other inmates in the county holding facility called after, "Good luck, Blondie," and "They gonna throw the book at you, drug dealer!" Inside Ronnie cringed, but she didn't look back, and she held her head high, as high as her five foot four frame could be in prison issued tennis shoes. She was hoping this would be the last time she ever saw a jail cell, yet fearing it wouldn't because she might not be able to make the bail. She knew real prisons from what she saw on the news and they were definitely worse than this.

After she was led out of the wing she was in, her thoughts once again turned to her predicament. Just how in hell had she gotten into this horrifying nightmare in the first place? Gary, she thought as her eyes narrowed suspiciously. The Sheriff's deputy turned her down another corridor and down a flight of stairs that took her to an underground passageway out of the county lock up. They passed several more guards who examined the paperwork without a word and let them pass. Signs and arrows indicated they were going to the Courthouse across the street.

Just a week ago she was laughing on a beach in Jamaica with her friends, and her boyfriend, Gary. Ex-boyfriend Gary, she reminded herself. God, she had misjudged him! Her mother indicated he hadn't called though she tried several times to reach him. Ronnie told her mother her suspicions of his possible involvement and Lou's shock had turned to anger. His family was powerful, and she knew her daughter's innocence would be even more difficult to prove. They both expressed those feelings, but Lou once again reminded her daughter that this is a fight they would endure to the finish.

Ronnie never should have gotten back together with him after their last break up. He had begun to bore her, and proved on more than one occasion that he was the spoiled rich kid who expected things to be handed to him on a silver platter. He fooled her at first though. But she had come back to school last year, lonely, still smarting over the "Nikko" affair that had tarnished her summer.

Gary, for all his faults, was tall, handsome, and athletic. He was Gary the hockey player who shared her interests and her love of the great outdoors. In the beginning anyway. As time went on, he turned into boring Gary, lazy Gary, help me study for finals, let me borrow your notes Gary, and spent more and more of his time playing video games and smoking pot Gary. But for their final year after the break up, he cleaned up his act a bit, needing to graduate he promised to focus on his studies and do better. He had a full schedule of courses he needed to pass. Hell, he wouldn't even be graduating from University in a week if it weren't for her help.

Then another thought occurred to her. Hell! Would she, she wondered for the first time. Surely, she would still get her diploma, all her course work was done, and she aced her exams! She hadn't done three years of schooling, and two summers worth of work, so she could graduate early for nothing, had she?

Oh God, she hadn't even thought about that until now. Would she get her Degree in Forrest and Environmental Sciences? Would she be employable as a forest or park ranger? The dry toast she had eaten threatened to come back up as she trailed behind the deputy Sheriff.

Gary! It all came down to him. Her anger rose, and she stiffened her spine as her rubber soles slapped at the parquet floors. What the fuck had he done! Smuggled pot, cocaine, and heroine on a cruise ship. What an idiot! And, the fuck-tard had stashed it in her belongings, her scuba gear! She was so level headed, planned everything out, and excelled in school, and outdoor activities. She prided herself on excelling, making the right choices. Dumping Gary the first time had been the right choice. Taking him back because he said he'd changed wasn't. Now, she was paying the price.

Graduation was just a week away. She'd obviously be missing it, but her god dammed diploma. She wanted that. She wanted her life back. Her future. Her head was swimming.

The Tampa Bay deputy, who escorted her out of her cell, suddenly stopped and she felt a slight tug on her restraints. Ronnie felt her release the cuffs, and then she turned her around and indicated to Ronnie to put her hands in front. The deputy then reapplied them there. She wasn't the least bit friendly about it either. And Veronica, Ronnie to her friends, couldn't blame her. She probably saw all kinds of losers and criminals if her job was escorting people from the county lock-up over to the Courthouse every day.

Ronnie didn't even try to engage her in conversation, let alone voice her innocence. She blew a stray pink streak of hair off her face. Hell, she never regretted her highlights until now, but she was rethinking them for sure. Her dirty blond hair, layered, and a bit messy and disheveled from her lack of grooming supplies in jail must look a fright! Added to that was the tangle of knots she had been unable to remove without a comb. Her pink streak would surely impress the judge, she thought miserably! Gad, she might fit the image of a drug dealer, supplier, mule, whatever, she thought, as lead filled her stomach. The charges against her, as told to her by the court appointed attorney, were numerous.

Deputy Morrison indicated with a tap on her shoulder that Ronnie needed to turn left at the end of the corridor. They were in some back entryway into the Courtrooms now. Ronnie could see the small plaques above the door indicating the numbered courtrooms, and a white board next to each door showed what hearings were being held. Ronnie made the turn the deputy told her to take, and one other orange jumpsuit clad prisoner sat on a bench outside the last door. This must be it, Ronnie thought, and knew she was right when she saw her name on the board.

"Take a seat. They'll call when they are ready for you." The deputy's voice was dull as dirt as she leaned against the wall next to another officer who apparently was with the other prisoner.

Ronnie sat next to the other female prisoner who just nodded at her, said nothing, and looked down at her shoes waiting for her own name to be called. Mere seconds later, Ronnie was startled by the squawking metallic box above her that she hadn't noticed earlier. It announced that prisoner Wanda Jones should be brought into the Courtroom.

The officer opened the door, and Wanda walked right in and turned to the right without being prompted. Hmm, Ronnie thought, Wanda had been here before it seemed.

An honor roll student with numerous awards for academic excellence, Ronnie was graduating a year early. She put the time in, taking extra classes, and doing extra field work. In just a week, she should be getting her Bachelors from the University of Maine. But no, instead she was attending a hearing to decide her future, probably would be unable to leave the state of Florida, and would be left to find a way to prove her innocence without anyone to corroborate or back up her story.

Ronnie waited, and then thought of the interviews she had lined up for the summer. She'd have to cancel them, and say what? Sorry, I'm standing trial for drug smuggling. What was this fiasco going to do to those chances? Her life, just a week ago, was full of possibilities. And now this, she thought dismally. She shook her head to force those negative thoughts out of her mind. Focus on the hearing. One day at a time. Breathe. Justice will be served. That's all she could hope for right now. Still, Gary came to her mind. He was the key. He'd have his time, she thought ruefully, brown eyes narrowing.

Her court appointed attorney had not given her much hope. He basically advised she confess, and throw herself on the mercy of the Court. New frigging lawyer, had been her foremost thought, screaming like a freight train in her brain. Luckily, her mother had been able to send her a message this morning that they hired the guy she had in mind; he was out of town, but would be flying in from New York. The message stated he couldn't be there for the hearing, to plead not guilty to all charges, and he would meet with her tomorrow at her mom's house after she made bail. Be stoic, not weepy; be polite, the message ended. It was crumpled in her hand in the pocket of her jumpsuit. Stoic. Polite. She kept repeating those words as the internal clock in her mind ticked away the seconds of her life.

When the court appointed attorney was told by her this morning that she wouldn't need his services after the hearing, that her new attorney would be meeting her the next day once she made bail, he just laughed. "Bail! Huh, good luck with that!" His scoffing mumbled remark was made as he snapped his briefcase shut, and his metal chair scraped against the concrete floor. Jail sounds were harsh, and everything echoed.

She felt as if the weight of all that concrete was pressing down upon her, that and the thoughts of facing jail time, long jail time, if her court appointed attorney's comments were accurate. He told her she could be looking at ten to twenty years for the amount of drugs hidden in her scuba gear.

Ugh, her thoughts returned to Gary. What had Gary been thinking? Drugs. She had no idea. She, who was usually so perceptive. A lot of drugs! What the hell could he have wanted with all those drugs?

And she knew it was him too. He had given himself away when the cops at the Tampa Bay Port Authority had come for her. Their friends, who accompanied them on this trip, had disembarked earlier from the cruise ship. They were leaving directly for the airport, while she and Gary had been going to stay with her mom for a few days, and then drive to Maine together for her graduation.

They had been in a large room, waiting for their luggage, when the police approached. Several of the passengers remarked on such a great number of officers all together and she heard the crowd begin to speculate. When she turned to look for Gary, she didn't see him immediately. When she turned back to the police they were already upon her.

"Veronica Louise Sears?" one officer inquired.

"Yes," she answered tremulously. She looked around for Gary again and saw him off in the distance, approaching the exit doors with his suitcase. He looked at her and shook his head, his eyes boring into her. She turned back to the police "My boyfriend . . ." she pointed.

"Is not our concern," the officer stated and turned her away from him. "You are under arrest for smuggling drugs into the United States of America." And that's when she knew it was Gary, and he left her holding the proverbial bag. But why had he done that, her mind screamed.

"Won't be much longer," the deputy muttered looking at her watch. Ronnie was brought out of her thoughts. "These things are pretty quick," she added.

Informative, wasn't she, Ronnie thought sarcastically. The long walk had been done in complete silence and now she wanted to be chatty. Stoic. Polite. The note tight in her hand, damp from perspiration. Ronnie wondered why the deputy gave her that information and gave her a perplexed look. She hadn't expressed any signs of sympathy before.

"I could tell you're a first timer; you look nervous, and you keep looking at everything like it's the first time you've seen it." Hmm, she might be light duty, but the cop had good instinct and was on her toes. Ronnie nodded, letting the cop know her assumption was correct, smiled demurely and swallowed the lump in her throat at the first sign of empathy she had been given be anyone other than her mother since this nightmare started.

Her hand fisted the note. God, she was nervous. She had no idea what to expect next. The internal clock was ticking. Her mom's last words to her yesterday replayed in her head. "Just a hearing, baby. We'll figure everything out once you're home." Ronnie shook her head. Her poor mother, what she must be going through. She never wanted to disappoint her, ever again. Her mother sacrificed so much for her, and now this.

She looked up at the deputy who was still watching her. "How much longer do you think?" Ronnie asked nervously.

"Maybe five minutes. Hearings don't take long." Just as she finished saying that, the door opened and Wanda was back.

"No bail?" asked Deputy Morrison.

"Not today," the other deputy replied while Wanda remained silent. "Judge Hitchcock seems a bit grumpy today; Wanda ain't got that kind of money. Ain't that right, Wanda?" she stated as she pulled her along.

"10 G's for car theft. He's crazy!" Wanda responded. "It was my boyfriend; I didn't even steal the damn car."

"Well, it was your second time around," her guard chastised.

"Yeah, I know, but I ain't no drug smuggler for god sakes," she laughed, smirking at Ronnie. Ronnie clamped her mouth shut. Her breakfast almost came up. "Let's get you back to your cell now. They'll be coming around for showers soon."

Ronnie's eyes widened in shock at Wanda's remark. Had she heard something in the Courtroom?

As if reading her mind when the guard and Wanda began to pass, she threw out over her shoulder, "Courtroom's pretty full, Blondie, and I heard the newsies talking. Big story, lots of press, college graduate, drug smuggler. Good luck."

And with her words fading, echoing down the corridor, the metal box squawked. "The State of Florida vs. Veronica Louise Sears." She was up. The nightmare was almost over, or had it just begun?

Chapter Two

The Hearing

As Ronnie walked into the crowded Courtroom and turned right, she immediately saw the galley was packed with paparazzi. Her public defender nodded at the seat next to him. She approached, but the quiet in the large room really surprised her considering the crowd. She saw a few flashes and pictures were quickly snapped as she made her way to her seat. When the barrage of flashes stilled, it took a moment for her to make out her mom and Jay sitting behind her attorney. Ana and Monica, her mom's closest friends, were sitting next to her for moral support. She loved those women, Ana like a second mom and Monica like an older sister. She gave them a tentative smile, and waved with her hands clasped together as best she could, the handcuffs jangling from her wrists.

Lou smiled and nodded, Jay winked, and both the woman gave her supportive looks.

She turned to the front of the room as the bailiff asked for all the attendees to rise for the Honorable James A. Hitchcock. A tall distinguished black man, probably in his mid-sixties emerged from his chambers by a door in the paneled wall that opened right behind the raised bench before her. He stood for a moment gazing out at the crowd and a hush fell as he silenced those who were still murmuring with a fierce look of consternation. There was a soft click from the paneled door as it shut. Then he sat. Order was called, they were told they could all sit except for the defendant and the attorneys. The judge was introduced again to be recorded by the stenographer, and the case number read. The attorney for the state and public defender were named and then called to the bench.

Ronnie remained standing, nervous, and unable to hear what the judge was saying to the lawyers or their responses despite the quiet in the room. The judge looked to her, when her public defender finished speaking, eyes narrowing.

His eyes remained fastened on hers, while her attorney returned to her side. When he and the prosecutor were once again facing the court, the judge began to speak.

"The case of The State of Florida vs. Veronica Louise Sears, case number 4733640, is now in session for the initial hearing. The accused is present?" Ronnie heard the court reporter, keys tapping softly below the judge's bench, and then saw her suddenly look at her.

Her attorney told her in a whisper to say yes.

"Yes," she whispered. It came out a croak, her throat being as dry as the desert. Stoic, and polite, she recalled, and added a "Sir," despite the sandpaper sound of her raspy voice. The judge's eyes narrowed further not leaving her face. He nodded, and looked down at the papers before him.

Ronnie remained standing, her eyes never straying far from the judge.

He glanced away from his papers, looked towards the windows facing the street, and then suddenly his eyes were piercing her own, brown and glittering hard like chocolate diamonds. While his eyes never wavered from hers, he asked the prosecutor to name the charges. He watched her for any possible reaction as charge after charge was read to the full court room.

The young attorney sitting across the aisle from her read the charges forcefully, punctuating each charge from felonies down to misdemeanors. He listed the drugs, their quantities, the method of transportation, the intents behind the amount according to state statutes, and Ronnie's brain swam with all the charges being filed against her. Her eyes became glazed as tears threatened to spill. She squeezed them closed tightly to stop them from rolling down her face, but one lone tear escaped, streaking down her cheek as it rolled quickly down to her chin. She swiped it away, her handcuffs rattling in the now quiet.

"How do you plead to these charges?" the judge asked, sounding bored.

She cleared her throat, licked her dry lips. Stoic, Polite. "Not guilty, Your Honor." Her voice came out clear, and firm, stronger than she felt. She was glad for the note of confidence that seemed to come through this time, but couldn't help but hear the sniffling behind her, her mom, and Jay shushing her. She turned and gave her mom a confidant smile.

"Eyes up here, young lady," the judge chastised, and she turned quickly back to the bench. "This is only a hearing, but I want you to realize the seriousness of those charges, and the possible outcomes if found guilty."

She nodded, and he continued in his firm tone, with a slightly pronounced southern accent. "You are looking at a minimum of ten years, and possibly up to twenty-five. You understand the seriousness of these charges?"

"I do, Sir." He nodded, and looked to the public defender.

"You are asking for bail?"

"Yes," her attorney replied. When the judge waited for him to say more and he said nothing, the Judge gave him an odd look, shook his head, and then his grey head swiveled to the prosecution's side.

"Arguments."

The prosecutor spoke up. "High bail. She is a flight risk. She lives in another state, although her Mother resides here. The investigation is ongoing and considering the amount of drugs, others may be involved, your Honor."

The judge turned to her attorney, who was looking out the windows, and the judge hearing no objection, shook his head again. He obviously disapproved of her attorney's lackadaisical behavior, but did not comment on it. His disgusted measured glances spoke volumes even though her attorney appeared not to notice.

He cleared his throat. "The eighth amendment requires bail be set in most cases in which there is no risk to the public. I think drug dealers are a public risk." He enunciated drug dealer, punctuating each syllable. Her jaw, which dropped at her own attorney's inattentiveness, just snapped closed, and she focused on the judge's words. She nodded, showing her understanding. Hell, she even agreed. She remained mute, knowing that judges didn't appreciate being interrupted, and that defendants should only speak when asked directly. The judge nodded at her. "But, the eighth amendment also clearly states that bail needs to be granted in order for the accused to be able to help in their own defense, and it also states it shall be set in accordance with the financial situation of the accused, it must not be set so out of reach, that you do not have the opportunity to work with your attorneys to gather the information you need to defend yourself which is difficult to do while in prison."

She nodded. This sounded good. Hopeful. But his next words dashed that hope. Squashing the reprieve he had set her up for.

"But I also agree with the prosecution, and think you pose a flight risk. You live in another state and may have friends and family there who will harbor you. And, you brought drugs into my State. The amount of drugs you have been accused of bringing into the country could have posed a serious risk to the public at large if they had been put out on the street. With that in mind, bail is set at 250,000."

The courtroom gasped. Cameras began to snap to capture her reaction. The judge rapped his gavel once and the crowd began to quiet. Ronnie felt like she was going to throw up. A quarter of a million dollars. There was no way her mom could come up with that much money. Impossible. She nearly fell, and swayed, and she felt Jay's hands grip her from behind, and hold her up. She regained her step, her balance, as a guard approached Jay, and he removed his hands quickly knowing she could stand on her own. She heard Ana say, "Don't worry baby girl, we've got this."

"Yes," Monica chimed in.

The tears were filling her eyes. They were going to help as well. She had a chance. But a quarter of a million dollars? She felt faint. Her attorney was speaking, saying something about her having to go with the guard until bail was made. Her mind was on her mother's friends and the fact she didn't know how they were going to raise that much money. She owed them all so much. She turned to smile at them to show her appreciation. She didn't know how she would pay them back, but she would.

The peril of the situation she was in was not lost on Ronnie. Her mind was doing the math. Despite the quarter of a million dollar bond the judge ordered, she knew that between her mom, Ana, and Monica they would be able to come up with the money, but it wasn't going to be easy by any means. Ana was a Ph.D., and although she worked for the state, she made a good salary and had a lovely home she put a lot of money into. Monica too, was a high school teacher, but lived modestly, and between her husband and herself they did well. Her mom, on the other hand, didn't have much, but she had a house, and Jay was an airplane mechanic.

But still, knowing the sacrifices they would all have to make for her, it humbled her. Tears were beginning to form again. She would prove her innocence and the bond would be returned. She would ensure that. She would have her day in court, and somehow, everything would all work out, she prayed.

She forced her mind to focus. The judge was speaking again, explaining how to pay the bond, and explaining the terms of her release if the bond could be raised.

Whispering behind her distracted her. It was Monica. "How much will you need?"

The voice that answered turned Ronnie's blood to ice. "My brothers and I agreed, we would take 10%, so 25,000 thousand dollars. We would also need the title to Lou's house."

Ronnie's head, of its own volition, turned to the sound of the husky voice she recognized. Nikko! Oh my God! She hadn't even noticed him sitting next to Monica. His eyes met hers and the blue glittered hard. The smile he gave her was just as dazzling as she remembered, but it was forced. The dimples in evidence. She swiveled back to the judge, as he called forcefully to her to give her his attention.

"Do you understand the terms of your release, Miss Sears?" he commanded.

She hadn't heard a thing. Her mind was a whirl. She nodded blankly.

The judge nodded at the bailiff who called for all to rise, and her guard, the deputy who escorted her in, began to approach.

She heard Ana. "Here is a check, Nikko. When will you have her out?"

"In an hour, or two, maybe four. It just depends on how many are being processed today. You never know. I'll handle the paperwork, no sense you all waiting around. Plus," he whispered softly to just Ana and Monica, "Mrs. Russell doesn't look well. But, I'll need the title for the house? Does she have it?"

"I have it," Ana stated. "I also brought my checkbook."

"Great. Then you all shouldn't wait here. As I said, it may take a while," he muttered. "I'll call when I have her out, and I can even drive her home. I'll have paperwork to file with the county where she'll be residing."

Ana was whispering Nikko's instructions to Jay and heard his firm agreement. He turned to Lou who tried to resist the orders to go home her new husband was giving.

***

Her mind was numb. Her mom's house! Nikko's confident voice giving them all directions. Her heart was racing. His was a face she thought she would never have to see again. Mortification set in, and not just because of her current situation, even though that should be enough.

The bailiff announced as the judge left that there would be a short recess before the next hearing. As Ronnie turned in the direction of the door she had entered from, photographers began to snap pictures again, and the flashes temporarily blinded her. She gave her mom, Jay, Ana, and Monica a smile.

"A few hours, baby," her mom whispered through her tears. Ronnie nodded, and caught Nikko's smirk.

He added, "Yes, I'll get you . . . out." His eyes barely hinted at the significance of the slight pause. She saw humor there too, eyes crinkling in his tanned and sharply angled face before she turned and was lead through the door.

Just before the door closed she heard Nikko again. "I'll drive her home. Lou, Mrs. Russell, you look exhausted. Take her home, Jay," he directed, "and as soon as I get all the paperwork done, we will be on our way."

"Thank you," she heard her mom murmur, and then there was the silence of the long hallway that would lead her under the street and back to her cell with nothing but time, until Nikko came for her.

***

The wait was longer than she expected and she was able to grab a quick shower. But, she passed on lunch thinking she'd be released soon. The congealed turkey on a slice of white bread with a scoop of cold mashed potatoes did not look appetizing at all. When the guard came to take her tray, she began to worry, but it wasn't for long. Her stomach growled and she began to regret her decision, but just then another guard finally arrived to tell her she made bail. She was immediately brought to a holding room. An officer, framed in a small window called her forward, handed her a large manila envelope, and told her to examine the contents and sign. The envelope contained her personal belongings from the afternoon of her arrest.

After she assured the guards the contents of her purse were all accounted for, she was lead to a room where she could change out of her orange jumpsuit.

She quickly stripped out of the hated attire, and opened up the large yellow envelope again that contained her belongings. Taking off the white cotton panties and bra she was issued by the county, she donned her own red silky panties. She planned to burn them later though as they were a gift from Gary at Christmas when they had gotten back together.

She slipped on the denim mini skirt she had worn off the cruise ship, and the rust colored tank top. She was a tomboy at heart, and rarely dressed up, or wore skirts and dresses. But on the cruise, she had gone more girly than her usual attire. She had been trying. For Gary. The schmuck.

Ronnie picked up her small purse again, and quickly scanned the contents. Her wallet was there, her keys, her small make-up bag, but her passport was missing. Taken by the Court, so she wouldn't leave the country she presumed.

She slung the bag over her shoulder and went out the door, leaving the jumpsuit and prison issued under garments lying in a heap on the floor where they had fallen. Good riddance. She hoped she had seen the last of prison grab.

"This way." Another guard indicated a large door just down the hall. "What about my luggage, my clothes?" she asked. Those had not been returned to her yet.

"Evidence," was the answer from the officer with a dismissive tone. She turned, shrugging her shoulders. She'd miss those items but felt she would receive them once she'd cleared her name. She had some things at her mom's anyhow, and they were practically the same size. It would have to do.

The massive door opened into a large open space with plenty of activity. Many officers were walking around, detectives too, and she saw the room to the right where she was booked, fingerprinted, and photographed. She shook off that horrible memory and began to look around, wondering what to do next. The guard who escorted her here had vanished.

Then, she saw him. Nikko. He noticed her right away, but was playing it cool. He stood next to a police officer, nodded in her direction, but made no move towards her. Apparently, he expected her to come to him. At first she was disoriented for a moment, and made no move towards Nikko. He was apparently her ride home. Her gaze swept the room, but she remained where she was, rooted to the spot. She heard the front doors open, saw a glimpse of the outside, and the Florida heat entered with the sunshine as a cop came in escorting a man in handcuffs. He appeared to be a vagrant, perhaps one of the city's many homeless. Nikko's attention was focused on his companion, still apparently engrossed in his conversation with the officer.

She began to fume. He was her ride home, wasn't he? He gave her another one of his smirks, and she smirked back. The ass, she thought. As soon as his eyes left hers, she made for the door. She wasn't going to wait around for him to shoot the breeze all day. He had taken his sweet time in getting her out on bail, and now he still kept her waiting. Waiting was not something she was good at, and she definitely wouldn't be waiting around for him. He had to know how anxious she was to get home, and yet he continued his conversation with the young officer. They were both laughing quite raucously and both glanced her way. The police officer gazed appreciatively at her, and Nikko laughed again. Her eyes narrowed. Nikko clasped the man on the shoulder and gave it one of those caveman type gestures. She'd had enough. He wasn't even looking at her now, and in disgust she marched towards the exit.

Just as she reached the double doors, she heard him. "Whoa, Ronnie! Trying to escape already, are you?" His husky tone was right behind her, in her ear as she pulled on the heavy doors. His voice dropped to a whisper. "You are awfully good at running away." She wasn't a fool, and caught the double entendre. Referring to their last encounter, their almost night together, when she fled from him in the parking lot at Pier Sixty on Clearwater Beach just made her anger more intense.

"Running!" she whipped out, turning on her heel. "I want out of here now, and my idea of now is not having to wait around for you and your buddy to finish swapping stories about your latest conquests." Two could play his game. Just because his brothers were now related to Monica, and they ran the bail bondsmen company that helped to arrange her release, didn't mean she was indebted to him, and had to wait around for him. They had a past, and that past couldn't be swept under the carpet because he had come to bail her out. He'd probably done it on purpose, offered to come, just to rub her nose in it.

His smirk softened. She thought she saw a glimpse of regret, maybe sympathy, in his narrowed blue eyes, before the disarming smile that was all charm was back in place. "Oh, Ronnie," he shook his head. "You haven't changed at all, still an ice princess one minute, then a scorching flame with a smart kissable mouth the next." A smart mouth he remembered well. One that tempted him with full pink lips. He couldn't resist putting her back in her place when she bit her bottom lip causing something inside of him to stir. "Well, except for the fact that you're a hardened criminal." He saw her nostrils flare, and her brown eyes flashed fire. But he couldn't help it. It was who he was. He liked to tease, especially ice princesses like her.

"I'm innocent!" She hissed back at him, her foot stomping the cement of the threshold to the police station. His blue eyes sparkled, and she gave him her fiercest glare, shook her head, and began her grand exit out the doors, but before she could take even one step, his hand was on her elbow, and the explosion the contact created almost had her stumbling down the steps of the police station right onto Eighth Ave.

"Not so fast, Ronnie! My little runner." He saw her expression and her fingers curling into a fist. He shook his head. "Come," he indicated with his chin over his shoulder, "You little minx, my car is in back anyway," he added when her gaze returned to him.

She turned on her heel, yanking her elbow out of his grasp, stormed around him, and made her way to the rear of the police station. She heard his laugh behind her, and inside she was fuming at the sheer frustration of the situation he seemed to find so humorous.

He laughed and passed her, his much longer strides in comfortable shoes, quickly overtaking her. He led the way through to the back of the building where his automobile was presumably parked.

Ronnie couldn't help herself. Her ire was up, and she didn't like him having the last word. "Never thought I'd hear you say, not so fast!"

Nikko just laughed and kept walking. Oh the man was still as cocky as ever and from her view of his backside just as fit and good looking. The only problem, the one that mattered, was that he knew he was a pretty boy and never failed to take advantage of opportunities thrown his way. Like Nancy.

Chapter Three

The Ice Princess

God, even in the Courtroom with that horrible orange jumpsuit, and her eyes all puffy, he felt the attraction, the pull to the little package that was Ronnie. And what a package, she was. *Cioccie!* That was the word his brother, Gio, would use to describe Ronnie. A real handful. His palms itched at the memories. The unflattering costume did nothing to hide the shape of that body underneath. The material strained over her breasts. More than a handful he remembered, as he stood up with the women and Jay when the judge entered. Her big brown doe like eyes never glanced his way, and it bothered him that she failed to see him, recognize him.

He'd recognize her in a paper bag. In nothing.

The proceedings went quickly, and smoothly, just as he and his brothers had foreseen. It wasn't until she was about to be escorted back to her cell, that she showed any signs of recognizing him. Her brown eyes narrowed in disapproval, her blond hair in disarray. She cast a him a mere glance before turning away to exchange sympathetic looks with her mother, and Ana and Nikko's new cousin Monica. He had come, volunteered to do this job knowing it would be an all-day thing. He wanted to clear the air, and hopefully offer her support in this difficult time. He hated to admit it to himself, but it bothered him that she did not seem to even notice him.

He cleared his throat in an attempt to get her attention, but she didn't look his way again. Ah! The ice princess, he remembered. But, he also remembered that she could be not so icy with a little liquid courage. In fact, she could be quite warm, and yielding with the right kind of encouragement. Yes, the ice princess had been a flaming inferno for a few brief moments. He regretted her misunderstanding the situation between them, and he normally didn't have regrets when it came to women.

He smirked remembering their too brief time together, and then shifted uncomfortably when his cock began to remember too. The proceedings were over, and the blond firecracker with the wild streak of pink in her hair, it had been purple last year, had often been in his fantasies this past year. She disappeared from his view, orange jump suit straining across her shapely ass. His hands itched to cup those cheeks again, maybe even slap them for running away from him, and not giving him a chance to explain last summer.

He groaned inwardly though. The ice princess was untouchable now. A Case! Albeit, he knew her somewhat intimately before this. His brothers would most assuredly disapprove of his thoughts, if they knew why he jumped at the opportunity to handle today's bail hearing. His brothers. Domineering, all of them, except perhaps Gio. He had a quirky, silly kind of humor at times. But Blaze and Andreas were serious, all of the time.

He led her to his pride and joy, his 1970 Black Cutlass. He and his brothers worked on it for years when he lived in New York, and now it was a classic he was proud of. It was what kept him sane after his parents had been killed, in the horrific double homicide that he himself had discovered. He was just seventeen when it happened, and he and his dad had picked up the junk car the year before. It had been their project, his and his dad, Frank. An early graduation present. After his parents were killed, his brothers each took turns working on it with him to finish it in time for his graduation from high school. It's what their dad would have done.

Ronnie didn't seem impressed. He opened the door for her, and she slid onto the black leather seats. He practically choked on his own air as he sucked in his breath when her skirt slid up exposing a great deal of her thighs to his line of vision.

"Boys and their toys," she muttered, glancing around the beautiful interior. The car was pristine, and she loved it, but she'd be dammed if she would let him know.

He slammed the door, rattling the car and regretted it immediately. This car meant a great deal to him. It wasn't a mere toy. But, he didn't expect her to understand. It was special. A connection. Her comment distressed him. He never liked to talk about the past, but he somehow wanted her to know. The urge to share his private hell, their family's tragedy overwhelmed him. But, he suppressed the urge to tell her. She had her own issues to deal with right now.

He made his way round to his side of the car, and got in behind the wheel. The steering wheel had been the last piece to be put in. Andreas had driven all the way to a junk yard in New Jersey to find it. It went in the day before his graduation.

He cleared his throat. Ronnie was sitting like a statue on the seat next to him. Hands clutched in her lap. He glanced her way, but she wouldn't look at him. "Seatbelt," he murmured politely reminding her, but when she made no move to put it on, he couldn't resist adding, "It's the law."

"I know the law, moron. It's stuck. I tried," she said as her head whipped around to him.

He quashed the urge to take the wildcat over his knees; he was trying to be sensitive after all, even though he didn't know why. He let out a sigh of frustration and leaned over to help her with it. He smoothly pulled the belt over her lap, and chest, and his arm brushed her breasts. She pulled back. The current went through his arm like a shock of electricity, and from her reaction he knew she felt it too. His arm tingled from where it made the contact among other places.

"Yeah stuck," he teased her as he righted himself in his seat. He forgot the passenger belt locked up on occasion. He rarely had people in this car. Normally he used one of the company's vehicles when he was transporting people, but he'd made the exception. For Ronnie.

"It was," she exclaimed, crossing her arms in front of her chest, and turning to give him one of her fiercest stares.

He looked back and could see the tough shell was anything but. He knew underneath she must be scared as hell. Hell, he would be too if he was in her dilemma. Accused of drug smuggling with the evidence stacked against her, and being just twenty-two, he felt some pity for her. He tried not to think of the other feelings he had for her. They confused the hell out of him. Thinking they'd go away on their own, he hadn't tried very hard to get ahold of her last summer. When he worked up the courage to try, she had already left Florida, and returned to school for her final year of college. But seeing her again, he had a pang of regret. It would have been good. Really good.

Down boy, he cautioned himself as he took one more look at those incredible thighs. The girl must run, or do a lot of hiking. He remembered her telling him last year that she was studying forestry and environmental sciences. She was a tomboy, she had joked. She sure as hell didn't look like one. Not in that mini skirt, and silky rust tank top that didn't leave much to the imagination.

Shaking his head, he started the engine, and the car rumbled to life. He loved the power of this car, and how it felt to drive it. He backed up, turned out of the lot, and in a few more turns he was on Nebraska Avenue headed down State Road 41 to her mom's house in Spring Hill. It was about an hour's drive. He could have taken the shorter route on the Suncoast Highway, but he wanted the extra twenty minutes with her. He wanted to learn some things about Miss Sears that he hadn't been able to last summer. His brothers told him to gather as much information as he could about her in case she ran.

Even though she was technically a friend of the family, they were still running a business. They always kept a close eye on all their clients, and did their research. Business was business. But given the state of their previous relationship, he figured he needed to soften her up a bit first. She wouldn't be very willing to confide in him so easily. So talking about himself first might make the transition smoother.

"My brothers helped me to build this car, put it back together, get it running, and we restored it to its original glory," he offered. When she made no reply and only stared ahead stonily he added, "My father bought it for me as an early graduation gift a year before both my parents were killed." He saw out of the corner of his eye that she sat up a bit straighter, and she turned to him slightly. She was listening. "Yeah, so it's not a toy to me. Just saying," he gave her a sideways smile. She gave him a small one in return so he continued. "My dad and I bought the car together when I was sixteen. We got the motor working but that was about it. Then he died."

She cleared her throat before speaking. She felt guilty for her earlier callous remark. "I'm sorry about your parents. Was it a car accident?" He mentioned them dying and wondered how.

"No, murder actually," he said nonchalantly.

"Oh my goodness!" she exclaimed. "I had no idea. I am so sorry."

He saw the sympathy in her eyes and a tell-tale guilty blush. He shocked her by sharing this information. Her arms relaxed though, and she was wringing her hands in her lap.

"Thanks. It was a long time ago. My dad was a cop, just like my brothers. And I was going to be a cop too, but they pushed me into going into forensic sciences. I had the grades for it, and got a scholarship and all. But after graduation, I went into the police academy anyway."

"You were a cop? All of you? How'd you all end up in Florida?" Ronnie asked with curiosity. Last summer, she assumed he was just a playboy who worked for his brothers in the family business. Interesting, there was more to this man than she thought.

"Yeah, for a while we were. My oldest brothers wanted out. They both wanted out of New York and were tired of the job. Blaze had just gone through a tough break up. I didn't want to go, but hell they were all going, so here I am," he answered her questions.

"Did they ever catch the person who killed your parents? If you don't mind my asking?" she asked tentatively.

Nikko didn't answer right away. He took a moment to compose his thoughts. "Hmm, well, no actually. He's still out there. Somewhere. Andreas hasn't given up. He never will. He got a few notes from him that first year, but then the case went cold." He paused and she watched his hands caress the steering wheel lost in thought. "He was a serial killer, a case of my brother's. The guy, he was the Rosedale Romeo."

Ronnie nodded as her heart rate picked up. She remembered hearing that name on the news when she was just a kid.

"Oh my god," she whispered.

He continued. "He came after our family because Andreas got too close to him. He took it personally. When Andy figured out who the guy was, the manhunt was on. They decided to release his name to the press and splash pictures of him all over the news, so there wouldn't be any more victims. The police descended on his family and the guy had nowhere to run. His name was Salvatore Erickson. The dude's wife said she didn't know anything. She was shocked that her husband had this secret life. Said she had no clue what a monster he was. Andreas believed her. The man was seriously twisted. She was put into protective custody, given a new name, a new life. They had kids and she took them too. They were all in hiding. Salvatore had no one else. He was furious. He was pissed at Andreas and blamed him for ruining his life. Not because he was a sick bastard who liked to torture and mutilate girls, but because he blamed Andreas for destroying his family."

Nikko paused again in his tale, and Ronnie waited patiently for him to continue. She didn't want to push, but she was definitely intrigued. She never would have guessed Nikko faced so much pain and horror so young.

He eventually spoke after glancing her way once seeing her waiting. "For a year, the trail was cold. A few notes promising revenge." He shook his head and she saw the cold look that crossed his face. "I was the only one still living at home at the time. I snuck out with my buddies one night and when I got home, I found them."

"Oh, how horrible!" Ronnie's hands flew to her mouth as she gasped.

"Yeah, it was pretty bad. I didn't want to go to school after that. Just wanted to finish the car that my dad and I started. But, Andreas moved back home. My other brother's lived in the city. Andreas was a detective, Gio had made detective too. Blaze was in law school. He did the police academy later. Like me. They promised to help me finish the car as long as I kept going to school. Each weekend one of them would work on it with me."

His voice sounded rough. She felt her own throat tighten, thick with emotion for him.

"You're close to your brothers," she commented to ease the tension in the car.

"Yes, I am," he stated. "They're pretty much all I got."

Ronnie nodded sympathetically. Her family was small too. And she cherished each one of them.

"How about you Ronnie? Got much family?" he asked, giving her a small smile and then he returned his focus to the road.

"Small too. It was just me and my mom, growing up. My grandparents are great; my granddad is one of my best friends. I have an uncle too, but he is somewhat of a recluse."

"My grandparents on both sides died long ago. I don't remember them," he told her. "I do have an aunt. My mom's sister, and a cousin too. Victor."

"Yes, Monica's husband." Memories of the wedding popped into her head. She couldn't find it in her to be mad at the moment. Not after all he revealed. "Monica and Ana grew up with my mom. So, they are like aunts to me. I love them a lot."

"I could tell you were close," he added. When they both remained silent for a while he decided to forge ahead. "What are your grandparents like? I don't remember much of mine. Always thought it would be cool to have them around."

Ronnie couldn't suppress a small laugh. She had never known her father. Her grandfather had been the one to fill those shoes. Her granddad was the best. "I love my granddad. He did lots with me. I was his constant companion, he was my babysitter, and I followed him everywhere. He used to tease me all the time too. He'd call out for me like I wasn't in the room, and then he would lift his shoe. I guess I was always underfoot," she used air quotes to emphasize her meaning. Nikko smiled and waited for her to continue. "He's the reason I studied forestry and the environment. While mom worked he would take me into the woods. We would walk, hike, fish, ride motorbikes. On the weekends we would go camping at his fish camp," Ronnie reminisced.

"He still alive?"

"Yes, both my grandparents and my uncle. They still live in Maine, in Presque Isle, about two and half hours from where I went to school in Bangor."

"That's nice that they were close," he offered.

"Yeah," Ronnie whispered and got quiet.

After a minute or so, he tried another avenue to get her talking again. "For the record, Ronnie, I feel bad for you and this situation."

"I don't need your sympathy," she muttered, stone faced. Her thoughts turned to her grandparents and how disappointed they must be.

Okay, he thought, what next? Another minute passed, and he hadn't thought of another way to get her to open up, so he decided to finish telling her about how they ended up in Florida.

"So earlier I was telling you why we came to Florida" he started. She looked at him blankly and he just continued. "I graduated with my forensics degree and Blaze decided to do the police academy. So we both did that together. As soon as we got out, and started looking for work, my brother Andreas announced that he had enough of New York, and that he and Gio were moving to Florida. My mom's sister and my cousin Victor lived here. They are pretty much the only family we had, so me and Blaze decided to come along for the ride. Blaze and I did about a year on the force. We were partners. Then, we moved here. That was two years ago," he finished.

"Oh," she muttered. "Interesting."

Again the silence. Ronnie was lost in her thoughts again. Well, he had gotten some information from her. He didn't think she would run, but any info he could get would be useful if she did. They rode in silence for a few more minutes when he heard the strangest sound. He looked at his console. Nothing appeared out of order.

He looked to Ronnie to see if she had heard it. She was squirming uncomfortably in her seat. He looked at his gauges again, nothing was going on there, and then he heard it again. It was definitely coming from her side of the car. He looked at her. She was pink faced.

"Um, was that you?" he asked tentatively.

He heard her sigh, and she covered her face with her hands in embarrassment and just nodded. He was confused as hell. And just kept looking her way, and then the sound came again. Louder.

"Well, what is it?" he asked, completely dumbfounded.

She shook her head in humiliation. "Believe it or not, that is my stomach growling. Prison food is not the greatest, and I hardly ate anything these last two days."

"Well, why didn't you say so," he replied, let out a sigh that nothing was wrong with his baby, and began to laugh.

"It's not funny," she pouted.

When her lower lip jutted out like that, he had the sudden urge to lean over suck it into his mouth, and kiss those lips. "Well first I thought something was wrong with my car, but if you're *that* hungry, I could just pull over and we could grab a bite. There's tons of good places to eat along this road."

"No thank you," she replied tartly. "Just get me home to my mom."

"Fine!" Women, he thought. He just didn't get them. If you are hungry, you eat. He drove on in silence, but not for long.

Her stomach was practically speaking. He just shook his head when he saw her place her hands over her offending organ. He couldn't blame her for wanting to get home to her mom, but something also told him, probably her tone, that she didn't want to spend any more time in his company than she had to. And, that bothered him.

When her stomach rumbled again he just had to ask, "You sure?"

One of Nikko's eyebrows arched up. And, Ronnie was hungry. There was no denying that. Her damn stomach betrayed her every chance it got. The advertisements along the road were just about killing her. But she had no choice. It was look at them or look at him. And damn him for looking so good in his white dress shirt, and dark slacks. He had taken his jacket off, and the tailored shirt fit him like a glove. The muscles bulging in his biceps as he handled the car smoothly was pure torture. She looked away from him, but could still feel his eyes on her. "Yes, now just drive!" she snapped, her eyes flashing his way, chest heaving in her sudden anger at him.

His eyes watched those breasts for a second too long. She noticed him staring and crossed her arms in front of them again and looked out of the side passenger window avoiding him.

"Okay," he growled. They drove a few more minutes in silence, her stomach occasionally reminding him of her hunger. Sometimes softly, other times fiercely.

They were half way to Spring Hill and he was looking at all the restaurants they were passing letting her stew in silence. The more places he passed and signs he read, he began to realize he was hungry too, and not just for the delectable little morsel by his side.

They passed several places advertising seafood, and barbecue. Popular choices in this area. He hadn't eaten much for breakfast, and it was past three in the afternoon now. He could use a bite, and that might also give him some more time with Ronnie. To question her, and maybe get a little more information.

They were stopped at a light. "Mmm," he teased. "That place looks good." He pointed at the sign advertising fresh seafood. Ronnie, couldn't help herself and looked. Her stomach growled in response. Nikko laughed, and lowered his window hoping beyond hope the smell of the place would reach them. The light turned green and he had to continue, but he left his window down just in case the aroma could entice her.

At the next stoplight there was a restaurant, well more like a shack along the side of the road. It was called Big Jimbo's Barbecue with a sign advertising all you can eat ribs. The aroma was pungent, sweet and tangy. He looked at her and gave her a conniving smile. Her stomach growled so loud it nearly surpassed the sound of his engine.

The barbecue did her in. "Pull over, asshole!" She gave him her dirtiest look. "And, you're buying!" she added for good measure when he burst out laughing and pulled into the parking lot of Big Jimbo's Barbecue.

Chapter Four

The Hunger

Ronnie was out of the car as soon as he had it in park, and he had to jog to catch up to her at the window of the barbecue shack. She was already ordering while he fished out his wallet from his back pocket.

"I'll have the sweet tangy ribs, an order of fries, some onion rings, and a strawberry milkshake." She turned to him and smiled wickedly licking her pink lips.

He wanted to taste them, but the ribs smelled good too.

"For you?" asked the scantily dressed brunette at the counter. She was getting an eyeful, and letting him know she liked what she saw.

Looking at her nameplate, he turned on the charm. "What would you suggest, Linda?" He gave her a winning smile and turned slightly to see if Ronnie was watching. She was. She didn't look pleased. That made him happy.

The brunette giggled. "Oh, the ribs are fabulous, but so are the pulled pork sandwiches. Those are my favorite."

"Well, Linda," he flirted. "If those are your favorite then I'll have one of those." He smiled and leaned on the counter getting closer to the brunette. Her white t-shirt fit her closely, suggesting that she too was more than a handful.

Ronnie turned away in disgust. Yup, this was the Nikko she remembered. A real man-whore. She walked stiffly to the picnic benches and sat with her back to the window. If Nikko was trying to put a show on, she wasn't going to give him an audience. Unfortunately, she could still hear them chatting. The man was an uncontrollable flirt.

"And what about to drink, Linda? What do you suggest I order?" His voice dropped huskily, but he kept his eyes on Ronnie watching her shoulders stiffen.

"You have to try one of our shakes, darling. Vanilla is my favorite."

"Mmm, vanilla," he drew out the word. "That does sound good."

His voice was practically a seduction, Ronnie thought. She recognized the tone. If she had a full stomach, she might have thrown up. She still might, if this went on much longer. Soon she could add the sound of dry heaving to her list of strange bodily sounds she shared with Nikko today.

"It is," Linda replied, her own voice taking on a sultry tone.

"But Linda, I'm not in the mood for vanilla today. I think I'll have the strawberry too."

"Whatever you want, darling. Whatever you want," she repeated.

Yup, Ronnie thought, I am going to puke.

"I'll be right over there, Linda. Call me when our order's up, and I'll be right back."

"Sure thing," Linda murmured, sliding the glass window closed.

Ronnie shook her head. The man was a pig. In the car, she briefly felt sorry for him, when he talked about his car, and his parents and brothers and all. But even though he had some tough times, the man was still the biggest Lothario this side of the Mason-Dixon Line.

She heard the gravel crunch under the soles of his shoes, and then she felt him behind her. The day was a hot one, but his body so close to hers was throwing even more heat.

"Ronnie, let's go sit over there in the shade. They've got a fan setup and it'll be cooler," he murmured behind her and touched her shoulder. Again, even despite her anger, her hunger, her frustration, she felt the current between them. She supposed he felt that way with every pretty girl he took to bed, and there must have been many. For her, this was something different.

But the fan did sound like a good idea, so she got up, and pulled her shoulder out from under his hand. The shade would be nice as well. She wished she had seen the spot earlier, but it was not in direct view of the front of Big Jimbo's Barbecue. She walked over and took the seat opposite him. They were sitting down, and no sooner had they sat, when miss long-legged Linda, in the tightest pair of daisy dukes on the planet, came sashaying out of a side door with two milkshakes in her hands.

"Oh, Linda," he teased. "You are fast."

"That's what they tell me," she laughed, not sparing Ronnie a look as she sat on the table her back to Ronnie giving Nikko an excellent view of her thighs.

"Nikko, if you want to be alone with this . . . this Linda. I'll go eat in the car," Ronnie smiled at him.

He looked from Linda's spread open thighs to Ronnie's face, and her words, said with as much disgust as she could muster, couldn't hide the emotion he saw there. Jealousy. He was slightly pleased, but didn't want to push his luck with her anymore today. "No, Ronnie. Stay. I really want to get to know you better. Sorry, Linda," he gave her a sympathetic smile. His way of letting her down easy.

"Oh, I'm sorry," Linda stated seemingly noticing Ronnie for the first time. She got up and brushed the debris, and dust from the table off of her backside. She acted confused for a moment, hurt.

Ronnie felt bad for her for a second, after all he had been flirting mercilessly, and she of all people knew what it was like to face the full effect of the Nikko charm.

"I'll be right back with your orders. Sorry, I . . ." she stammered, "misunderstood." Then she was sashaying back to the cook shack much more quickly than she approached the table. When the door shut with a clang of screen door hitting metal frame, Ronnie shook her head.

Nikko shrugged his shoulders, "What?" he asked, playing the innocent when Ronnie continued giving him a dirty look.

"You are a reprehensible flirt. That girl thought you were hitting on her."

"Was I?" He continued to play coy and she wasn't buying it for a second.

"Seriously Nikko." She rolled her eyes at him, just shook her head, and began to fiddle with the wrapping on her straw. She popped it into the top of the Styrofoam container, and then took a sip of her strawberry milkshake, a long one.

He watched her curiously. He knew he had been flirting, but only to make her jealous, and realize what she missed out on last summer by running from him. He began to peel the paper off of his own straw when she finally came up for air. He wished those lips were sucking something else. His cock was enjoying the thought immensely. He was grateful the table was hiding his powerful erection.

As Ronnie took another pull on the straw she saw Nikko squirm on the seat uncomfortably as he tried to get his straw unwrapped. "Oh yes!" she whispered huskily and licked her lips. She put the straw back in her mouth to suck a little more of the frothy, creamy concoction into her mouth. Two, could play his game, she thought, as his jaw hit the dirt. She could make more out of her enjoyment of the milkshake than she really felt and give him a little dose of his own medicine. She released the straw and then darted out her tongue to lick the tiny bubble of ice cream that appeared on top. Nikko jammed his straw into his own mouth and looked at her fiercely. Smiling and then ignoring him, she popped the straw back into her mouth sucking greedily.

Nikko's mouth dropped at the sight of Ronne's lips on the straw, sucking. And her words practically had him shoot a load like he was a teenaged boy again. His blood was pumping in his veins. The wrong veins, or maybe the right ones. He felt his cock in his pants stir against the constraints. The second, no maybe third time that day, she'd made him harder than the Rock of Gibraltar. He shifted on the wooden seat uncomfortably. His balls would be blue in no time if she continued her little sensuous torment much longer. He knew what she was doing, but that didn't, couldn't stop his reaction to it.

He finally took another sip of his own drink needing the coolness of it to tame the flames she was fanning. It was good. "Oh yes," he teased her back saying it breathily. "So good!" he purred and went in for another sip.

They exchanged glances over their straws and then both of them couldn't help themselves, they burst out laughing simultaneously.

They laughed, and for Ronnie it felt good. It was the first time she had laughed in days, and had not thought about all the things she had to face. For Nikko, it was startling. He realized he loved her laugh, and would like to hear her do that more often. Like last summer, he realized there was something about this girl who made him want more than just a roll in the hay. But, he couldn't think of that now.

"Ronnie, I'm sorry about earlier." She just shook her head, and looked at him. "I know I can be a flirt, but I was just trying to make you jealous. And for the life of me, I don't know why!" he told her. *Honesty. How different that felt.*

She gave him a quizzical look and then smiled softly. "It's okay," she shrugged, trying to brush it off like it was nothing. "I know what you . . ." and her words were interrupted by Linda and the screen door again, but this time she carried a large tray laden down with food.

Nikko wondered what she was about to say, but thought better of asking her to finish it. He somehow knew it wouldn't have been something he wanted to hear. She had her long awaited food, and he didn't want to spoil the joviality of her current mood.

Both of their laughter slowly trickled off as Linda set the tray between them. Nikko handed her a fifty dollar bill, and told her to keep the change, and she nodded politely and walked away, a sad regretful smile on her face.

Ronnie couldn't wait any longer, and neither could Nikko. They dug into the feast set before them. Ronnie grabbed the paper basket containing a pile of the aromatic ribs. Her mouth was watering as she sunk her teeth into the most delicious ribs she had ever eaten. She couldn't help the groan of pleasure that escaped her lips as the food slid around in her mouth, and she swallowed her first bite.

Nikko loved watching her eat. She dug right in, and paid no mind to the barbecue sauce on her fingers, or the little bit that dribbled just past her bottom lip. He shook his head and reached for his sandwich as she nabbed the onion rings, and popped a smaller one into her mouth.

"Oh God! Now this is good," Ronnie moaned not faking anything this time.

"Are we doing that again?" he teased. He set down his sandwich which was quite good, and reached for her French fries.

"I can't help it! Nikko. These are really good," she said biting into another pork rib. "And stay away from my fries," she warned around her mouthful of food while shaking her rib at him.

He laughed and held up his hands in mock surrender but couldn't help adding, "Or what?"

She just laughed, took another bite, and they ate for a while in companionable silence. Good food seemed to have brightened her mood. After her onion rings were half gone, and half her ribs, she pushed the containers away and reached for the French fries. He finished his sandwich, and enjoyed just watching her while he sipped his milkshake.

"Try them," she offered. "I'm all done with them."

He normally didn't eat greasy fried food, but the smell, and her words earlier had him curious. He picked up a large onion ring sinking his perfect white teeth into it. They were great. The flavor of the crispy batter and the sweet Spanish onion exploded in his mouth. He finished it while she smothered her French fries in ketchup, and he wrinkled his nose at the gooey mess. He had never liked ketchup masking the taste of his food.

"Don't knock it," she teased, lifting a smothered French fry to his face. Food from her hand, he couldn't resist, and opened his mouth just enough to take a small bite, but she still had to reach to get the food there.

Ronnie's mouth suddenly went dry as Nikko's eyes flashed and dared her to feed him the fry; the man was just too damn sexy for his own good. He couldn't go ten minutes without flirting. She waved the French fry in his face daring him to take it from her.

He saw the glint of mischief in her brown eyes. She squinted just a bit before she put the fry to his mouth, and pulled back before he could bite it.

"Tease," he whispered huskily.

She smiled in return, and brought the French fry close again. But this time, just as she pulled back he took her hand, grabbing it in his own as he guided it to his mouth. Her hand trembled under his pull, and her air left her, as he took the fry into his mouth all the way to her finger tips, just barely biting the tips. It sent shock waves through her. She stopped resisting him, and relaxed as he then licked a dollop of ketchup off of her finger. She literally shivered despite the heat of the day, as her pussy clenched in response to the sight of his tongue. He licked it, sucked it, and when her finger was bathed by the warmth of his mouth he slowly released it.

"Delicious," he whispered, drawing his tongue across his lips.

She was speechless, and desire so intense pooled in her. She felt her panties getting wet, and a throbbing ache began to possess her. Looking down at her hands and the finger he briefly sucked on, she shook her head again. She grabbed a wet nap and ripped the package open to finish cleaning her hands, lost in the aftershocks of the sensations he evoked in her. She needed the time to compose her thoughts and regain control of her senses. That, and she was a bit too ashamed by her reaction to look up just now.

Nikko watched the play of emotions flit across her face, from wonder, to shock, and confusion. He would love to know what she was thinking. His next words snapped her out of her delirium.

"Thank you Ronnie, lunch was quite enjoyable," he whispered, not wanting to break the spell of the moment.

Ronnie forced her mind to clear, shook her head and got up.

"I'm done. We better go."

He rose as well but more reluctantly. She was still cleaning her hands with the wet nap as he untangled himself from the picnic bench.

"Yes, Ma'am. Let's get you home," he assured her when she began to move.

He tossed the remains of their late lunch onto the tray, dumped it into the closest trash can, and then he quickly caught up to her just as she opened her passenger side door. He intended to open it for her, but she had been too quick. When she backed up she backed up right into him, and there was no denying his arousal. The hard long ridge pressed up so intimately along her backside immediately set her body on fire again.

Ronnie turned in his arms and the look on her face took him by storm; it was what he was feeling, shock and desire, and he swept his arms around her pulling her into them, doing what he wanted to do since he first saw her in the Courthouse. The kiss was fierce. There was no foreplay. This was no gentle kiss. He plundered and she opened without hesitation. She wanted this as much as he did.

Beyond the taste of barbecue was Ronnie, all sweet and giving. Her breasts were crushed against his chest, and he could feel the tiny buds hardening as she began to return the kiss. He was getting his fill and his arousal was pushing against her, between them. He felt her hands grasp at his back as she clung to him, her nails digging in and scraping him through the material of his cotton shirt.

He moaned his pleasure, and one of his hands of its own volition strolled downwards to grasp her ass and lower even, to the back of her leg, skin to skin below the mini skirt she wore and then back up again. He gripped her barely covered ass cheek in his hand, gently squeezing the flesh. He groaned again, and she pushed herself against his cock, getting closer. He was about to burst into flames. He had to stop this insanity, his mind told him, but he couldn't resist this woman.

Ronnie was lost. This man haunted many of her dreams, but she never expected to see him again. When his hand began to massage and squeeze her ass, she was almost a goner. The ache she felt was like nothing she had ever felt before. It was insanity, she thought. She couldn't think, couldn't breathe. Then she was pushing him away.

"Stop. Please stop," her voice was near panic as she turned her head away from him.

He felt the loss. Nikko pulled his hands away immediately and took a step back. Her hands were covering her face in shame, and he hated to see her like this. He slowly reached up to pull her hands away. In his mind, she had nothing to be ashamed of.

"Nikko, we can't," she whispered, looking into his eyes hoping to see understanding there.

"Why?" he asked, needing to hear the explanation but afraid of it at the same time. He knew what she was going through, but he could provide her support, comfort, and be by her side if she would let him. He waited for her answer.

"Nikko," she sighed, knowing he wasn't going to be put off. "I'm not in a place right now to start something." When he started to shake his head, she went on. "Listen, we can't do this. That's it. Nikko, please don't do that again, I just can't. These charges, Gary, my mom, I just need to focus on this right now. I won't have my head in the game, and it's not fair to you or me. Please try to understand," she asked, slipping her hands out of his. Especially because she knew she would just be another notch on his bedpost. With this man it would matter to her, she hated to admit to herself. When he remained mute staring down at her in confusion, she turned and got into the car.

Nikko knew she was facing a lot, but he also knew she didn't have to face it alone. He wanted to help, to be there. He didn't know why, but he felt it was the right thing to do. He knelt and touched her cheek. He could see tears forming there. He felt like such a jerk and didn't want her to think he was all about sex, all about his baser needs. He knew she must going through a gamut of emotions and didn't want to complicate things further for her, but he wanted her to know he would support her decision, for now.

"Ronnie. Please look at me." When she looked at him, eyes shining, he lost a little bit of his heart and the words just came to him. "I'm sorry. I know you must be going through a roller coaster of emotions with what you're facing. I shouldn't have done that. But Ronnie," he took her chin in his hand so she couldn't look away. He wanted her to hear him, really hear him. "There is something between us. Ever since last summer, and you and I both know it. This something is definitely unfinished between us, and it needs to be." When she started to shake her head to deny it, he used his thumb on her cheek to caress it, and added. "I'll give you space. The last thing you need right now is some lecherous fool like me making advances every time you accidentally brush up against me, or vice versa. I want to help you get through this, Ronnie. I will help you if you'll let me. Then, when we get your name cleared, and we will, then maybe we can see what this is between us, see what it really is. Okay?" His eyes searched hers looking for something.

What else could she say? The man was persistent. She doubted there would be a follow through, but right now more than anything, she just wanted to get home. "Okay." The word came out shaky, but it was enough for him for now. He kissed her softly on the cheek, stood up and shut her door.

When he got in, he noticed she her hand on the cheek he kissed. It took his breath away. When he hesitated to start the car, she looked at him. He noticed she wasn't wearing her seatbelt. "Seatbelt?" he asked.

"Oh, that," she laughed nervously, and reached behind her to tug on the strap, and it stuck again.

"Want some help?" he asked leaning over carefully.

"Um, no . . . thank-you," she said as she tugged even harder in vain. Stupid seatbelt, she thought. She didn't think she could deal with another close encounter with Nikko.

He hid the grin that threatened to spread across his face. He reminded himself not to fix that seatbelt for the second time that day. But being sensitive to her needs, he was careful when he reached over to assist her. Cautious not to brush against her, he pushed her hand out of the way gently, and smoothly he pulled the belt loose of its mooring. It slid effortlessly across her chest. Lucky belt. He clicked it into place, and then straightened and did up his own seatbelt. Both he and Ronnie let out a soft frustrated sigh as he started the engine. They were on their way.

Chapter Five

Out . . . on Bail

The black Escalade skimmed down the highway going precisely nine miles over the speed limit and a very angry Andreas Marino was at the wheel.

"Anything yet?" he snapped, clenching his jaw in frustration.

"Nothing," Giovanni replied from the shotgun position, putting his phone back in his phone case and clipping it onto his belt. He was nervous as hell. Nearly four hours ago their brother picked up the girl to bring her home. It should have been an hour's drive tops. His hand reached up to push a stray lock of dark hair out of his face. His brother Andreas was angry. He was worried.

"You?" Andreas asked, glancing in the rearview mirror at his younger brother, practically a mirror image of himself, only seven years younger at twenty-eight years of age.

"Nope. Not a thing. His cell is dead or off," answered Blaze yawning in the back seat, trying to get comfortable in the cramped quarters for someone six foot tall. All the brothers were six foot, or more.

"Hell. I knew something was up. He offered to handle this a bit too quickly. It's not like him to volunteer for the hearings. You sure nothing went on between him and the girl last summer?" Andreas was pissed. Nikko, his youngest brother by nearly nine years, was the most reckless, the one who had to be reined in at times. This case was just too big, too important. Fuck! He should have handled it himself. But when Nikko offered, it had taken him by surprise. He thought the talk he had with him a week ago, might have sunk in. That he was willing to learn all the avenues of the business, and not just what he considered the exciting stuff.

"Calm down, biggie," Blaze rumbled from the back seat. "He and Ronnie never. He told me so." Blaze was the serious one in the family, the one who never exaggerated. He was closest to Nikko, being not quite two years apart in age. He was also the peacekeeper in the family when the brothers became over heated. He was the one who could be counted on to get Nikko to toe the line when it was needed, and usually settled the disputes between them all.

"The police sergeant I spoke with said they left the station around one o'clock, but he wasn't sure because he saw Nikko talking to someone for a while. They may have stopped to get something, gas up, eat, who knows. He'll get her there."

Andreas just grunted. Blaze was probably right, but still. He should have called or sent a text. He should have kept his damn phone charged. God, he just hoped everything was okay.

"He should have driven her straight home. Her mother and friends are blowing up my phone. Christ! Why doesn't he just do what he's told!" he slammed his palm down on the steering wheel, and turned off the highway onto State Road Fifty only fifteen minutes from the girl's mother's house."

Gio shifted uncomfortably in his seat. He knew to keep quiet when Andreas was on one of his tears about Nikko.

"He'd better be at Lou's place when we get there. He'd just damn well better," Andreas spoke grimly, as his phone notification indicated he had yet another text, probably from the girl's mom again.

He grabbed his phone and gave it to Gio. Just three years younger than him at thirty-two. Gio was fiddling with the phone, and finally read the message to him. Gio smiled and let out his held breath. "What's it say?" Andreas commanded.

Gio half turned to include Blaze in his announcement. "It's Louisa. She says they finally called. Had a flat tire, and just had it changed at a garage on Forty-One. Phone was dead like we thought. They waited for the tow-truck, and called from the garage. He will be dropping her off within the next half hour or so."

Andreas let out a sigh of relief. He didn't want to lose this bounty. He wanted the girl to wait for her day in court, and do what was expected of her. They had a lot of their own money tied up in this one. A favor to Victor. He was still pissed at Nikko though. Making the mother wait, not calling. His notification went off again.

Gio read, "They stopped for lunch too, she says. She wants to know if we are still coming." Andreas didn't answer so Gio continued. "Are we still coming?" he asked.

Andreas nodded. "Might as well. We are nearly there anyhow. We can explain the situation to Miss Sears, what's at risk, and Nikko is still not off the hook as far as I'm concerned. And what the hell was he doing on Forty-One? That's the long way!" Gio nodded next to him, and sent the mom a quick text letting her know they were all on their way.

From the backseat, Blaze chimed in his two cents. "Andreas, dude, take it easy on him. It could have happened to any one of us."

"I seriously doubt that. I keep my phone charged and so do you. There is a charger in all the vehicles. No excuses. Taking her out for lunch, and a joy ride. What the hell is that all about?" he shook his head in apparent disgust. "The girl's in serious trouble, and he is taking her out to fucking eat. Can't he think with his head for once?"

Blaze tried to suppress a laugh from the backseat. Andreas looked at him in the rearview mirror eyes narrowing. "Thought you said nothing was going on?"

"Nothing went on . . . *last summer*," he added after a significant pause and laughed again not bothering to keep it in this time. Blaze caught Gio's smirk out of the corner of his eye.

"Shut up," Andreas cautioned his brother when his glance in the mirror told him Blaze was about to make a rude comment about the kind of thinking Nikko liked to do and with what body part.

His face turned pouty. "Hey, I was just going to say maybe she was hungry," Blaze offered, trying to sound innocent. Andreas gave him a look in the rearview mirror that ended all further discussion on that topic. The eldest Marino was most certainly the toughest. Hard and hard to please.

***

When Lou heard the next car pull up, she knew it had to be Veronica. She jumped out of her seat at the kitchen table and headed straight for the door. Jay, Ana, and Monica were all at her heels. The Marinos, who arrived a few minutes earlier, remained where they were sitting in the living room, but Andreas did stand up to peer over their heads out the open door. He recognized his brother's classic black Cutlass in the driveway. He relaxed. Slightly. Figured. One of the company's cars never would have gotten a flat. His tires were puncture proof. It also explained why his phone wasn't charged.

"Veronica, baby. You're home," Lou called and engulfed her daughter in her arms.

"Mom, we were fine," Ronnie muttered breathlessly from within the embrace. When Lou pulled back to look at her daughter, to give her the maternal once over, Ronnie added, "Nikko would have called, but his cell phone battery died. Mine hasn't been charged in days. We called from the garage."

"I know," Lou stated and pulled her in for one more hug before releasing her. "I mean I'm just so glad you're here, you know . . ." Her voice trailed off, unsure of how to finish.

"I know what you mean, Mom," she ducked out of her embrace and steered her mom back into the house.

As Ronnie made her way inside, she was engulfed by Ana, and a very pregnant Monica as well. She thanked them profusely for their help in securing her release.

"Wouldn't have it any other way, baby cakes," Ana muttered against her cheek, and let her go.

She turned around then to face the room full of grim faced Marinos. They stared at her, and then Andreas' voice boomed out over head. "Nikko outside, now."

Ronnie turned to see that Nikko just entered the house, but he gave her a small smile before turning on his heel and heading back outside. She did notice as he turned that his smile quickly disappeared. Apparently the eldest Marino was not too impressed with his baby brother's delivery being four hours delayed.

Ronnie was ushered to a seat in the living room, the recliner Andreas just vacated, and Lou was bringing her a coke. She just made out Andreas' words as the door shut behind them. "What the hell were you thinking?" He hadn't even bothered to lower his voice.

The other Marinos looked around uncomfortably, but no one moved to leave or follow Andreas out. "So . . ." Ronnie started and left her statement unfinished.

Blaze was the first to speak. "Yeah . . ." And he let his sentence go uncompleted too. Gio laughed and it broke the mood, and soon she found herself explaining what transpired again, but all the while wondered how the conversation outside was going.

"You took her to eat, didn't charge your cell, got a flat, and God knows what else. Nikko, it shouldn't have taken you four hours to get here. What the hell?"

"Hey, you told me to talk to the girl. Get some information in case she ran. Places and such she might go. I took the longer route figuring she would be uncomfortable talking to me at first. I was just doing what you told me to do. How was I to know that road would have a ton of construction and I'd pick up a nail?"

"Why would she not want to talk with you?" Andreas's hands raked his hair as he paced the gravel drive.

He immediately seized on the one part of Nikko's explanation that made no sense to him.

Nikko never told his brother about last summer. Shit! And, he wasn't about to go there. "I . . . figured the girl just got out of jail. She might need some time to loosen up. It's maybe twenty, thirty minutes longer."

"Okay, but why stop to eat. You could have gone through a drive through window for Christ sakes." Andreas' wasn't buying this story. He had seen them dance at the wedding, and although Blaze had said nothing transpired, he still wasn't sure.

"Okay," Nikko held up his hands. "Yes, we could have. She was opening up, and then she asked to stop and eat, she saw the barbecue place. What was I going to say? No. The girl was talking." He didn't tell his brother he practically forced her to eat by teasing her with the aromas when he rolled down his window. He would definitely be keeping that little tidbit of information to himself.

Andreas looked at his brother hard. "The phone?"

"The car doesn't have a phone charger. The heat at lunch, outside, must have drained the battery. By that time, we were only MIA an hour and half. How the hell was I supposed to know I'd pick up a nail, and get a flat? Come on bro, you really going to rake me over the coals for this. I was doing my job. We called as soon as we got the Cutlass to the garage. Ronnie offered to help me put the bubble on, but then a tow truck came by. I didn't want to drive her on the bubble, and knew we needed to call so I figured getting the new tire would give me more of a chance to get Ronnie to open up."

Again Andreas looked at his brother hard. It all made sense. It did seem Nikko had been doing the job, circumstances had just gotten in the way. "So, what did you find out?" he asked abruptly.

"I got names of some friends. I got places she hangs out. A cabin her granddad has. That sounded like a likely place. She mentioned loving it there."

"Okay, good. That's good." Andreas nodded. Maybe Nikko had listened to him last week about taking on more responsibility. He nodded at his brother. He'd let him off the hook this time. But, there better not be any more screw ups.

Nikko held up his hands in surrender. "We good?"

"Yeah, we're good. Let's get back in there. Since I'm here, I still need to go over some things with Louisa and . . . Ronnie, is it?" He arched one eyebrow up gauging Nikko's reaction to the girl's nickname.

"Yeah, she likes to be called Ronnie. Only her mom calls her Veronica, I guess."

"Okay, Ronnie it is." Andreas turned on his heel, and Nikko followed him back into the house clapping his hand on his big brother's shoulder.

Just maybe, Andreas thought, his brother was maturing. He liked that thought. After moving here two years ago from New York, he had been partying a little too hard. But maybe things were changing now that he had settled down in his own place, and now that he was working more. Maybe the responsibility of the job was just what he needed. His brother was twenty-seven now, maybe he had been treating him like the kid brother for too long, he thought, as the door shut behind him and all eyes turned towards him.

"All is good," he rumbled.

Ronnie let out a breath she didn't realize she was holding. The man was a taller, stronger looking, older version of Nikko. Very handsome. But very intimidating too. In fact, these two brothers looked the most alike.

"But, we do have some things to discuss, that we didn't get around to Louisa, when you called. So, if you don't mind." He indicated the sofa next to Ronnie.

Lou made her way towards it and sat at the edge closest to her daughter. She took Ronnie's hand in hers. Jay, her husband, came around behind her. A former soldier, tatted up, he looked menacing, but everyone knew what a softy at heart he was.

"Yes, go on," Lou stated, once she was comfortable. She gave Ronnie's hand a reassuring squeeze for good measure. Perhaps to bolster her own confidence, Ronnie wasn't sure.

Andreas didn't sit, but when all was quiet he began. "Okay, so Ana and Monica came up with the twenty-five thousand for the bond. That, of course, is our fee for insuring the bond. We work with a few insurance companies to secure the bond. It was paid, and you will make arrangements, I assume, to pay your friends back because that is forfeited to us. Our fee for arranging the remainder."

"Yes. I understand. I will do what I can to pay them back." Lou's face was grim. Having to borrow this much money from her friends terrified her. She and Jay, newly married, were just starting out, and with what they had going on, what no one else knew yet, not even Jay, well, it would complicate matters even further. But this was her daughter, and she would do whatever it took to get her out of this mess.

"No, Mom. I will," Ronnie interjected. She witnessed the play of emotions across her mother's face. She knew this expense could break her. It made her feel even guiltier for ending up in this situation.

"Honey . . ." Lou interrupted trying to assuage her daughter's fears.

"Mom," Ronnie started firmly.

Then Ana was speaking. "Monica and I were going to do something for your graduation. We talked about it, and we don't want either of you to worry about this." Monica was nodding her agreement.

"No, it's too much," Ronnie stated forcibly. Lou was nodding her agreement. "This is more than a graduation present. Hell, who knows if I'll even be able to graduate now."

"Hush now, Ronnie. We won't hear of it. And of course you will graduate. You completed all the course work, passed the exams. The ceremony is only a formality. I didn't go to mine," she added when she saw Ronnie wince.

"But," she started. She hoped that was true. Still, this much for a gift, she just couldn't accept it. "I . . ."

Andreas interrupted. "Ladies. Why don't you discuss this later? We don't want to keep you, and we just have a few other things we would like to clear up."

The women all stopped talking and looked to him. Ana's eyes narrowed slightly. Something about this man rubbed her the wrong way, Monica's new cousin or not.

"Yes, go ahead," Monica prompted, effectively ending this conversation for now. When the women settled down he began again.

"Okay, so this is how it works. If you go to court, and show up for your case, and do what you are told by your lawyers, no harm no foul. You have your day in court, and hopefully get acquitted."

"Yes, we understand." Jay interjected.

"Good. But, there is more . . . If you don't," Andreas paused, and his blue eyes, so like his brother's, and his cousin Victor's, pierced hers, "your mother loses this house. Do you understand that?"

Ronnie gulped. Her eyes registered panic. Good, he thought. He watched her watching him.

The man held nothing back. His eyes were so much like Nikko's, but icier, fiercer. She nodded. "Anything else?"

Andreas had to give the girl credit. She was tough. She didn't waiver, or look away. Most women did. "Normally, we need collateral, in the amount of the remainder. But, since your mom didn't have it, and Victor's our cousin, we accepted what she had. With the house, and Jay's motorcycle . . ."

"You didn't?" Ronnie asked with astonishment, her head whipping up to peer at Jay. He just shrugged, sheepishly smiling at her, then looked with nothing but love at her mother.

"Yes, he did. Now what you need to know is that if you show up on your court date all is good. You will have your day in court, and hopefully get acquitted. Your mom and your step-father will be able to keep their house and motorcycle. So, you need to listen to your attorneys, and do what they tell you." Andreas paused for a moment and all eyes were still on him. "Now, we work with some insurance companies, and they back our bonds. We have a good name and a good reputation. We want to keep it that way. The bail was a quarter million. Your mom's house and the motorcycle weren't even close to what we needed. But Victor's our cousin. So we took this, and left it there. But if you run," he pointed at her, stared her down with the bluest eyes she had ever seen. "Your mom loses the house, your step-father his motorcycle. I am out 150K. And, I won't be happy. I'll be pissed." The room was quiet despite the number of people in it. "See my brothers?" he indicated the three other Marinos in the room, Gio, Blaze, and Nikko, standing along the kitchen counter, wearing similar cargo pants, similar black t-shirts except Nikko. She turned and looked back at Andreas, and nodded again. "Well, they will be pissed too. And we will come after you. We will find you. And we will bring you straight to jail. No passing go. No collecting anything. *Capisce*?" His eyes narrowed and searched hers. She swallowed again and nodded one more time.

Still staring her down, he indicated the door with a shake of his head, and two of his brothers began to move. He got up, turned, and began to leave. Monica was already standing by the door. He paused to say his goodbye to her.

Patting Monica on her belly, he asked, "So when are these little guys due again?"

Monica shook her head and laughed. "Two months, the doctors want me to go another month at least."

"We can't wait." He smiled down at the beautiful brunette his lucky son of a bitch cousin managed to snag. She was sweet, and loved his cousin to the ends of the earth.

"Victor too," she smiled, reaching up to give her big cousin a hug. "Every time the babies kick, he practically jumps out of his skin."

He smiled fondly at her envying his cousin's good fortune in finding such an angelic soul-mate. "My place this Sunday," he reminded her. "I love it when it is my turn to cook. Gives Aunt Mary a break."

"Nothing spicy, please," Monica chastised rubbing her belly. "That Shrimp Fra Diablo about did me in last time."

"Sure, sure," he laughed as he turned to leave. He was followed out the door by Gio, and Blaze.

"Nikko, out now," he called from the doorway when he noticed Nikko was still rooted to his spot in the living room looking like he was a fixture. Nikko nodded his goodbyes, and followed his brothers out also stooping to give Monica a brief hug.

Ronnie watched Nikko leave, trying to keep the look of disappointment off her face. She had hoped to speak with him one more time before he left.

The door banged shut behind them, and Jay was the first to speak. "That's some family, Mon."

"I know," Monica laughed. "They look tough and menacing, but they are really great. Really!" she added to the silent grim faced group assembled in Lou's living room.

"Don't get me wrong, I am grateful for their help, but that older one has a chip on his shoulder, and I might just have to knock it off," Ana added to the room at large that still remained quiet in the wake of the Marinos. She was pensive. Ronnie turned to the red head, her mom's best friend. Ana was looking at her as well, curiously.

Chapter Six

Worry

Outside, Nikko stood by his brother's Escalade wondering what his brother had to complain about now.

"Nikko, I want you to stay in the area. Get a hotel. I saw one down the road. Check in on the girl tomorrow."

"What?" he asked, completely taken aback by Andreas' request. That was the last thing he was expecting. "You're kidding, right?"

Andreas was no fool. He knew there was more than a passing interest between these two. After sizing them up in the living room, he felt it might work to their advantage having Nikko close by. Nikko looked at the girl like he wanted to eat her, and she did the same. He could tell the girl was no felon, no junkie, no drug dealer, but she was proud. Having Nikko nearby might distract her from having some crazy ideas like trying to prove her innocence on her own.

"Yeah, you ever hear of good cop, bad cop, Nikko. Well, I was just bad cop. Now, you swoop on in and be good cop, *Capisce*? In fact, stay a few days. Pop over, and oh, I don't know, apologize about me being an ass or something. Then get some more info from the girl. Stick close to her. I got a feeling about this one. I couldn't get a good read from her. I don't know if she is a runner or not, but she's proud. The girl wouldn't look away when I tried to stare her down. Tough. Independent streak, I got from her. Sometimes those kinds get ideas. You know what I mean? Get more info. Check in with me every day."

"I've got no clothes." He was still flabbergasted. That was the first thing to come to mind.

Gio laughed and made some off-handed, off-colored comment under his breath that sounded like 'no clothes . . . no problem' that got him the evil-eye from Andreas. Blaze just smiled and nodded knowingly.

"Use the business credit card. Get yourself some things. Get a charger. And here," he stated handing him a manila folder with some papers in it. "File these, let the county cops know what is going on. She is not to leave the state, and I'd prefer it if she would stay in the county."

He turned to his vehicle and opened the door. Once inside, he started the car, and Gio made his way round to the driver side, and got in. Blaze held back, as Andreas rolled up his window.

"Is he kidding?" Nikko asked his brother, the brother not quite two years older than him.

"Nope, he's not. But, it seems like he wants you on point for this case, so don't let him down. You better check in every day. And hey," he added as he reached for the door handle to the rear seats, "What a case?" he teased, gesturing with his hands the old age expression for a stacked lady, "*Poppe!*" he gestured with his hands in front of his chest. "If you're lucky she'll be *stracciamanici.*"

Nikko just shook his head at his brother who wished Ronnie might prove to be insatiable, and gave him a dirty look as Blaze got into the car laughing the whole way. Before he had even taken three steps, he heard the crunch of gravel, and his brother's tires spinning in it. He stopped to give the boys a wave and then began to reach his own car. Looks like he'd be sticking around a few days. Surprisingly, he didn't mind the assignment, as an image of Ronnie's "*poppe*" flashed into his head. He enjoyed the thought just as he heard the door to the house open.

It was Ronnie.

"Hey, I'm glad I caught you before you left," she muttered as she jogged towards his car, her *poppe* bouncing enticingly. The sun was beginning its decline and her hair looked like a halo of gold around her, temporarily blinding him.

"Hey, what's up?" he asked, squinting in her direction. He put his hand against his forehead in mock salute to block out the sun. She came into focus.

"Just wanted to say thanks for the ride, and well, tell you maybe you're not the ass I thought you were," she teased.

She'd think differently if she knew what he was thinking in that moment. He laughed. "Oh, gee thanks. Actually, I'm staying at the hotel down the road for a few days," he told her. Better to let her know ahead of time.

"Why?" she asked curiously, suddenly suspicious.

"Big brother just informed me, actually. I have some papers in this county to file." He held up the folder.

"Those about me?" she asked, peering at the file folder in his hand.

He just nodded gloomily.

"Okay, well bye," she said as he began to turn.

He needed to stop her if just for a moment. "Hey if you don't mind, maybe I'll stop in to say hello while I'm here now and then." He wanted it to appear nonchalant.

She stopped, and turned. From the expression on her face, she wasn't buying it. "Checking up on me?" her eyes searched his face looking for the truth.

Again he nodded. He felt the urge to reach up and touch her hair.

She just shook her head a little sadly and shrugged her shoulders. "Sure. Why not? It beats hanging out with the folks and talking to attorney's all day. Why not?" And with that, she turned again and headed back inside.

Nikko waved to her retreating figure, and when the door closed softly, and she was safely tucked inside, he headed to his car. He had some shopping to do. He also needed to get a charger for his phone.

***

Ronnie woke up Saturday morning to the sounds of birds outside her bedroom window. Missy, her mom's Golden Retriever, sat at her feet watching her from the side of the bed, big brown eyes waiting for a sign of movement. Ronnie allowed her arm to slip out from under the covers. "Missy!" she exclaimed softly, and the loyal dog was there licking her fingers.

In the joy of the moment, she almost forgot the charges she was facing. This had been her dog from childhood. Missy was getting old, and she enjoyed each precious moment with her.

It was still early, the sun just rising. It was quiet, but she knew her mom would be up, always an early riser. She might as well get up and enjoy some quiet time with her mom.

Plus, Missy's tail was wagging furiously, and if she didn't get out of bed soon, the sweet dog she had gotten for her twelfth birthday would give her away.

"Okay, sunshine. I'm getting up." The dog yipped happily as she sat up swinging her legs to the side of the bed. When Ronnie's feet hit the floor, Missy was doing circles in the small space of her bedroom. Ronnie shook her head. Always happy. The simple life of a dog. If only it could be that easy. It seemed the weight of the world was on her shoulders despite her fairly decent night's sleep.

Her mom's friends stayed late, providing moral support, trying to keep her and her mother distracted from their worries. She slept well despite her circumstances because it had been the first night in a real bed in quite a few days, longer if you considered the cruise ship's bed. The jail cell had not been conducive to sleeping with the night sounds and her own worries, and the cruise she had taken had not been very restful.

Her long t-shirt she slept in still on, Ronnie grabbed a pair of gym shorts from the top drawer of her dresser, and slipped into them before venturing into the hall. Missy still hot on her heels. A glance across the living room told her she had been correct. Her mom was sitting on the sun porch drinking her coffee, watching the sun rise over the horizon. She shook her head sadly at the worry she must be causing her mother and slipped into the bathroom before she faced her.

In the bathroom, Ronnie took care of her most pressing need, brushed her teeth, and finger combed her hair. All her toiletries had been confiscated by the police and were locked up as evidence. She was told most of the items would be returned to her, but that hadn't happened yet, and wasn't likely to happen anytime soon. She would need to make a stop at Walmart and get some things, she thought dismally, as she raked her waves into some kind of order. It was the best she could do. She didn't want to go through her mom's room to her ensuite bathroom and risk waking up her step dad.

Well, time to face the music, she thought. She reluctantly turned the nob, and Missy was waiting patiently for her. A glance told her that her mother was still waiting outside. Ronnie was shocked to see a cigarette in her hand. She had quit years ago, and Ronnie knew it was because of her and the stress of the whole situation, that her mom apparently picked up the habit again. The guilt pressed in on her. Not wanting to be caught catching her, she coughed and crossed to the kitchen not looking her mom's way. She made for the coffee pot, a mug already set aside for her, and prepped the coffee just the way she liked it, light and sweet.

From the corner of her eye, she could see her mom had crushed out her cigarette and stashed the cigarettes in a side drawer of an end table along with the ashtray. Ronnie took a long sip of the delicious brew. She loved her mom's coffee, so much better than the concoction served in prison with one creamer and one packet of sugar.

She gave her mom another moment before "seeing" her. Her mom waved at the air to disperse the cigarette smoke, and took a sip of her coffee. Turning towards the Florida room, Ronnie "saw" her mom, nodded and began to approach.

Her mom was out of her seat opening the sliding glass doors. "How'd you sleep, sweetie?" She spoke the words softly. Jay was still sleeping. He and Victor, when he'd shown up to bring Monica home, had a few drinks. Monica had done the driving.

"Good actually," Ronnie muttered, pressing a kiss to her mother's cheek and couldn't help but wrinkle her nose.

Lou saw and blushed, but made no comment other than to tell her to sit. Lou also managed to give her a sheepish smile.

Ronnie nodded and sat next to her mom who placed her hand over hers in what was meant to be a comforting gesture. Ronnie sighed and looked at her mom's eyes noticing they were quite puffy. She turned her hand over under her mom's and grasped them, squeezing them and bringing warmth back into them.

"Mom, I love you! Thank you for doing this all for me." She made her voice upbeat, confident, trying to restore her mother's usual confidence.

"What else would I do? You're my heart."

Ronnie saw the tears welling in her mother's eyes. Of all that was going on, seeing this pain, this worry on her mom's face practically undid her. Her mom did not look well at all. Her skin was paler than usual, she'd lost weight, and her eyes had dark circles around them.

"Mom," Ronnie chastised, "I am so grateful. Really, I am, but I really need you to be strong for me. I need you to take care of you. I am innocent. And, I will clear my name," she stated with fervor. "But if I see you sad, crying, Mom, I just can't see you that way knowing I have put this fear in you. The smoking? Please!" she begged her mom with plaintive eyes.

Ronnie's plea touched Lou. She was trying hard, but old fears resurfaced. She bought the cigarettes yesterday. Had only lit two, thinking they would help calm her nerves. Help her relax. She hadn't even inhaled them or touched them to her lips. She wouldn't dare. But it had been the need to have a sense of calmness that had driven her to buy them. They hadn't helped in the least.

"You're right doll face." Lou shook her head. Although she was terrified for her daughter, and her future, she wasn't worried at all about the house, or the money. She could start over. Again. She's done it many times, but a mother didn't want a child to have to go through these struggles. And now she had another child on the way. No one knew yet. She wasn't far along. It was also the reason she hadn't really smoked the cigarettes, but she wasn't willing to share that news just yet.

The morning she had gotten the call from Ronnie at the police station, before Ronnie had called, she had taken a pregnancy test. Thirty eight and a new mother again! Her mind reeled. She looked forward to telling Jay that night. And even though he would be shocked at first considering his history, she knew once the shock passed, maybe even a little guilt, he would be over the moon with happiness. He would love this child, and worship the second chance at a family he had been given.

A glance at the drawer where she hid her stash of contraband, made her guilt return even more. She needed to take care of herself and this child. Ronnie was right about that. She needed to take care of herself for Ronnie, and this new baby. For Jay. She got up and opened the drawer, grabbed the cigarettes and lighter and threw them in the trash.

"It was a stupid momentary weakness. Don't tell Jay, please. He despises smoking," she winked at her daughter conspiratorially. "I won't lapse again."

She gave her mom a smile. Her tone was stronger and just that gave Ronnie hope. She needed the resilient woman her mother had always been by her side in this fight. Her mom had always been a rock her whole life and she needed that more than ever.

"I need you to fight, Mom," she voiced her concerns. "I need your faith, and I need your strength. I hate that I am causing you this worry. But, I hate to say this; I need you now more than ever."

"I'm here for you. Always. And as for my faith, and strength, you have that too baby girl!" Steel was in Lou's voice now, and as the words left her mother's lips, Ronnie was engulfed in her embrace and it was like iron.

Momentary weakness gone, she told herself. Strength and courage were what they both needed now. Her daughter would not have to ask her twice.

Chapter Seven

Why Can't We Be Friends?

Nikko was up early, but waited until nine o'clock before leaving the hotel. The place he was staying at was near Ronnie's and her mom's, and a nearby bakery was convenient. He didn't want to show up empty handed. His momma had always told him never to pop in on someone without a friendly gesture.

Leaving the Italian bakery, his box of goodies by his side, he was surprised at how much he was looking forward to seeing Ronnie again. It hadn't even been a day.

Nikko laid on the accelerator pushing his classic Cutlass just slightly above the speed limit in his haste to get to Ronnie's house. He pulled into the gravel driveway, the tires crunching and announcing his arrival. As he got out of the car, he saw Louisa peek through the curtains, and she had the door open for him by the time he reached it.

"Well, this is a surprise," she called out in greeting, eyeing him suspiciously, especially the white boxed baked goods.

Nikko gave her a flash of white teeth and his most winning smile. "I told Ronnie I'd stop by while I'm in town. I am stuck here until Monday or Tuesday," he answered her simply.

Louisa gave him another guarded look, but opened the door wider allowing him entrance. "Ronnie's in the shower, but she should be out shortly. I'll put on a fresh pot of coffee. We are expecting her lawyer, Ronald Stimson, later on this morning."

"Oh! He's good." Nikko recognized the name. Knew he was an excellent defense attorney from one of the finest firms in Tampa, and one of the most expensive. His eyes widened in surprise.

"He's somewhat related to one of my dearest friends," she offered in answer to his unasked question while she began to set up the coffee pot for round two. Nikko took a seat on one of the stools at the kitchen island setting down his box of goodies. He heard the shower running and would have to make nice with Ronnie's mom. But the sound of the water running, and knowing Ronnie was in there naked, had his mind wandering.

"When will he be here?" he asked, trying to make casual conversation.

"In about an hour." She glanced at the wall clock in the kitchen as she set out the cups while the coffee brewed. His thoughts kept flying to the bathroom. He was having a hard time concentrating, and that wasn't like him. Lou spoke, suddenly interrupting his shameful thoughts.

"What are you really doing here, Nikko?" she demanded. The edge in her voice threw him momentarily off guard, that and his wayward thoughts.

He was at a temporary loss, but quickly recovered. "Really?" he sighed, giving her a sheepish grin. At her nod, he continued. "I have to submit some papers to the court here in the county regarding this case. And here," he used his finger to indicate her home with a circular gesture, "Because I genuinely like your daughter, and thought she could use another friend around, distract her. Keep her company, give moral support. We met last summer, you know," he gently reminded her.

Lou looked at him sharply. "I don't know about the distraction part, but yes, she could use all the *FRIENDS* and support she can get right now." Nikko clearly got the message. "Are you watching her for business purposes, too?" she added without a pause.

The woman was sharp. He'd give her that. "Yes." He, too, answered without pause.

Honesty was the best policy. He didn't want to make an enemy of this woman especially since he wasn't sure about his feelings for her daughter.

"When my brothers and I post bond for someone, we do like to stick around for a while. See the client's routine, hangouts. That sort of thing. But, Mrs. Russell, I really am here this morning as a friend. She is more than just business. I like her. Ronnie will go stir crazy staying put, doing nothing but worrying. If I can help to keep her spirits up, then that's what I'd like to do."

Lou's eyes narrowed, but she nodded, and gave him a small smile. She turned to retrieve the pot of coffee, and then poured him a cup.

"Okay, Nikko Marino. I agree she could use a friend, someone to keep her mind off all this, all the time. But she, and I want to be clear, needs only friends right now. I don't think it would be fair to you or her to complicate matters if you know what I mean?" Her eyes searched his for something. Understanding.

He took her pointed reference and stress on the word friend for a second time. "I understand, Mrs. Russell. I don't want to complicate the situation for her. I really don't."

Just as he finished speaking he heard a door open. Lou looked past him, eyes widening, and made a shooing gesture with her hands. He couldn't help but turn to look behind him. And there she was, dripping wet, in nothing but a towel, a rather small towel. God help him, he thought, he definitely wanted to be more than friends with Miss Ronnie Sears. He was glad a rather tall counter separated him from the girl's mother.

"Oh!" Ronnie gasped in surprise. "I didn't think anyone was here. Jay left for work, and . . . oh, I'll just be out in a jiff," she responded, holding her towel closely, water dripping over her shoulders from her unwrapped hair, down her throat and chest.

He could see the rivulets of water, wanted to trace the same path down her skin with his tongue. He was all of a sudden very thirsty as she quickly ducked out of sight into her room, and shut the door.

Nikko reluctantly turned from the vision that just vacated his sight; he kept his eyes downcast, and reached for his cup of coffee. He took a slow sip. When he did look at Lou, her eyes were wide, and she was watching him closely, very closely. He felt the heat creep up his face. He couldn't hide it.

"Well," he offered, drawing out the one syllable word uncomfortably. He tried to add a bit of humor to the word by exaggerating it.

"Friends," she reminded him, narrowing her almond shaped brown eyes.

"Yes," he reiterated his promise, felt himself blush under her scrutiny. "Friends." Very good friends! Intimate friends, he hoped despite Lou's advice to the contrary. He wanted to be a lot more than friends. He lifted his coffee to her, and took a sip noticing she hadn't poured herself a cup.

"Not having any?" he asked.

"No, I had one this morning. I'm trying to cut back. But Veronica will have one with you, I'm sure." Her tone was slightly sarcastic. Then more kindly, "She drinks the stuff all day. But, I think I will have one of these," she said pulling the box of goodies towards her and inspecting the contents. She pulled out a massive bear claw confection. "I shouldn't though," she looked down to her trim waistline.

Nikko laughed. Women were so concerned about weight gain. "Please, Mrs.

Russell. You aren't one of those women, are you? Worried about every calorie?"

He was trying to tease her, lighten the mood until Ronnie returned, then added.

"Although when I had lunch with your daughter yesterday, I noticed she could really pack it in."

Lou couldn't help but laugh at the eagerness on this young man's face. She could tell he was smitten with her daughter. She just hoped her warnings were heeded and he proceeded with caution. Although very suspicious of the young man's intentions, especially after last summer, she knew her daughter needed some friends her own age. So despite her misgivings, she wouldn't voice her concerns any further. Ronnie would need friends. Even if it was just someone to vent to, or distract her. Goodness knows this young man was quite good looking, and charming, and although he might prove to be a little too distracting, she mused, he might be an additional support for her daughter. She wouldn't deny her that. And, Ronnie was grown after all. She made good decisions, well most of the time. Gary was another matter altogether.

"Ronnie has always had a good appetite. Lucky girl, burns calories while sleeping. She's always been blessed with a great metabolism. But, she has always been very active and athletic. She runs, hikes, and is always keeping busy. I, on the other hand, have a desk job." She smiled at the young man. Lou picked up the flaky pastry, and bit into the tender layers. "Mmm," she moaned. "Delicious."

"Enjoy it," he laughed at her simple pleasure. "I could bring more of those tomorrow," he teased, as she stuffed her face with the pastry for a second time.

Lou chewed and swallowed, moaned her pleasure, and couldn't resist adding, "If you show up with these again tomorrow, I'll slam the door in your face."

He laughed liking this side of Mrs. Russell very much. He now knew where Ronnie got her sharp tongue, and quick wit.

Ronnie wasn't much longer. Both he and Louisa had finished their pastries and he his coffee when she emerged from her bedroom looking fresh and clean. She wore denim shorts, and from the way they stretched across her rear he could tell they were probably her mothers who didn't have the curves her daughter had in that particular area. She also wore a simple black tank top. Her hair was towel dried, and lay in long wavy layers framing her oval face, the few pinkish highlights looking darker when wet.

"This is a nice surprise," she said as she approached and her mom poured her a coffee. Her smile was pure mischief as she looked from her mom and back to Nikko again. Mother and daughter exchanged looks, Ronnie looking all innocent, and her mother all-knowing. She peered into the box of pastries and selected a rainbow cookie and put it on a napkin before her.

"I mentioned I'd pop in," he laughed indicating her mom with a nod of his head. His eyes said back me up on this.

She laughed before answering. "Yes, yes you did. Really, Mom. Should have mentioned it, sorry." She gave her mom her innocent smile, and then turned to Nikko, "Too bad my lawyer's on his way. Should be here in thirty minutes or so," she added before sinking her little pearl white teeth into the small cookie. "Delicious," she pronounced before taking another bite.

"Your mom was telling me," he put in, and continued. "I have heard of him. Very good." He wanted to offer her encouragement. "A lucky break he is family to your mom's friend. He is in demand. He actually got a few of our clients off, but pricey." From Ronnie's reaction he could kicked himself. Definitely not the right thing to say after last night's ordeal. From Lou's expression as well, it appeared to be a double faux pas on his part. Lou in fact, blanched, and Ronnie's head swung to her mother.

"Don't worry about it Veronica," her mom cautioned, giving him a sharp unappreciative look.

Ronnie was about to speak. She'd forgotten about the attorney's fees. Hells bells, one more thing to weigh on her mom, and her. She closed her mouth, not wanting to worry her mom or upset her. She looked pale, and again

Ronnie couldn't help but notice it looked like she'd lost weight recently.

"Veronica, one day at a time. Now, if you'll excuse me, I have some paperwork to take care of in my room. I'll let you visit with Nikko until your lawyer gets here." Before either could protest, she was half way out of the room making a hasty retreat. The pastry was about to come up, and the last thing she wanted her daughter and her friend to see was her throwing up.

"Shit, Ronnie. I'm sorry," he quickly apologized. "I wanted to provide support, be a good friend, and it seems I upset you and your mother by mentioning the cost. I really didn't mean to do that." Nikko's face showed his concern.

Not wanting it to spoil their visit, she shrugged nonchalantly trying to ease his worry. "Don't worry about it," she smiled popping the rest of the rainbow cookie into her mouth. Nikko smiled back, and when he smiled at her like that, her stomach fluttered. Damn, he was just too good looking.

Over her coffee, Ronnie eyed her visitor. Dressed down in jeans and a simple grey t-shirt, he looked delectable. His blue eyes popped and sparkled against his tan face. The man was beautiful, she thought again. What he saw in her petite, overly curvy stature, she would never know.

"Fo'getta bout it," she added letting him off the hook. Ronnie couldn't help but laugh at her horrible imitation of a New York accent. They both did.

Nikko sputtered over the last sip of his coffee. "That's bad, Ronnie, real bad. Good thing you didn't take up acting," he teased. The tension evaporated.

"Come on. Let's go out in the yard. I hate being indoors and cooped up," she stated as she got up from her stool. He had no choice but to follow.

It was still early, the breeze off the water kept the heat of the Florida summer at bay. Missy followed them outside, and Ronnie was throwing a purple something, that resembled a monkey of some sort, a chew toy. He couldn't tell.

He stood beside her and watched her interact with the aging dog. "Hey, I'm sorry about earlier. If it's any consolation, this guy is good. He has one of the highest success rates in Tampa of any defense attorney. And, I'm sure being almost family through your mom's friend, you'll get a great discount." He gave her his boyish innocent smile, and she returned it.

"You're probably right. Don't worry about it. I guess I'll cross that bridge when I get to it. I'm glad Ana was able to get him to represent me." Missy chased the purple mess, and came loping back. Ronnie threw it again, and continued. "Thanks for coming though. I feel horrible for my mom, and every time we are alone together the guilt just gets to me."

"Glad to be a distraction, milady," he bowed and she laughed at the noble gesture.

"I just need time to not think about it sometimes too, you know?"

"That's what working on my car was when my folks died," he offered softly, taking the purple monkey from her and throwing the next pitch.

She could still see the pain there. He did understand. But when their hands touched, the current passing through them was instant. He stepped back.

Ronnie made eye contact with him, knew he felt this energy too, but was trying to restrain himself as her breath nearly left her.

"I'm sorry you lost them so young, but I'm glad you understand." She took a step closer to him, needing to be near his energy again.

His heart rate picked up with each step. What he saw in her eyes thrilled him.

"It's nice to have a friend who understands," she practically whispered.

"A friend, Ronnie. I like that," he teased as she got closer. "Hey, can we be friends?" he joked softly, using the title of an old song as her body came to within an inch of his. He knew that word was meant to remind him of something, but only God knew what it could be in that moment.

She was so close, and it just seemed so natural to take her into his arms, and that's what he did. Forgotten were her mother's words. Forgotten were her pleas from yesterday. When she looked up to him within his embrace, he bent to press a kiss to her forehead. But when she lifted her face higher, the kiss they shared was as natural as breathing. Both of them held the passion in check but it was there, under the surface, waiting to be unleashed.

Chapter Eight

The Best Defense... Is a Good Offense

Nikko and Ronnie were still in the backyard, talking at this point, when Ronald Stimson showed up in his silver Lexus, parking next to the classic Cutlass, and behind Louisa's Audi.

He recognized the girl from her mug shot, and Ana's description. He waved at the young couple sitting at a picnic bench in the backyard. She'd have to do something about her hair, and her clothes, he thought, as he continued on to the front door of the small house. The young couple had risen and it seemed would greet him inside entering from the rear although it appeared they were in no rush.

Louisa Russell opened the door, and he remembered the well-endowed brunette from the reception his mother-in-law threw for Teddy, and his new bride upon their return from Las Vegas.

Ronald greeted Louisa warmly, but with a professional demeanor. "It's nice to see you again Mrs.

Russell, albeit I wish it were under better circumstances." He gave her a nod of sympathy.

"Oh, please call me Louisa or Lou, and thank you so much for taking this case, Ronald. We didn't know who to call, and when Ana suggested . . ." she rattled.

"You are quite welcome," he interrupted. "My wife, Ebony, dotes on her baby brother, Teddy, and she'd have it no other way. The whole family adores his wife, Ana, and you are her closest friend. She may not have even married the poor man and put him out of his misery if it weren't for your help I hear." He made small talk as he passed through the open door, and looked around the modest, but comfortable looking home.

Lou was a working woman; she worked day by day, and week by week to get by. Her new husband was a mechanic, worked on airplanes at a local, small airport, and he had only been working there about a year. He turned to face her when she started to speak again.

"Well, no matter why you accepted, we are just thrilled you did. I have heard nothing but great things about you. I feel we really have a chance," she paused looking to see his reaction.

He could hear the fear beneath the surface of her false bravado. He mentally applauded the courage she was attempting to show. A father of four boys himself, he knew what a parent's love and worry meant, and the toll it could take on a person.

When he continued to give her his most professional perusal, she forged ahead.

"And about your fee?" Lou asked getting right to the point.

"Oh, well," he muttered, not expecting her to broach the subject so soon but was spared from answering by the young couple and the dog entering from the sliding glass doors off the living room.

"Mom, I will take care of his fee," Ronnie stated strongly as she led Missy to her bed. Making her way to her attorney, Ronnie extended her arm to shake his hand. He took it, and she shook firmly. The girl was confidant and had an air of strength about her. He felt an instant connection, and despite the clothes, too tight, and the hair, too colorful, he doubted very much that she was a drug dealer, a smuggler. But, it was going to be hard to prove. The evidence was stacked against her. He had his personal assistant fax everything to him about the case before leaving New York yesterday, and he read the file on the airplane and again last night before heading to bed. He couldn't wait to interview her. Hopefully, she would give him some information he could use to begin developing her defense.

"My fee," he started awkwardly.

"I have some savings bonds. Gifts from my grandparents. I've managed not to touch them through college. They are yours, about eight thousand. Then I can make payments, I presume, once I'm working," she stated with firmness, trying to negotiate the matter. He had to smile at her naiveté though she tried to sound worldly.

The young man behind her looked uncomfortable. Familiar too, Ronald thought giving him a once over trying to place him.

"Um, Ronnie," Nikko started and she tossed him an annoyed look over her shoulder to silence him. Nikko placed his hands up and allowed her to take the lead. He was there for support, he reminded himself.

When Ronnie turned back to Mr. Stimson, Nikko just shrugged his shoulders and smiled at Ronald, and that's when he recognized the young man, he was one of the Marinos. His firm used them, Andreas mostly, the older brother, on occasion to do some digging for them. He correctly assumed Marino's Bail and Bonds must have posted her bond, and this young man was her watchdog. But from what he had seen in the backyard, this young couple seemed to be more than casual acquaintances.

The oldest brother was smart. Hopefully, this younger one was as well, and did not mix business with pleasure.

"Ronnie, my friends call me Ronnie too, but at work I go by Ronald. As for my fee, and what Mr. Marino may have been trying to tell you, is I am quite, quite expensive." His repetition of the word had been intended. She would be getting a break, but he wanted to let her know ahead of time this was a serious matter, not to be taken lightly.

Clients tended to be more cooperative when they knew what they were getting, and the worth.

Her false bravado wavered slightly, but nearly a breath later, "How much?"

I usually ask for twenty-five thousand up front for costs. My retainer. As my expenses incur, I begin to bill for my services and my time as I accrue it, and then when I go beyond the retainer, I usually expect similar payments to be forthcoming. My hourly wage is three hundred dollars." He hated to scare the woman, but the proud daughter needed to know these things and the seriousness of the case.

Lou gasped, and her eyes widened.

"I guess we will have to look elsewhere," Ronnie mumbled less confidently, and began to turn away from him.

"No need," he reported when Louisa was about to protest Ronnie's dismissal, "My firm expects each attorney, myself included, to do one pro bono case a year, something big and splashy that will bring us some publicity. Lucky you, I haven't taken my case yet, and sorry, this case is big and splashy."

"What?" Ronnie asked afraid to hope, but not believing all the lucky breaks she was getting so far could extend to free attorney services from a greatly respected defense lawyer. "Can you repeat that?" she asked, fearing she hadn't heard right.

Nikko was behind her; he reached for her hand, took it, and squeezed it reassuringly behind her back. She had heard correctly. He knew Ronald Stimson was a shark. This man fought hard, and knew the law, all the loop holes, and the system. If there were flaws in the case he would find them. Reasonable doubt was all he needed.

Not giving Mr. Stimson a chance to explain, Lou piped in. "Really?" Her stomach had done multiple flip flops, between her nerves and the baby; she didn't think she would be able to deal with the stress of trying to find a decent attorney she could afford. His words had an invigorating effect on her. She felt like she could breathe again.

"Yes, Mrs. Russell. I know it may sound strange under the circumstances, but your timing was lucky." He turned to Ronnie, and added, "But there may be some fees my firm won't condone, and I'd like to have the eight thousand you mentioned as a retainer for those costs." Also, having a nervous young woman with access to that much money was never a good idea.

A thought occurred to Ronnie as she watched her attorney spot the kitchen table and began to head in that direction. She had a puzzled expression. "Not that I'm ungrateful, Mr. Stimson, but since you will be representing me pro bono, why would you need the eight thousand?"

Yes, the girl was quick, he thought. Mr. Stimson set his briefcase on the table slowly and deliberately before answering her. He looked down on her as he got ready to sit. "Well, Ronnie, and is it okay if I call you that?" he asked, looking at her quizzically. At her nod, he continued while pulling out his chair. "We usually do pro bono for people without any means. If the firm sees you have funds they might suggest I reject the case. Also, having eight thousand dollars available to you, worries me, and frankly I'm sure it will worry the Marinos as well."

Ronnie looked sharply to Nikko, and he confirmed her attorney's words. She nodded her acceptance. "Fine, I'll go to the bank this week." Her arms crossed over her chest defensively.

"Good, now please sit, we have a lot to discuss today." He indicated the seat across from him. He placed a pair of glasses from his breast pocket on his face, and popped open his brief case. Taking out quite a large stack of papers in several manila folders, he placed them on the table before him. He closed his briefcase and set it on the floor to make more room for them at the small round table.

Ronnie sat, as did Lou. The attorney looked to Nikko still standing. "Is Mr.

Marino staying?" he asked.

"It's Nikko, and should I leave?" he asked in a tone of innocence. He had been hoping to stay, and hoped no one would ask him to leave. But, Mr. Stimson was too sharp to let something like client-attorney privilege go unnoticed. He didn't miss a trick.

"Honestly, I don't mind," Ronnie looked at her attorney. "I have nothing to hide and I'm innocent. One-hundred percent innocent. And Nikko, is a . . . friend," she added softly.

Mr. Stimson gave them a prolonged look, and lifted an eyebrow at Lou. She simply shrugged her shoulders and nodded. "Well, okay then. That's fine with me, but please sit, Marino. I don't like people towering over me. I often use your brother to do some digging for me, and may call upon him for this case. So, it's fine by me. But this conversation is protected. Understand?" At Nikko's nod, and while he got comfortable, Ronald added, "No interruptions either please." He ruffled through his paperwork and pulled out the police report.

Ronnie saw her mug shot lying on the top, and cringed at the bewildered and frightened expression she wore when that photograph was taken. Remembering that moment, her stomach rolled.

"As to your innocence, well the good news is all the evidence is circumstantial. I can make a case easily that the drugs could have been planted and probably get a jury to buy it. The blood test performed on you showed no signs of drugs. That is excellent, although the prosecution will argue that dealers don't normally do drugs."

Lou nodded, and reached over to pat her daughter's hand. She was relieved her daughter hadn't experimented as many high school and college students did. "I've always stressed to my daughter the dangers of alcohol abuse and the dangers of drugs. Even marijuana can be a gateway drug and lead people down the wrong path." Stimson was scribbling away on a yellow legal pad.

"Good, I may call you on the stand to testify to that. We will need the names of several people to use as character witnesses."

Ronnie gave him the names of the few friends she had made locally, Margaret and Brad. She also gave him the names of some professors, and friends back in Maine who could attest to her drug free lifestyle.

Her attorney wrote a bit more after she was finished then asked, "Ronnie, have you ever used narcotics?"

"No, never." She was firm.

"Will pictures surface showing you in an ill light. Facebook? Instagram? Twitter? Drunk, using drugs, smoking cigarettes, hanging out in places with less than respectable people."

Ronnie's stomach lurched. She nodded.

"What kinds of pictures?" he asked. "I need to know. The prosecution will find them, probably has them already, and I'll need to find a way to explain them without putting you on the stand."

"I'm not worried about going on the stand," Ronnie interjected defensively. "And as to your question, I think there may be one or two pictures of me drinking, hanging out around a campfire with some friends, and there may be people in the background smoking."

"May be? And smoking what?" he asked, sharpening his focus on her.

"Yes, smoking pot. It's far enough in the distance that we could argue it is just cigarettes. But, I don't smoke pot, and I have never smoked a cigarette in my life. Yes, I have had a drink or two on occasion, at parties, but I respect myself and my body and what I put into it."

"Okay, Ronnie. I get it. But on the stand, you can't blow your top and get defensive like you just did, juries don't like it. It makes you appear belligerent, rude, and angry. Let me worry about what to argue and make the decision on whether or not to put you on the stand. Plus, the police can simply find these people in the pictures, and ask them. If they have any arrests for drug use, well, forget about it. That will look bad, very bad for you that you hang out with people convicted of drug use."

As he talked, Ronnie knew this route wasn't a good one. She had to tell him. "Shit, Joey, my ex-boyfriend's friend, was the one in the background. And he was once arrested for possession. It was a small amount, but . . ." she trailed off realizing how that would look for her. Guilt by association.

"Not good," he confirmed. "I'd say remove the picture, but I'm sure they already have it. The prosecution had two days last week, and with young people they go straight to social media to begin their search. Teens incriminate themselves constantly with the stuff they put on the net. On Instagram, Facebook, and Twitter." He shook his head at the stupidity of youth. Even with all the warnings and precautions, kids these days revealed way too much via the internet.

He shuffled through some more papers, and pulled out another report. "Let's talk about the drugs the police found inside your scuba equipment and snorkeling equipment. How did it get there do you think? Their case revolves around this. If there is any plausible way to explain it and provide proof to back it up, they will have to throw out the case. It could have been planted by anyone, cruise ship personnel, customs, wherever you had your tank, and equipment serviced, a drug dealer, anyone, but can you think of someone in particular."

This is where Ronnie didn't hold back. "Absolutely. It was Gary. I know it without a doubt," she added.

All eyes turned to her. Mr. Stimson was looking at her with new interest. Nikko was shocked by this new bit of information. He had assumed someone she didn't know had planted the drugs. The scumbag.

"How do you know it was this Gary fellow? I see no mention of him in the reports other than he was your boyfriend and the two of you shared a cabin. No drugs were found in his belongings." Mr. Stimson shut his file, and picked up his pen.

"Gary Caldwell. My ex," she stated vehemently looking downcast and away from Nikko. "I know it was him because when the police were approaching, and the people in line began to murmur their suspicions because there were so many officers and custom officials with dogs, I turned to Gary, and he looked terrified. He was already backing away."

"Really?" Her attorney's voice sounded pleasantly surprised. "Tell me about

Gary?"

"I told this to the police, but they didn't seem interested," she confessed.

"They wrote nothing about that in the police report. That I find strange too. I will most certainly be calling the prosecutor today about that. What else should I know about Gary?" Mr. Stimson didn't sound pleased that the police ignored putting this information in their report of their initial interview with Ronnie. He was taking notes while she spoke.

"Well, he does smoke pot, or did. And his family is connected. They don't know about him smoking pot on occasion though. Well, not that I know of. But, I have seen him do it a few times. I'd thought he stopped. In fact, I had demanded he stop. It was one of the reasons we broke up last year. His grades were slipping and I suspected he was using again this year. I nearly ended it, but he swore he wasn't using right before our trip. But, I'd noticed these last few months he had been sleeping more, missing classes, in fact he never would have graduated without me."

"You didn't cheat?" her attorney asked, looking up from his pad of paper.

"No! I wouldn't do that. But before tests and exams I'd review with him, orally tell him what I knew and what I thought would be on the test. He scraped by. I'd also read his papers and give him suggestions."

"Okay, this is good. The prosecution can of course argue you were a mule for your lover."

Nikko winced at those words, but tried to hide it when Ronnie looked over at him briefly before returning her attention to her attorney.

"Has he been arrested that you know of? I need his address, and the location of his hang outs."

Ronnie gave him the information. To her knowledge, he had never been arrested. Her attorney asked about Gary's friends and family as well. He was there over two hours and time flew as he quizzed her more about Gary and his friends. He took copious notes, his pen flying across the yellow legal pad.

Nikko, too, was listening quietly filing it all away so he could report in with his brother. This Gary Caldwell sounded like a real ass, and he cringed at the thought of this guy being Ronnie's lover. The slime ball, pot head, let his girl take the rap for his stupid attempt at scoring some cheap drugs and having his own little stock pile. Fucking ass bag. What a no good mother fucker!

Nikko gave Ronnie a supportive smile when the attorney asked about her spending habits. Wanting to know about them in case the prosecution discovered she had more money than she could explain through college loans and scholarships, and her tutoring. When she told him about her frugal lifestyle, he seemed quite satisfied.

"Well, I think I have enough of a start here," Mr. Stimson concluded as he began to pack up his papers, reaching for his briefcase.

Lou got up, and thanked him as he rose. Nikko and Ronnie followed suit both standing as well, stretching their legs after sitting so long. Mr. Stimson clicked shut his briefcase.

"If there is anything else you think of, call me." He handed her a card with his office number, and his private cell phone number circled. "The best defense, Ronnie, is a good offense. And you have given me a lot of information. One, I'm going to hire someone to go to Maine and dig into this Gary Caldwell. Two, I'm going to roar like a lion down at the police station as to why the arrest reports make no mention of this Gary fellow you were traveling with, and your other companions for that matter. I'll threaten bringing the press on to that fact to make them use some police monies to look into that route. They hate the suggestion of police ineptness getting leaked to the media, so I think they'll hustle there. It's all about planting reasonable doubt, Ronnie, and there is a lot of that in this case. And number three, I'm going to customs at the Port of Tampa, and get some video footage of that sneaky bastard leaving you in the lurch. That just might be our best piece of evidence yet."

"Oh my God, that would be great. I hadn't even thought of that," Ronnie exclaimed as Lou's hand squeezed her shoulder.

"I can't promise the angles will be good, or quality, but if we get anything showing him slinking away, that will definitely be an ace up our sleeve." He winked at Ronnie while he shook Lou's outstretched hand.

"Won't you have to release that evidence to the prosecution?" Nikko interrupted for the first time.

"By all means, and if it's good enough video evidence, they'll start digging too. I'll punch holes in their case until they drop it, or in court I will make them look like a bunch of bumbling keystone cops who dropped the ball. Either way works fine by me." He shook Nikko's hand and began to head towards the door reminding Ronnie to call him if she thought of anything else.

She promised. When he left she felt better than she had in a long time. She had a defense. He was planning a great offense. And she had a smart attorney too.

Chapter Nine

Distractions

When Ronnie's attorney left a little after noon, Lou suggested they have a light lunch. Ronnie looked at Nikko eyes asking him if he wanted to stay without words, and although it looked like she wanted him to stay, he felt she probably needed some time to herself to process all that had happened. He also didn't want to push his luck with her mom.

"I'd like to, really, but I need to go make some copies of the paperwork my brother left with me, and I do have a few phone calls I'd like to make." He softened the look of disappointment that crossed her face by winking mischievously and adding, "But how about, I pop in tonight, maybe take you out for a milkshake!"

Ronnie tried to contain it, but burst out laughing despite her mother's confusion. "Really? A milkshake! That's the best you can come up with." She rolled her eyes at her mom, who just smiled politely and went to the kitchen. Ronnie walked Nikko to the door after he waved goodbye to Louisa across the expanse of the living room.

"I'll see you later, I guess," Louisa called out shrugging her shoulders and began to fix a sandwich plate for her and her daughter. She watched Ronnie follow Nikko outside.

Lou could tell these two had some kind of connection, and although she was worried Ronnie would be tempted by the handsome young man's charms, she seriously hoped she wouldn't fall for the guy. The timing was just not right for this. But on the other hand, he was also a distraction, and perhaps she thought more glumly, as she peered in the refrigerator for the fixings for a salad, he could get her mind off her problems every now and then. Her daughter had a rough road ahead of her. She just didn't want to think about what she could possibly face, so set to work chopping the vegetables for the salad. She needed to eat healthy, keep up her strength and had not one, but two children to consider now.

Ronnie followed Nikko outside. She was still laughing at him.

"Well, what else could I have said?" he teased back, "The truth? I want your daughter, Mrs. Russell. I want the chance to be alone with her. I'll pick her up later; I'll take her for a ride in my car, and see how far I can get. A milkshake seemed more innocent, friends going out for a sweet treat. Your laughing at me, I'm sure, made your mom quite suspicious. Now she'll figure milkshake is code word for 'I'm taking your daughter out for a night of passion, and I'll bring her home sore and tired, but feeling great.'"

At first Ronnie was shocked by his blunt manner and took a step back. Then laughed at the ludicrousness of the entire situation. Here she was, contemplating his offer, a man whom she had sworn off last summer, and yesterday. But a good night's sleep, a couple of refreshingly honest conversations, had her seeing Nikko in a different light.

"Is it the truth?" she asked huskily.

Nikko heard the question, but her tone threw him off. His pulse beat a little faster. He didn't want to push. And hell yes, it was the truth. "Only if you want it too," he answered holding back. She just looked at him, brown eyes staring into blue. Seeing him for the first time.

She was tempted. God, help her. Her mouth was suddenly dry. But his statement, although said in jest, reminded her he was a playboy, a very handsome one whom she found way too attractive. The kiss this morning had been a mistake, one she initiated, and maybe now regretted. He was getting harder and harder to resist.

If they had consummated their passions last summer, who knows where she'd be now. She never would have taken Gary back. She questioned why she ever had. In their small circle of friends, it had been more for companionship than anything else. All of their other friends were already coupled up, and it had been convenient. She'd been planning to break up with him after graduation, find a job far away, and just break it off cleanly. He'd never leave Maine, or his family. His father owned a lumbering company that cut down trees and prepared them for sale, and he was planning on pursuing that as was expected of him.

She shook her head, if only. Nikko was looking at her curiously. He was waiting for an answer. Yes, if only . . . he wasn't so damn handsome. She needed to remind him of her situation.

"Well, although a milkshake does sound yummy," she rubbed her belly mocking him, to make the blow of her next words easier to take, "you could have just said, I need to go fill my brothers in on all the info I got from sitting in on the conversation between lawyer and client, and then I'll be back to keep a vigilant eye on the possible flight risk." She was stalling. His invitation was there, clear as day, open and waiting. All she had to do was say yes.

His eyes narrowed in disappointment. Too soon, he thought. He saw in her eyes she was shutting down again. The ice princess was back. Damn, this girl ran hot and cold, and switched gears so fast he couldn't keep up. But he couldn't fault her now, not with the situation she was in. He gave her his most stunning smile and also gave her the truth.

"Yes, I do need to speak to my brothers, true. Do I think you're a flight risk?" He paused long and hard to let her wonder. "No, I don't think you'll run. Your mother would lose her house. And, you wouldn't do that to her." He already sensed how important her family was to her. They shared that.

Uncomfortable under his gaze, Ronnie looked down at her feet momentarily. When she looked up, his smile was replaced with an expression of regret. A warm feeling welled within her chest, and she decided to be honest with him.

"I'm sorry Nikko, my emotions are just all over the place. I shouldn't have led you on. I know I kissed you earlier, but we really shouldn't…" She sighed and ended abruptly, not sure of how to finish.

He didn't even give her the chance though. "Why?" He asked point blank. His blue eyes searched hers. She just stared at him blankly not knowing what to say. He began to approach her, still staring into her brown eyes. His hands went up to skim her arms, and she shivered under his touch. He was mere inches away. "Why?" Again the question. He dropped his voice down to a husky whisper, making her skin feel warm and cool at the same time. "Why?" he asked again in a breath that mimicked the whisper of the summer breeze.

"Because," she stammered. She couldn't think with him so close, so near.

Gary never made her feel like this. Gary never . . . And that was it. With Nikko . . . she couldn't think clearly. She pushed herself back from him.

"Because, I need to have my head and wits about me, and with you around, I can't think straight. You confuse me. Just your nearness. And, to you I am just another conquest, a notch on your belt, like the redhead I saw about to give you a blow job in the parking lot. Like Linda from Big Jimbo's, and however many countless others there may have been. And honestly, Nikko," she begged him to understand what she was trying to say, "I'm not that kind of girl. I don't have casual affairs." She turned abruptly to head back into the house.

He reacted by instinct and stopped her even though she had thrown him for a loop, a real curve ball. He was confused. With his hand on her shoulder, she stopped and slowly turned to face him as he spoke, "What? Wait. Last year?" he asked. He saw what looked like a flash of pain cross her eyes, but wasn't sure. It was gone in an instant, replaced by anger.

"Yes, when you and I were going to meet up later, but you found someone else. If I am being really honest about it, I was hurt. I mean stupid. I don't know. I thought you liked me. Thought we could have a fun summer. I know it was just one night, but damn, an hour later and you're fondling someone else, and letting her . . . " Ronnie winced and looked away not able to meet his gaze any longer.

Nikko's eyes widened in horror. "Whoa, letting her! I was trying to push her away. She was drunk, and she was all over me. Not the other way around. I wasn't interested in her in the least. I was, I still am, very interested in you. And, I know you are a good girl." He took his hand and lightly cupped her chin to bring her eyes to him. "And Ronnie, if I have to be honest here, I've never been THAT interested in anybody before. And so you know, I also went home that night, alone and very frustrated. Very disappointed. I tried to get Monica to invite you over when she returned from her honeymoon, but she and Vic had so much going on when they got back. Then Ana came by with her newly adopted daughter, Jessica, nearly every other day. They mentioned you were leaving soon, and so I let it go. Please believe me." His words were said so sincerely, they threw her for a loop.

He watched the play of emotions cross her face, and when her eyes were once again focused on him she asked tentatively, "Y-you did?"

He nodded not breaking that all important eye contact. "Yes, I did. By the time things settled, you were gone, and that was that."

"Wow," she breathed still clearly confused, still taking in all this new information.

He gave her a few more moments to process it all. "I like you Ronnie. WE have chemistry. I would like to see where this can go. I know the timing is all wrong, but now or later, I will pursue this. But, I need to know some things too." His tone was earnest.

She just stared for a moment longer, then asked, "What do you want to know?"

He looked nervous suddenly. She saw him swallow. "Yeah, well, um, so is there any reason why I shouldn't pursue you for more than just sex. Gary? Do you still have feelings for this jerk?"

She was taken aback. "Oh my God, No!" was her vehement reply. "I was breaking up with him anyway. As soon as I found work outside of Maine. The past six months it was just more like convenience to stick together until after graduation. No, no, that relationship was never going to end well."

A look of relief crossed his face and he immediately gripped her shoulders. "Good!" He pulled her close and just held her for a moment.

Her heart began to beat faster, and she felt his heart thudding in his chest. When he pulled back just a bit to look down into her eyes, she saw a storm brewing in those icy clue eyes. His next words both shocked and thrilled her.

"I'm glad Ronnie. Because I want you. I want you like I have never wanted anyone before." And then he descended upon her to claim his prize. His lips sought hers and demanded a response. It was brutal and crushing.

Reacting with equal vigor, Ronnie was lost in him. It wasn't noon under the Florida sun. She wasn't charged with countless crimes. She wasn't facing a trial and a possible long jail sentence. Her life wasn't in shambles. She was simply a woman, a woman who felt desired by the man of her dreams, and she reveled in it. Soon, Ronnie was pressing herself against a very aroused Nikko enjoying all he had to offer and taking what she could get. She was so aroused, and when his tongue began to tangle with hers in an intimate dance, she felt a chain reaction of emotions. Her nipples tightened, and her core pulsed and clenched of its own volition. She felt a wetness in her pussy and knew she couldn't get enough of this man.

When it ended, they were both gasping for air. But he held her until the world settled. She brushed her cheek against his chest, and listened to his heart thunder. Her own heart was beating a similar tattoo.

"Well," he managed to croak out.

"Well, what?" she asked, her breathing beginning to return to normal.

"Any other barriers to my pursuit? Is there anything else I should know about?" he asked when she tilted her head to look at him again. He nipped her chin, his lips making their way to her ear. He swirled his tongue around her lobe.

She groaned her pleasure and then answered. "Other than me going to jail for a very long time?" she whispered as she leaned into the sweet delicious sensations he was evoking within her.

"Yes, other than that?" he asked whispering in her ear.

"No," she moaned.

"Good," he murmured as his lips found hers again in another punishing kiss that had her reeling.

This kiss left her breathless. She soaked it in. It went on and on, both of them so hungry for each other.

He did eventually end it, but held her pressed to his body for a few moments longer.

"We can't deny there is something there, Ronnie. I admit it is not good timing. But you shouldn't deny yourself a little fun, the chance to feel, or to experience pleasure. I don't know what this is Ronnie; I'd love to find out, but I'll respect your choice. I promise though, if you are worried about it still, you are not a one night stand to me. Even last summer. It never would have been then, either."

Ronnie was too choked to speak. If only . . . . She was glad he was still holding her and couldn't see her face at the moment. She burrowed deeper into him hiding her thoughts.

"Ronnie?" He asked wanting, no, needing to know what she was thinking. He felt her arms tighten around him. Nothing ever felt better in his life. But, he still craved those words.

He heard her clear her throat. She was getting ready to speak. "So, um, a milkshake then. Later, if your offer is still good," she whispered into his chest.

Ronnie felt the laughter before she heard it. It expanded out from him. The rumble of it made her squeeze him, and he returned the embrace.

"Oh Ronnie baby, that offer is most assuredly still good. I'll take you for a milkshake any time." He kissed the top of her head, and whispered, "Anywhere."

***

Jay walked in exhausted from a long day at the airport around six o'clock, but it was nice to see Lou looking happy making dinner with her daughter. He'd been very worried about his wife since this mess started over a week ago. Actually, he'd noticed some weight loss, and despite her ample breasts she didn't have a whole heck of a lot of weight on her. But seeing her smiling and laughing made him feel better. He worked at the airport on Saturdays, but had Sunday and Monday off, and he planned on pampering Lou. Between her job and her daughter's crisis, he could see the stress was taking its toll.

"How're my girls?" he asked, setting his keys and baseball cap advertising the Oakland Raiders on the table by the door.

"Very good," Lou imparted and put down the knife she was using to chop vegetables for the salad. She started towards him.

He met her half way. "Glad to hear it," he murmured against her cheek, planting a soft kiss just in front of her ear. "Mmm, smells good."

"Me or the pasta?" she teased, softly kissing him in return.

"Both," he laughed, patting her rear when she turned back to the kitchen.

"Veronica wanted pasta, fettuccini, and we also made a salad. I've grilled some shrimp too," she laughed as he trailed her to the kitchen, jacking a shrimp from the platter and popping it into his mouth.

"Hey, now. Wait for dinner," she chastised as she turned to the refrigerator and got him a bottle of Michelob.

He popped the top and sipped at it, leaning up against the counter as the girls finished up the salad. He couldn't help but notice Ronnie appeared a little too dressed up for a causal dinner at home, but he didn't say anything. The blue peasant blouse she wore was extremely cute, and revealing. The stretchy grey material of her skirt showed off her assets. He wondered if they were having company tonight. She also had on a bit of makeup which to him was a dead giveaway. God, help Nikko. He had his hands full, literally and figuratively.

"You look nice," he remarked.

She smiled and thanked him. "I'm going out later," she answered, proving his assumptions correct.

Jay looked over her head at her mother whose eyes widened, but shoulders shrugged.

He couldn't help himself. He never could. He was known for his smart mouth and his incessant teasing.

"Oh, really," he drawled out. "With that Nikko fellow I presume. The one I almost caught you with in the bushes last summer?" he tormented.

"Jay! You said . . ." she protested, eyes widening and looking nervously at her mother.

Jay just laughed. "That was last summer, baby cakes. Plus, I've already told your mom about it a long time ago. She suspected anyway the way you moped around last summer, and I can't keep secrets from my wife." He held up his hands in surrender.

Her eyes narrowed angrily, but a glance at her mother showed her smiling. "Really?" she asked, fully facing her mother now.

Lou nodded. "Ronnie, I was young once too. Mom's sometimes don't like to admit they know what is going on when they really do. I know you're responsible. I trust you. But, are you sure you want to go . . . with him," she asked, leaving most of the question unasked.

"Mom, I know the timing sucks. But, he made a good point. I'll go crazy just sitting around all the time. I do like him, too," she added, blushing slightly.

Lou looked at her daughter. She didn't want to interfere, but she had to know if her daughter was aware of all the talk that circulated around Nikko Marino. "He's got quite a reputation you know. Monica's mentioned it."

Ronnie knew what Nikko was all about, and knew her mom was just worried about her, but the thought of being cooped up, confined to the house for however long, just got her ire up. Rolling her eyes, she let out her frustrations.

"I know, Mom. I knew last summer too. I don't want you to think I am entering into this with blinders on. I'll be careful. But, I'm not getting serious. He isn't. I know that. I know my limits. I have made them clear to him. It's just fun. I even called Margaret, and Brad. Let them know I was in town. It could take months for us to even get a trial date. I can't leave Florida. Might as we'll hang out with some of my friends. You'll be working. You can't babysit me every minute of every day. I'm not staying home twiddling my thumbs. I'm not in jail yet!"

"Whoa, sorry," Lou interrupted her daughter's mini tirade. "I know you're an adult. But I also just can't stop being your mom, can't stop worrying. I know Nikko is nice. I like him too. He is very charming. I just don't want you to get hurt." The concern was evident in her tone and in her eyes.

Ronnie felt guilty for going off on her. She apologized. "I know Mom, I'm sorry too. It just feels like I've already been sentenced. I don't know," she muttered.

Finishing his beer, Jay interrupted, "Honey, you're not in jail yet. Have fun. Just watch out for your heart is what I think your mom is trying to say. With guys like, Nikko, and as young as he is, he's just not the settling down type. Not usually anyhow. That's all."

Ronnie turned to Jay. She loved how he could read her mom so easily. "I understand Jay, I do. I will keep that in mind. I promise," she muttered for her mom's benefit.

Jay smiled broadly. "Okay, good. No more fighting. Let's have a nice dinner, and I'll try to keep the teasing down to a minimum. Just let me go wash up first. Plus," he added half way across the room, "I want to hear about the meeting with the lawyer."

"That went very well," Lou called out to him. "He's got some great ideas to pursue. Go, we will get everything on the table," Lou urged when he paused by the door to their bedroom.

Jay went, and the ladies set to the task at hand. Butterflies persisted in Ronnie's stomach, however, because she had made a decision about tonight and now she was beginning to have some doubts. If what Jay was saying was true, a leopard didn't change his spots. And Jay would know. After all he had been a confirmed player for quite some time before he met her mother.

Chapter Ten

Attraction

When Nikko showed up around eight o'clock, the sun was just beginning its descent over the Gulf of Mexico. As he pulled into the driveway of the secluded cabin, Ronnie opened the door and waited for his car to come to a complete stop before she made her way to the passenger side. He quickly got out, hustled around to her side, and reached for the handle of the door just as she did. He didn't want to screw tonight up.

The electricity from the contact of their hands gripping the handle at the same time was intense. It shot through him like lightning. She looked absolutely mouthwatering in the peasant style blouse, one shoulder completely revealed. Her skin was bronzed from the sun. He could see the pulse at the base of her neck beating, and the urge to press a kiss there almost had him doing just that. The skirt, some type of clingy material, fitted her generous hips, tapered then flared out just above her knees, the grey and white diagonal stripes subtly accentuated her curves. It revealed her shapeliness. He wanted to touch her, everywhere. She wore her wavy hair down, just below the shoulders, and her scent was citrusy. Fresh. He wanted to taste her. Everything about her he found exciting. He didn't know if he could be a gentleman, and on his way over he vowed he would try to show her a different side of him.

She slid onto the seat and smiled up at him, lips plump and pink. Again, he had the urge to kiss her; he wanted to bite that bottom lip and take it into his mouth. He also suspected he might have an audience. He knew her step dad was home now and didn't want to give him another peep show by attacking his step daughter in the driveway. Nikko knew even one small chaste kiss would set him aflame, so it was better to resist the urges of his body altogether, for now.

"You like nice, Ronnie," he said softly, admiring the picture she made against the black leather.

"Thank you." Under long eyelashes that hid her desire for him, she admired his attire as well.

"Do you need help with your seatbelt, Ronnie?" Nikko stepped back to give her room to close the door, but couldn't resist asking as she reached for the handle.

"I got it, Nikko. But, thank you," she murmured, eyes still downcast, suddenly shy, remembering the last time he helped her, and also knowing where tonight was headed.

Yes, she thought, this could be a nice distraction, a diversion from all her worries. She held no hopes for a future with a man like this. But she also couldn't help but believe him—she wasn't a mere flash in the pan, a notch on his post. Her trial would be months away, and with his brother's investment in her, they had time at least. Four months she figured. That was a long time, and anything was possible, wasn't it?

He gave her that crooked smile that showed his dimples as he pressed the door closed, and she reached for her seatbelt. She watched him walk around the car, and just enjoyed the view. He was like a panther in his movements. Sleek. Sexy as hell. She imagined him dating models, not short girls with curvy figures. But she knew he was attracted to her, just as much as she was attracted to him. Why not take advantage of it? It would be one helluva ride.

When Nikko was in the car, the electricity between them was intense. There was static in the air. He turned the car's ignition over and smoothly backed up out of her mother's driveway. Soon they were cruising along State Road Fifty headed into Spring Hill.

He reached for her hand and held it on his lap, while he steered with one hand. He used one finger to trace small light circles on the top of her hand, constantly in motion. It was comforting and did crazy things to her. She enjoyed the intimacy of the small gesture.

"So, ice cream, a milk shake?" he reminded her softly and broke the spell.

She gave him an 'are you absurd look' and he laughed. Who were they kidding? "Um, no," she replied just as softly. Her heart rate picked up.

"No?" he questioned lifting one eyebrow and looking at her sideways before returning his eyes to the road. The look on her face set his heart to beating faster. His mouth suddenly went dry. *Where did she want to go?*

A slow smile spread across her face. "No, Nikko. Let's just go to your hotel, and do what we have both wanted to do for a long time." Honesty was refreshing. She didn't want to play these games any longer.

He looked at her suddenly, and she saw the fire in his eyes. His nostrils flared. His grip on her hand got tighter, and his foot hit the accelerator. He spoke no words, just searched her eyes for a moment, saying nothing.

He saw the need in her eyes mirrored his own. It thrilled him. Pure passion. Wanton desire. He couldn't wait to sink into this woman, claim her as his. He wanted nothing more than to possess this tough as nails ice princess and make her melt. Not saying anything, he released her hand; he needed two hands now so he could drive faster. The hotel wasn't far, not far at all.

***

The Quality Inn Nikko pulled into was close to Lou's place, and was the newest hotel in the county. The sun was just dipping below the tree-line, as Ronnie followed Nikko through the lobby, her hand in his as he crossed directly to the elevators. He handed her his key card and told her to go to room four hundred and twenty-five. He would join her shortly. He wanted to get something from the bar.

He pressed a kiss to her lips. It was chaste, but firm and she felt the heat behind it. The promise.

* * *

Ronnie walked into the mirror and oak paneled elevator, and by the time she turned she could already see Nikko's retreating figure half way to the entrance to the hotel lounge. She hit the button for the fourth floor, and the doors slid shut as she watched him rush toward the bar, not looking back once. He appeared to be a man on a mission.

She felt the elevator lurch and begin its ascent. It didn't help her already queasy stomach. She just hoped her hunch about Nikko was right.

When the elevator stopped and the doors slid open, she didn't have far to go. Nikko's room was directly across the hall indicated by the brass plate showing room four hundred and twenty-five. Two large double doors of deep mahogany gleamed directly in front of her. It must be a suite, she assumed. She slid the key into the electronic box and it flashed green. Pulling the card out, she quickly opened the door, and stepped inside onto a very plush chocolate colored carpet.

Yes, it was definitely a suite. The room she entered was a foyer, and directly in front of her was a large curved sofa facing a flat screen TV, and then beyond that a table big enough to seat six comfortably in a dining area. There was also a large wet bar fully stocked. She passed through the two rooms and off the dining area was a small bathroom on the right, but on the left was a massive stone archway carved intricately in a fleur-de-lis design. She passed under and walked the few steps down the hallway which opened up to a tastefully decorated bedroom. A very large bedroom with a king sized bed. The decor was done in browns and tans. The furniture mahogany. Again above one of the dressers in the room was a large flat screen TV, and there was also a small desk in the corner, and Ronnie noticed it had a guest computer built in. Ronnie set her purse down on a divan, and turned around in the room taking it all in. The Marinos must be doing well to take such luxurious quarters, she thought absently running her hand along the quality furniture as she passed through the room.

She knew there must be an ensuite bathroom, and looked for it. She saw the door and peered inside, amazed by the grandeur. The stone theme continued. There was a glass enclosed massive shower, and a raised hot tub. Very impressive. Very tempting.

She checked her teeth in the mirror, and satisfied with her appearance, turned back towards the bedroom. Nikko wouldn't be much longer.

***

When Nikko entered his suite with his other key card minutes later, he carried a bottle of chilled champagne, and two crystal flutes. He hadn't planned for this, but wanted to make this night special. Yes, he hoped to bring Ronnie here, but hadn't counted on it. He wanted to offer her more than the hard liquor supplied in this suite. He rarely drank, but when he did it was usually a beer. Occasionally he drank a glass of wine with dinner.

He didn't see Ronnie right away, and thought she might be in the bathroom, but when he entered underneath the arch he found her already on the bed. She was curled on her side facing him. Waiting.

Shit! When she made her mind up about something, she didn't hold back. He laughed nervously, and lifted the champagne to her in the way of explanation. She nodded at him.

He set the flutes down on a nearby dresser, and then popped the champagne over the trash can to catch the flume. He was quick, grabbing a glass, and filling it, letting very few drops escape. Setting that glass down, he filled the other. He set the remainder of the champagne on the side table, and then he picked up both glasses and made his way over to Ronnie. What a sight she was. He knew she didn't know just how beautiful she was. That was something else he liked about her.

Ronnie sat up, just as he reached her, and took the proffered glass. She touched the rim of her flute to his after he gestured her to do so.

"To you, Ronnie. A beautiful, remarkable, strong woman. A woman I desire a great deal. The only woman I have fantasized about for over a year," he winked at her as he touched his glass to hers, and they both lifted their glasses to take a sip.

The sweet fizzy liquid was delicious. He set his glass down on the bedside table, but Ronnie took a second sip before setting her glass down besides his. Nikko just stood there watching her, giving her time to really be sure she wanted this as much as he.

Ronnie felt naked under his gaze and the intimacy of the moment was just too much to bear. She needed to act. She got up, but he was close, very close. Her body slithered its way up to meet him. She reached his shirt, and he allowed her to pull it up, helping her only when she couldn't reach any higher. His bronzed chest lay fully exposed to her sight. She pressed her hands against the great chiseled expanse before her and immediately felt the iron like muscles ripple beneath his silky skin. She used her hands to explore this fine specimen of a man. Gary had been fit, from years of playing hockey, but not defined in this way. Nikko was surely a treat for the eyes. A work of art.

Nikko allowed her just a few moments more to explore him, but his hands itched to do the same to her. His hard on pressed tightly against the fly of his cargo pants. He wanted to see this beauty he had only briefly been able to feast on once before.

Her hands just finished exploring his pecks, when he stooped down to press a kiss to the exposed nape of her neck. He watched her pulse beating there and yearned to taste it, to feel her blood pumping faster through her veins under his lips, for him. He did so, and then trailed kisses along her neck to her shoulder as her head arched back to give him greater access. Her little murmurs of pleasure made him even harder if that were possible. Her breasts pressed firmly into him titillating his own senses. He could feel her nipples like pebbles scrape across his chest. Nothing ever felt better.

His lips reached the edge of her blouse, and using his teeth, he tugged it down to reveal more of her cleavage and he couldn't help it, but a groan of desire and frustration escaped his lips. This woman, he remembered, had the most amazing tits he had ever seen. Not only were they full, and large, but they were one hundred percent real. His hands snaked across her back, and he found the clasp of her bra, and cleanly unhooked it. He knew what he was doing. He pulled back, and grabbed the hem of her blouse, and in one fluid motion pulled it off. Her bra came with it, and her large breasts were fully exposed to him.

His mouth descended. He couldn't hold back any longer. He captured one nipple in his mouth, and bit it lightly then sucked it until her nipple was even harder. His other hand toyed with her other breast noting the weight of it in his other hand.

Ronnie adored the sensations of Nikko's teeth, tongue, and hands on her breasts. She felt the intensity of it shoot from her sensitive nipples straight through to her pussy which began to involuntarily clench in anticipation of what was to come. Her legs began to shake and she felt weak and dizzy with her own desire.

Sensing her need, Nikko scooped her up into his arms, biceps flexing, and placed her onto the bed reaching to the center as far as he could. Her brown eyes half closed, he could see her pleasure would come fast. He kicked off his shoes, quickly unfastened his pants, and pulled them down along with his black boxer briefs.

Her smoky eyes widened in surprise at the sight of him fully engorged, and sprung.

Ronnie's mouth began to water. Nikko's cock stood fully erect, reaching his navel. He was huge, and wide. She squeezed her legs together feeling her clit yearning for friction. Her hands reached for him, and slid along the satin smoothness of his cock, wanting it inside her. All of it. Kneeling on the bed beside her, he trembled when her fingers claimed his dick, and slid around it, holding him.

"Oh, Ronnie, I don't know how much of that I can take," he rumbled from deep in his chest. Her hands on his cock was just too much right now. His voice was harsh, guttural. "I've got to be inside you soon."

Ronnie felt her need coursing through her. His reaction increased her desire tenfold. Her pussy clenched at his words, and she felt the wetness seep out. She released her grip on his cock, and dug her heels into the mattress to lift her ass in order to pull off her skirt. She wanted him, badly.

"Nikko, I want you too," she urged. Seeing her dilemma, he helped her pull off her skirt, and then she lie before him, in nothing but a thin scrap of cloth. His hand reached for her waist, slid down her abdomen, and then below the piece of black lace to her pussy. He found her well-groomed, and groaned his pleasure as he slipped a finger into her opening. She was hot and slick. He found her clit protruding and already unsheathed for him. He circled it, and her hips bucked at the intensity of that first touch. She pushed herself onto him. He rubbed across the top with the one finger applying just a bit of pressure.

Ronnie's air escaped sharply through her teeth in a hiss of pure pleasure. "Please," she begged. "Nikko!"

Her throaty response was all Nikko needed. He plunged his finger into her and she clenched around it. She was tight. He withdrew as she raised herself to meet his thrust. He plunged in again this time with two fingers and again her body reacted. He pulled out, and plunged in again with those same fingers making her ready to receive him.

Ronnie was panting her pleasure. This was good, but she wanted more. Her nails scraped along his rib cage as he settled beside her to continue his teasing and this oh so torturous foreplay.

"Please, please," she begged, thrusting up her pelvis to meet his hand thrust for thrust. Her clit needed the friction.

Hearing the hunger in her voice, and knowing he wanted this, her, all of her, more than anything in this moment, he pulled his fingers out of her hot pussy, and grabbed the bit of cloth, and tore it right off of her, the fabric giving way easily.

"Please, please," she repeated her need.

He was on his knees between her legs, at her opening. He paused for a moment and reached for a condom he had placed beside the bed. She hadn't even seen him place it there. He made quick work of it and then he held his cock in his hand, felt the blood pumping in his veins, and held it to her opening. He pushed into her, just an inch at a time wanting to watch her face as he claimed her. He felt her pussy clench trying to take more of him, and she turned her face from him.

"Ronnie, I want to see your eyes," he murmured huskily holding his passion in check.

"Babe, I want to see your face while I take you. Can you keep your eyes open for me?" he asked, panting at the strain of holding back when he wanted nothing more than to ram his cock into her over and over again. But, they would only have this moment once.

She turned and looked into his eyes. Ronnie could almost feel the burn from the intensity of his gaze. She couldn't look away from those eyes right now if she wanted too.

He liked her answer, and gave her another inch. He felt her stretch around him. She was tight. That intensified his pleasure. "Keep them open," he reminded her, when instinct made her waver. He urged her, and stroked one of her firm thighs as she opened her legs wider for him. He pushed in again, one more inch.

"Oh God, yes," she moaned and started to thrust upwards to take more of him.

"Don't," he ground out, wanting this to last. He gripped her thigh and sliding down on his knees a bit, took her leg and placed it over his shoulder so he could achieve maximum penetration. He released his cock, but held his position. He gave her another inch, feeling her tremble and quake beneath him.

His blue eyes practically glowed silver with fire. Molten liquid silver fire. Another inch. She could feel his cock pulsing inside her, and wanted it all.

"Now, Ronnie," he grunted, as he seated all ten inches into her, and plunged his cock to the hilt. He saw stars as her heat enveloped him. His cock, as hard as granite, filled her hot flesh and she took him, all of him. He muttered the only words that came to him. "Your mine now, Ronnie."

"I'm yours," she repeated mindlessly. His cock slid out briefly, and then back in again. He took his time rubbing his shaft along her sensitive clit. In this position, he controlled it all. She took it. He began to move faster but each time he plunged, he deliberately assaulted her clit with his cock putting just the right amount of pressure to keep her completely aroused and at a complete loss for coherent speech.

"Oh, fuck, fuck," she urged, enjoying the deliberateness of his every movement. She twisted beneath him enjoying each and every stroke.

His pace began to quicken. "Oh, Babe, fuck," he grunted and then she felt herself begin to come apart at the seams.

"Don't look away," he grunted. His movements began to become rhythmic, as he pummeled her pussy with his cock.

"Oh, my God," Ronnie screamed, "Yes, yes! Yes!" Her screams pierced the night. "Nikko!" she screamed as wave after wave of pleasure coursed through her.

"Your mine now, Ronnie. Mine," he grunted as he found his own release. His cock pumped and pumped in and out of Ronnie until he was spent, and milked dry. He collapsed beside her, finally releasing her leg. *"Mine,"* he repeated and pulled her body onto his, holding her while their hearts thundered in their chests.

Chapter Eleven

Satisfaction

Nikko passed out briefly. When he woke fifteen minutes later, Ronnie was still asleep, half on top of him. His arms instinctively circled her in a protective gesture. He was surprised about how he reacted during his taking of her for their first time together. He wanted to possess all of her. He felt more connected to her than he had ever felt before. He not only wanted to fill her body with his cock, but wanted her to feel his claim upon her.

He still hadn't been able to muddle through his thoughts when she began to wake beside him. Her tight little body rubbed up against him, and it had his need for her stirring again. She shifted her head and with eyes half closed looked up to see his blue eyes gazing down fiercely into hers.

She opened her eyes wider and he smiled down at her. She felt his hands slide up her hip, across her ass caressing it and then his hands brushed the side of her breasts.

She felt his cock hardening under her leg and so she moved it slightly to give him space. But instead of space, he put his hands under her arms now and pulled her up, so she was lying completely atop him.

"Nikko?" she asked.

"Again," he murmured seductively. "I've not nearly had enough of you yet, Ronnie." His lips a breath away descended on hers.

His tongue slipped into her mouth, teasing her to do battle. Soon his hands were back on her ass squeezing her cheeks, and then he forced one of his knees between her thighs so she was astraddle him. His cock was at attention between them as he leaned up on an elbow not breaking the kiss. He reached for another condom and handed it to her. She tore open the package greedily, and slid the sheath onto him.

"Ronnie, I want you, now," he murmured. "Say it," he breathed while biting her bottom lip.

"I want you too, Nikko" she murmured, as his tongue darted into her mouth again.

He broke the kiss moments later, grasped her hips and guided them to his cock. He wanted to ram his cock into her, over and over again until she begged him for release. But instead took his time. He wanted her to control the pace this time. He urged her to sink onto him slowly. She complied, taking him in an inch at a time until she was completely impaled by his throbbing member. Using his fingers, squeezing her hips, he encouraged her to move. With a knee on either side of him, she began to move, rubbing her already swollen clit along the juncture between them. Her excitement had her wanting to move faster, but he kept the pace slow. His fingers dug into her.

Her head began to thrash in her excitement with her impending explosion. "I need to see it, Ronnie. Look at me when you come undone. It's me making you come, baby," he grunted, holding back his own release as her slick pussy slid up and down his shaft.

She looked at him, and his look of ownership, did her in. "Fuck me, Nikko. Fuck, I am going to come." She intensified the speed despite his fingers sinking into her hips, gripping them tight. She kept her eyes on him. "Fuck, fuck, fuck, damn, yes, yes," the words spilled from her lips with no logic, just the words of her release. "Oh my God, yes, Nikko, fuck!" She drew out the last syllable as the explosion came.

Jerking his hips, he slammed into her hot wet pussy as her eyes went wild, and rolled to the back of her head. His explosion came too, just as intense as before. He spilled his seed into this ice princess, but damn if she wasn't the hottest most wanton creature he had ever been with. Her hair hung limply around her, sweat dripped down between her breasts. Her body—she smelled of sex. Their sex, and just as he finished unloading into her still quaking pussy, he no sooner thought of how he could have her again. And again.

There were a lot of things he wanted to try with Ronnie.

***

Driving Ronnie home was the last thing he wanted to do, but it was nearly midnight, and Ronnie expressed she didn't want her mother and stepfather to worry about her on their first evening out.

The drive was done too quickly as the conversation didn't lag. Ronnie invited him over for dinner the next night after he suggested coming over the next day. Not wanting to seem eager, but knowing he was facing one heck of a boring Sunday, he reluctantly agreed. Dinner with the folks was something he normally didn't do. But Ronnie's circumstances were different. He figured he could make his calls to his brothers tomorrow, and fill them in. In fact, he'd sent them a text reassuring them he would do that and all was well when Ronnie escaped to the bathroom after their third sexually acrobatic session was over.

When he parked in her driveway, he turned off the engine figuring they could talk for a while longer, but were both surprised by the massive hulking figure in the window of the car that emerged suddenly out of the darkness. Recognizing the tattoos lacing down one arm as her step father's, Nikko reluctantly rolled down the window. Their ears were immediately met with the massive man humming a tune that was popular a few years back, "My milkshake brings all the boys to the yard".

"How was the milkshake?" He laughed, leaning into the window putting his massive forearms onto the frame of Nikko's Cutlass.

"It was great," Ronnie piped in not hiding her sarcasm. Her step father had no filter. When he thought of something clever to say, it came out, and usually embarrassed everyone except him. In fact, he rather enjoyed it. She couldn't help but add, "I'd say it was better than yours, but I'm afraid you'd tell me otherwise, and that's just something I really don't want to hear." Jay was wonderful, but hearing about the sexual activities between him and her mother . . . well, it was wrong on so many levels. But it never seemed to stop him.

Instead of laughing Jay just sighed. "No, I'd agree with you tonight, Ronnie. Your mom is just not feeling well again."

"What's the matter?" she asked full of concern leaning even more towards the window so she could see his expression more clearly.

Jay shrugged and answered. "She said it must be something she ate, but god dammit, she didn't eat a thing tonight. You saw that. She really just picked at her food."

Nikko thought to the bear claw she had wolfed down earlier. He hoped that hadn't made her sick. He groaned inwardly. Maybe the cream in it had unsettled her stomach.

He wasn't about to fess up to this giant of a man, but felt guilty anyhow. Way to go, he chastised himself.

"I better get in then," she murmured hastily as she reached for the door after a pressing a chaste kiss to Nikko's cheek.

"No. No hurry, Ronnie," Jay retorted, stilling her with his words. She turned back to face him. "She's actually sleeping. I brought Missy out one last time. I'm heading in now, to give you a little time to . . . shall we say . . . say goodbye," he teased and made kissing faces and smooching sounds at them.

"Real mature, Jay," she called out after his retreating back, Missy at his heels.

"Yeah, I know. But you love me anyway," was his flippant retort made over his shoulder. "Nice seeing you, Nikko," he added, still with his back turned then the sound of the door closing.

"Interesting man," Nikko muttered under his breath.

"He grows on you," Ronnie laughed.

"I'll take your word on it," he laughed in return as she scooted closer to him on the bench seat of his classic car.

His arms were open, waiting, when she pushed into them, against him. "Tomorrow then," she murmured against his lips.

His answer was a groan of pleasure as her tongue slid into his mouth. For the next few moments all he could think about was his hot little ice princess making him very uncomfortable in her parent's driveway. When her hand slipped to gently squeeze his massively hard cock, he had to stop her.

"No my little ice princess, a man can only take so much." He took her hand off his crotch.

"Ice princess?" she laughed, arching one eyebrow.

He laughed and nodded at his own term of endearment. "Mmm-hmm. That's my nick name for you. You're sending me on my way with blue balls baby. That's pretty cold," he teased.

She was already sliding along the seat to her door. She opened it. Laughing hard, knowing Jay was rubbing off on her in a bad way, she couldn't resist adding, "Well, there is always the five finger salute, babe. I hear boys are pretty good at that." He had no chance to reply, she was out the door, skipping to the porch.

His window was still open. "You'll pay for that, Ronnie," he called. She was still laughing softly when the door closed behind her. Oh, you'll pay he thought.

He spent the drive home thinking of ways to make her pay, and it did nothing to alleviate the tension he was feeling at the moment. Or his blue balls.

***

Ronnie was working her magic in the kitchen with Lou's help. She hadn't done much cooking during college, but in high school, her mom had taught her quite a few dishes. Tonight, for Nikko, she was making chicken Parmesan, and a tomato salad with cucumbers, basil, and fresh mozzarella that she would sprinkle with red wine vinegar and olive oil. She knew Nikko was Italian, and was missing his family's Sunday dinner because he was assigned to be her watchdog. But, there were perks to him staying here, she mused.

Jay was puttering outside on his motorcycle and enjoying his day off with Missy while the women cooked.

Popping the chicken breasts that had been pounded down to thin layers and coated lightly in bread crumbs into the oven, Ronnie turned it to bake while her mom lowered the flame on the sauce to simmer. Everything else was set.

Ronnie retreated to her room to freshen up, change her clothes, and get ready for Nikko's arrival. She'd been surprised at how much she missed him today, but she wanted to stay home with her mother. Despite eating a decent lunch, her mom still did not look well.

Their talk had been about the trial, her attorney, and the fact they felt it would be trying, but they were both confident of success with Mr. Stimson on the case. He had even called to tell them he had gotten a judge to sign orders to have the Tampa Bay Port Authority release video tapes to him. He would be watching them on Monday, which was the next day. He'd promised to call her and fill her in on what the tapes revealed.

When Ronnie emerged from her room, she caught Lou and Jay having a small dispute.

"Louisa, I want you to go to the doctor, baby."

"I'm fine, Jay, really. It's just stress."

"Honey, you started losing weight before this thing with Ronnie. Now you are throwing up every day." He reached up to put his hands on her shoulders. "Listen, just humor me. Get some blood work done. Something," he pleaded.

"Fine. I'll call Monday and make an appointment," Lou gave in. She knew what was up, but wasn't ready to tell Jay just yet. She needed to see her doctor anyhow to confirm the pregnancy, and get a referral to an obstetrician.

"Thank you," Jay breathed a sigh of relief. "I know Ronnie's got you worried, but you're no good to her if you don't take care of yourself." After his mini tirade, he pulled her in for a hug, holding his much frailer wife gently in his massive arms. Ronnie ducked back into her room, as Jay's head dipped down for a kiss. She wanted to give them some time alone and not intrude on this tender moment.

***

Back in her room, Ronnie fiddled with her hair feeling even guiltier than usual. But she too was worried about her mom's health. If Jay's words were true, this illness began before her fall from grace. That scared her even more. What if something was seriously wrong? Her mom was tapped out. Please let it be something simple, she prayed. Her mom had just found this happiness, a place of her own, and Ronnie didn't want to lose the only parent she ever knew.

When enough time had passed, Ronnie emerged from her room, with a cough to indicate her arrival. Lou was alone, however, setting the table for dinner.

"Where's Jay?" Ronnie asked. "I thought I heard him."

"Oh, he's taking a quick shower, baby," she murmured, setting the plates down tiredly. Ronnie noticed, and took action.

"Mom, why don't I finish this," she said, approaching her but not revealing her concern. "Why don't you go get freshened up as well, lie down for a bit. I've got this," she stated firmly, taking the remaining plates from her. "Nikko won't be here for an hour, and we've been at it in the kitchen now for a while. You've cleaned the house from top to bottom today and you look tired."

"You sure?" Lou looked around vaguely as if she were trying to think of what to do next.

"Yes, go Mom. I've got this."

Her mom gave her a gentle smile and nodded. "Okay, I might take a nap." Lou began the trek to her room. This pregnancy was tougher than the last one. The nausea lasted all day, then at night the heartburn was keeping her up, that and her fears. Yes, she thought, going to the doctor was definitely a good idea.

***

Soon after Lou departed to her room, Ronnie finished setting the table. Everything was nearly ready. Missy was curled up on the floor by the sofa enjoying a nap, and Ronnie decided to step outside and get a bit of fresh air. She loved Maine, loved the seasons, loved the cold, the forest, but she was finding more and more to like about Florida too. Yes, it was hot in the summer, but near the water you didn't feel it as much. You always had the breeze. The beaches were magnificent, and she even thought about looking for work here in the Everglades, or the Keys; and then, there were even some jobs she could apply for at the many botanical gardens, and parks the state had to offer.

But thinking about applying for jobs right now was out of the question. She kicked a large stone in the driveway into the Florida scrub. Sighing, she realized in just three days she would have been walking onto a stage to accept her diploma. It would have been her graduation. She would miss it. She had been looking forward to walking across the stage with her mom, grandparents, and uncle in the audience cheering her on. Well, no use moping around, she thought. She had a defense to work on. Her name to clear.

She heard Nikko's car before she saw him. Turning, his car, sleek and shiny, pulled up into the driveway. Cutting off the engine, he quickly got out of the car, looking scrumptious to her eyes, in fitted Levis, and a simple grey V-neck shirt. Yummy. Her mood lifted immediately. He approached her, and she him. His cologne, Burberry, enveloped her, and so did his arms.

"Mmm, Ronnie," he mumbled against her lips. "I'm starving," he breathed before pressing a kiss to her lips.

"Good," she murmured when he pulled back. "I cooked up a storm."

"I meant for you," he whispered, and bit her lip teasingly. His straight white teeth tugged on her bottom lip before releasing it.

"Didn't get enough of me last night?" she laughed.

"No way, not nearly," he chuckled and began walking her to the door. "Maybe I can convince you to come back to the hotel with me after dinner."

"That might be a possibility," she laughed in return, grabbing and squeezing his ass possessively as she walked beside him.

Chapter Twelve

Reaction

Dinner had been a success. Nikko proclaimed his enjoyment of the Italian feast she prepared. Her mom ate heartily to Jay's delight, and the two men got along well, which pleased both of the women.

Knowing her mom needed to work tomorrow, the night ended early, and Ronnie made the excuse to accompany Nikko for a ride not wanting to sleep so early, and announced she would return in a few hours.

Jay made faces at her beyond her mother's back, but she kept her face expressionless as she was getting used to his antics. The man was a beast, but a teddy bear at heart, who loved to tease everyone mercilessly, one target at a time. She was currently his. She liked that part of him.

With a spare key in her purse, she announced they shouldn't wait up. Jay's quick reply was, "We won't." Then, they were off.

The ride to the hotel was silent. The ride up in the elevator wasn't. As soon as the doors slid closed, and they were alone, Nikko pulled her to him. She had been standing in front of him, and he ground his already painfully swollen cock into her sexy ass. "Fuck, Ronnie, you have a great ass," he murmured as he dipped down to press a kiss along her neck from behind. "I've thought of all kinds of delicious things I could do to it."

"My ass?" she laughed, enjoying the sensation of his cock at the apex of her rear. She pushed back into him increasing the pressure. It caused her muscles in her pussy to contract.

"Damn, that feels so good," he murmured as a bell dinged indicating the fourth floor, and the doors slid open. He passed her quickly in the hall, key card out in a flash, and the door of his suite pushed open. She was right behind him passing under his arm. She hadn't taken two steps when he swept her into his arms, and took five more steps and they were in the center of the living room. He set her down behind the sofa that faced the large screen television.

"Get undressed, Ronnie," he commanded. He wasn't wasting any time. Neither was she. She unbuttoned her blouse, and he already had his T-shirt off.

"In a hurry," she teased, allowing the soft silky shirt to slide down her shoulders to the floor.

"Yes, I want to bury my cock in you, baby. Fuck you until you scream my name." His pants were undone, and he was pushing out of them. Ronnie kicked her heels off, and he stood only in his boxers.

She wasn't fast enough for him though. His arousal and desire for this woman was almost painful, and he was taken aback by it. He missed her today, and for him it had been unsettling to say the least. Ronnie still wore her skirt, and he wasn't waiting any longer. Taking her by the shoulders, he turned her away from him, and at first she seemed to resist, but his hand slid between her legs from behind. He found her core, cupped her pussy, and pushed her legs apart. He slipped his hand around the front and tugged her panties down off her hips. She instinctively bent over the back of the sofa. He finished pulling them down her firm thighs, and she stepped out of them. His left hand stroked upwards until he cupped her again, holding her womanhood, feeling the heat. He could feel the muscles inside trembling. His right hand pushed her down more, so she was bent over and holding herself up with her arms on the seat cushions. He coaxed her to bend all the way over. He slid a finger inside her, and was delighted she was already wet for him.

Her moans encouraged him, and her breathing began to increase in tempo. He felt her relax, and then he hitched up her skirt higher, so he could see her lovely ass, his palm itched, and he had the urge to slap it, but instead caressed it. He didn't think she would be ready for that yet. But someday, maybe. He let his hand slide up her back again, all the while finger fucking her with his left hand, in an and out, slowly.

"Oh, yes, Nikko, that feels good," she murmured when he stroked her back and then stroked back down to

her ass. Her ass began to squirm, and move, to undulate. He needed to be in her. Needed to feel her pussy squeezing his shaft. Releasing her ass with his right, he lowered his boxer briefs enough to let his cock spring free. He took the condom he removed from his pocket and quickly put it on. He grabbed himself, and ran his cock along the crack of her ass, and felt her tense nervously; yes, that would be later too he thought, and then trailed his cock down to her pussy. He put the tip inside but just the entrance, getting it wet. Then he rubbed it along her ass cheeks, and then back down again.

"Bend down, more, baby," he encouraged, and she complied needing him to be inside her as much as he needed it. Her legs were beginning to shake in anticipation.

"Fuck me, Nikko," she began to beg. "I need it." Like she needed air.

He was willing to comply. Not knowing if she was ready or not, Nikko, placed the tip of his cock at her entrance, and charged. She took him, all of him. In one swift stroke he slammed his cock into her and quickly pulled out, and slammed in again, balls to the wall.

The noise that came out on those two thrusts from him was garbled, but his cock swelled from the heat and the tightness. She was snug, and he loved the feeling of her pussy around him, sucking at him on the withdrawal, and pulling at him on the re-entry. He couldn't control his need, and just kept plunging and fucking, thrusting as she rocked back against him, joining in the frenzied rush to reach climax.

He knew he was going to come, and come fast, but he could also tell she wasn't close yet. "Ronnie, I'm going to . . .," he tried to warn her, but too late. Clenching her hips from behind with both hands now, he thrust into her, holding her tightly, probably leaving marks on her, claiming her, he spilled his seed as his balls clenched and tightened until his release was spent.

Not wanting to leave her without her release for long, he pulled out, and flipped her around. The look on her face was frantic, she hadn't had her orgasm, but he would soon rectify it. Lifting her onto the edge of the sofa, he planted her there, and taking his hand, he inserted two fingers into her. He felt her pussy grip his fingers, and her eyes go wide, as his thumb made contact with her clit. He fucked her with his hands, applying constant pressure. Her breathing quickened, and she began to moan.

"Open your eyes, Ronnie. I want to see your face when I make you come," he murmured as he began to stroke faster.

Her eyes flew open. He wanted to see her beautiful brown eyes dilate when he did this to her. When she came because he made her. His obsession with seeing her eyes was also something new to him. Perhaps because he hadn't been her first, he didn't know. But each and every time, she came, and he knew he would make her come a lot; he wanted her to know it was him bringing her to orgasm.

"Oh Nikko," she began to shake. "That . . . feels . . . fuck!" Her scream tore at his soul. He kept flicking her clit, getting every last bit of tension to leave her body, until she collapsed from the intensity of it into his waiting arms.

Nikko picked up a very spent Ronnie, and carried her to the bed.

***

Ronnie was beat by the time she returned home. And, she had an early day. She needed to use her mom's car, and therefore, she needed to rise early and take her to work. She was also nervous, expecting a call from her attorney as he would watch the tapes today.

Waking up when her phone alarm chimed, she was still quite tired, and sore, she admitted to herself. Nikko was unlike her past experiences. She was definitely learning some new things, new things she quite liked.

Ronnie grabbed a pair of sweat pants and threw them on quickly. Knowing she had to wake up early and drive her mom to work if she wanted to keep her mom's car for the day to run some errands, she showered last night, with Nikko. Brushing her hair to get the tangles out, she was still smiling with those memories, as she clipped up her hair into in a messy knot. She would take care of it later, before she ran her errands, but definitely after taking her mom to work.

She could hear her mom in the kitchen. Louisa had always been an early riser. Not wanting to make her mom late, she came out of her room to grab a quick cup of coffee for the road; she would eat later, but stopped dead in her tracks when she saw her mom sitting at the table. She looked green.

"What's wrong?" she asked going to her.

"Not feeling well. It must be the flu," Lou mumbled, foregoing her usual cup of coffee for ginger ale.

"The flu?" she questioned, touching her hand to her mom's forehead. It felt cold, and clammy, not warm. "You're not still going to work are you?" she probed with concern.

"No, sweetie. I've already called in. I'll just tough it out." Her mom sighed and picked up her glass of ginger ale taking a small sip.

"You should see a doctor." Ronnie voiced her opinion.

Lou heard it from Jay earlier, before he had gone into work. She nodded her assent and took another sip before speaking. "I will call when the office opens up later." Lou stated, taking yet another sip of her flat ginger ale to settle her stomach. Jay had been out the door practically, when she had lost her cookies, and returned at the sound of her retching. She wouldn't be able to keep her pregnancy from him and Ronnie for too much longer. Someone was

bound to figure it out sooner or later. And she'd rather tell them than let them figure it out on their own.

Jay's worry was apparent, and she hated not telling him. But her concern for Ronnie overshadowed that. After seeing the doctor today, ensuring everything was fine, she would tell him tonight first, and then her daughter. She made her decision this morning when another bout of morning sickness had her running to the bathroom.

After convincing and promising Jay she would go see a doctor, and letting him witness her calling in to take a sick day, he had finally gone into work. Normally, he had the day off, but had been called in when his boss announced the Blackhawk choppers at the airfield would be performing afternoon drills, and he was needed to finish some routine maintenance before the pre-flight routines could be handled. Two others had called in sick, and since he was low man on the totem pole he really needed to go. But, he also made her promise to call him after she left the doctors. He wanted to know what was wrong right away.

"I think you should just go, and be there when they open," Ronnie suggested. Her mother looked pale.

"Yeah, that might actually be a good idea. Jay is so worried, and I hate for him to worry when he has so much going on at work today. They open at nine. I'll go get ready, but unless my stomach settles, I don't think I should drive myself," she informed her daughter, silently asking her to take her.

"I'll drive you, Mom. We've got time. I can always do the things I need to take care of after I bring you back, and see you settled down and resting." Ronnie was relieved her mom was agreeing so easily. She wasn't one to miss work, or go to the doctor. She hoped it was a simple flu bug like her mom thought. But, she had a niggling suspicion this, whatever it was, wasn't a simple flu bug.

***

With her mom getting ready in her room, Ronnie retreated to her own bedroom to make herself look more presentable. She needed to go to the bank, and take care of some things her attorney asked her to do. She also needed some money, and had a bit left in her savings account. She didn't want to ask her mom for money for personal items, and didn't expect Nikko to always treat her. Then, she wanted to do a bit of shopping since her luggage still had not been returned to her from evidence.

Within an hour the women were off. Lou suggested Ronnie complete one of her errands so as not to waste her day while her mom waited at the doctor's office to be seen. Leery of leaving her mom, who still looked unwell, she eventually agreed when she saw how agitated her mom was becoming, and because she was insistent. Reluctantly she agreed to drop her off at her doctors, but promised to be back within the hour, only going to Walgreens on the corner to shop for some essentials with what little cash she had.

She would need to go to the bank for more, but thought that would take longer, and wanted to be done by the time her mom was ready to go home.

At Walgreens, she purchased a bit of make-up to replace her own that had yet to be returned, some feminine hygiene products, a hair brush, and curling iron, and her own toiletries. Her mom was waiting outside on a bench when she returned and to her relief looked much better.

Her mom walked to the car just as she pulled into a parking spot. "What did she say, Mom?" Ronnie asked with concern.

Her mom gave her a bright smile. "Everything is fine. She did blood work here in the office, and all looked well. And she gave me something for the nausea."

"But what's causing it?" Ronnie asked not convinced. There was something her mom was not telling her.

"It could have been flu, my nerves," she shrugged. "But she gave me some tablets to take until it passes." Lou didn't mention the prescription for pre-natal vitamins she had given her. She was further along then she had thought. The doctor did an ultrasound to calculate how far along she might be, and that's why the nausea was so bad. Four months. Even with Ronnie she hadn't started showing much until her fifth month. She'd fill her prescription tonight after she told Jay, have him get some ginger snaps, not wanting to take the tablets unless absolutely necessary. The morning, noon, and night sickness would soon pass. She stopped being sick with Ronnie when she started her second trimester, and according to the doctor she was there now.

Ronnie gave her mom, a suspicious look, out of the corner of her eye, hoping her mom wouldn't keep something from her just because of her own circumstances. Her mom didn't notice though as she seemed lost in her own thoughts.

The ride home didn't take long and Lou, feeling even more revived, encouraged Ronnie to go finish her errands. Even though Ronnie felt weird about it and still felt strange leaving her, she really needed to take care of some things. She did promise to hurry.

Lou promised to settle in on the sofa, and rest, enjoying her day off. She would text her if she needed anything. Ronnie wasted no time. She wanted to return as quickly as she could.

***

Unfortunately, as quick as she could took much longer than Ronnie hoped. The bank took hours, but she had her eight thousand bond cashed, and for good measure she took five hundred out of her savings knowing she might not get a second trip to the bank soon. Plus, she needed to turn the eight grand over to her attorney, Mr. Stimson.

After the bank, was Wal-Mart for under garments, and the mall for a couple of outfits that fit her a bit better than those she borrowed from her mother. She also made a quick detour into Victoria Secret. She wanted to treat herself and Nikko to something new.

Then, on her way out of the mall, she ran into Margaret, her one and only friend in the area, and also her hairstylist when she was in town. She and Brad, one of her employees, hung out a few times last summer and had hit it off.

The pretty young blonde, just twenty-three, had started her own salon, called Mavericks, on the four corners in Spring Hill, and catered to people who wanted a unique style, blending new with the classic. The name of the salon was just one indication this woman went her own way. She liked her, a lot, and had always managed to spend a couple of days with her whenever she was in town. They had a cup of coffee and caught up. Margaret, was a sweet woman, professed her faith in Ronnie's innocence, and told her to come hang out at the shop if she was bored, or just needed to vent. She even went so far as to offer to be a character witness for her.

By the time she returned home, it was four, and she was surprised to find Jay was home early. He never arrived home from work before six. Figuring he had probably come home to check on Lou she didn't think anything of it at first, but then fear set in. Perhaps her mom had gotten ill again, and called him instead of her. She rushed to the door, but stopped dead in her tracks, when she heard a strange sound coming from inside. It sounded like a pained animal crying out, but somehow she knew it was not Missy making that sound.

Tentatively, Ronnie turned the handle on the front door and it gave way. The sight she was met with was even more frightening to her than anything she could have expected. Her mom was still seated on the sofa, Jay perched on the end, and tears were streaming down his face. That sound was coming from him as a look of pure pain crossed his face, and his sobs were gut wrenching. Staying absolutely still, the door only slightly open, she heard Jay croak out after several more fearful moans, in a guttural whisper. "The doctor told you that. Really?"

"Yes, my love." Lou stroked his arm, giving him encouragement, strength. Ronnie remembered all the times her mother had done that for her when she was upset, trying to instill the courage in her to get through a difficult time.

"Four months?" he questioned. His back was to Ronnie now as he had pivoted on the edge of the sofa to fully face Lou. She saw her mom nod with a sad smile, watching for Jay's reaction. She didn't notice Ronnie at all. A lump formed in Ronnie's throat, and her imagination ran wild with what her mom could possibly mean by four months.

"She's sure," Jay croaked out. The earlier cries of anguish had subsided to soft moans.

"Yes, Jay. Darling. She ran the test twice." Louisa reached out to cup his face. He reached out and held hers.

"Darling, please tell me what you are thinking." Lou broached tentatively. Knowing this news shocked him, he had lost his wife and his only child just weeks before birth. He hadn't ever expressed a desire to have children, even indicated he felt having another one would be disloyal to the baby he lost.

"Oh my God, Lou. I love you so much. I don't know if I can handle this," she heard him say between his gentle sobs.

Ronnie wanted to cry too, knowing all Jay had been through. Now, this. Her mom, sick. Just four months *to live?* Panic set in. She wanted to run to her mother, comfort her, comfort them, but the scene before her was too poignant, too painful for her to watch. She needed to give them this time alone to figure out how they would cope, and so her first thought was Nikko.

She needed to talk this out with someone, and Nikko would do. Surely, he would be done at the county clerk's office, and the sheriff's department by now. They talked about possibly meeting up tonight. He would be headed back to Tampa Tuesday or Wednesday, and promised to return on the weekend. Surely, he wouldn't mind her company a bit early. She needed someone.

Ronnie backed out quietly, and closed the door softly. She picked up the packages she hadn't realized she'd dropped, and went back to her mom's car. Driving up the block, she pulled over to send her mom a quick text. She didn't want her to worry about her prolonged absence, and wanted to give Jay and her some privacy. It would be soon enough, and heart breaking enough for her, when Lou had to break the news to her daughter. Let her mom deal with one crisis at a time. She punched in the message.

Ronnie: Popping in on Nikko. Hope it's okay. Be home in a couple of hours.

Waiting on the side of the road to try to suppress the tears that were on the verge of making it impossible for her to drive, she heard the tell-tale beep of her mom's response.

Lou: Take your time, sweetie. Jay came home early. I'm fine, feeling much better. But do come home. I have some news for you, oh and your lawyer called.

Ronnie dashed at the tears coming down her face. Her mom, always trying to protect her. Her mom, always putting other's first.   Her mom going through this nightmare, whatever it was, still wanted to protect her. Her lawyer had called too. It mustn't be good. The tapes must have shown nothing of significance or else she would have mentioned it in the text. She felt her world tilt on its axis.

She cried violently sitting in the car on the side of the road. Angry at the world, at fate, at herself for trusting Gary. After her mini-breakdown she fought the tears back. She needed to get off the side of the road. Traffic was getting heavier at this time of the day, and someone would be bound to stop and check on her. She stopped her tears, and held the breakdown she knew was coming in check. It could wait until she got to Nikko's hotel. She just had to get there.

Putting the keys back in the ignition, she started the car, and pulled back onto the road repeating the words, don't cry, don't cry, not yet. It became her mantra. The hotel was just a few miles away. Please be there, Nikko, she whispered. She hoped she could find her solace in him.

But even that was way too much to count on. When the world decided to put Ronnie Sears on its shit list, it held nothing back. As Ronnie pulled into the parking lot, she had her second, no, third shock of the day. Walking out of the hotel was Nikko, and by his side was the fucking barbecue bimbo, Linda. In a blind rage, and not knowing if up was down, Ronnie hit the gas, and sped out of the parking lot tires spinning. She had no idea where she was going. She had no idea what the hell she was going to do. Her world was crumbling down around her, and she had no one to turn to, nowhere to go. As she drove down the highway, the tears coming, the only thing she knew was she had to get the hell out of here.

Chapter Thirteen

And Down Comes the Hammer

Ronnie was just driving. She was too upset to think straight. First this mess with Gary. Then her mom, then Nikko. What more was going to be dumped on her before she would break?

She just drove. She didn't know for how long. Time just passed and when she realized she was near Mavericks, she stopped. She needed to talk to someone. Anyone. And even though she had just seen her hours earlier, Margaret would have to do. She was her only other friend in this area. And, she also knew she would be on her side.

Pulling into the shopping complex on the corner of Spring Hill Drive and Mariner Blvd., Lou quickly got out of her mother's car, grabbed her purse, and locked the doors.

She was relieved to see Margaret wasn't busy when she opened the front door to the small salon. There was only one woman there getting her hair colored by another stylist. Those two, and the girl who worked the counter were the only other people in the place. Brad had the evening off.

"Long time no see," Margaret teased when she saw her friend walk in. But as soon as she saw Ronnie's face, saw the fear and pain there, she uttered, "Oh my God, what happened in the last two hours? You look a wreck. Come," she ordered, leading Ronnie to the back room, where Margaret had a break room for her employees that also served as storage. "Sit."

Ronnie complied. She felt lost. The tears just came. Margaret was quick to sit next to her to provide her comfort. She reached for her hand and ordered her to spill. Ronnie did. It all came rushing out.

Margaret's grasp on her hand got tighter when Ronnie told her about her fears for her mother. Margaret's look got angry when Ronnie explained where she went after leaving her mom's and finding Nikko walking barbecue bimbo, Linda, out of the hotel.

"What am I going to do?" Ronnie flatly asked. Her tears had stopped. She was still distraught about her mother, but she was also so extremely disappointed in Nikko. He promised, well somewhat, that he would be additional support for her through this ordeal. He'd also implied he would be monogamous, hadn't he? Her mind couldn't wrap around it all.

"First of all, lose the loser, Ronnie. You're better than that. He doesn't deserve you. Obviously last summer the little parking lot scene was probably what it was. Him leaving the hotel with this Linda chick is proof of that. Once a player, always a player. The guy is no good. He can talk a good game, charm the pants off of you, but once out of sight, out of mind." Ronnie nodded numbly. She should have trusted her instincts. Nikko, with his looks and charm, could have any girl he wanted, and apparently did. She didn't want to be anyone's fool. First Gary, and now him. What the hell had she been thinking to get involved with such a ladies man even if she knew it was temporary? He'd made her think he'd be different with her. So stupid. Was she that desperate to put her faith in him? She was just so stupid when it came to men. Obviously, her two times at bat was telling. Did she need to be clobbered over the head or something? Did the universe have to hit her over the head with a hammer?

"You're right," Ronnie agreed. "I really feel like such an idiot. I hate being played. I just thought he'd . . ." her words trailed and she let the rest go unsaid.

But Margaret finished her thought. "You thought he'd be different with you. You were attracted to him. The guy is hot. I'll give you that. So, you had a few hook ups. But get out now. Don't let him drop the hammer, girlfriend. Beat him to the punch. Put your focus on your case, and your mom, and kick this guy to the curb."

Her mom! Her case. That's what mattered now. That's where her head should have been all along. She felt the coils of strength beginning to return. She needed to focus on herself. She vowed she wasn't going to let anyone else use her—ever again. If her mom taught her anything, it was never be anyone's doormat. She wasn't about to be Nikko's. Hell no! The coils burst into small licks of flame. Ronnie glanced at the clock. It was just five. The flames grew higher. She did want to get home. But there was one thing she wanted to do before she left. A plan was starting to form.

"Margaret?" she asked. Her eyes narrowed with determination.

Margaret saw the change come over her. "What do you need, honey?" Margaret was relieved to see a bit of the Ronnie she knew coming back. There was a tiny spark in those baby browns. Ronnie just needed a push, and then the tough spunky girl she befriended a few years ago would emerge. "What's on your mind? Whatever you need," she reiterated her earlier promise from the mall squeezing her friend's hand one more time.

Smiling up at her very talented friend, her eyes showed the determination that was so much a part of her character once more. "My hair." Margaret smiled knowingly. Nodded, arched her eyebrow, and got up.

"Ab-so-lute-ly!" She enunciated each syllable. "Nothing like a new hairstyle to light a fire under someone." And Margaret knew exactly what she was going to do. This girl needed to be reminded each time she looked in the mirror if anyone messed with her, they would be burned.

Ronnie followed Margaret to her station inside the salon prepared to let her have her way with her. She had a few ideas, but she'd leave the creative parts to the professional.

***

Margaret was just finishing up with an amazing new hairstyle for her, and it was close to seven when Ronnie heard her phone notifications indicate she had a message. Swiping at the screen to activate her phone, she saw two missed texts. One was from Nikko, and the other was from her mom. And as hard a she tried not to, she glanced at Nikko's first wondering what the ass hat wanted. He had some nerve. Afternoon delight with Linda and now he was looking for his nightly booty call. Smirking, she tapped his name and read his message.

Nikko: We're still on for tonight, right? What time do you want me to come get you, babe? :)

Never. Asshole!

Reading over her shoulder, Margaret just made a disgusted sound in the back of her throat and set to work cleaning up her station giving Ronnie a little privacy. She quickly tapped out her response. She had been formulating a plan, but hadn't shared the details with Margaret.

Ronnie: Not tonight. Something came up.

She had been tempted to say she had a headache, but did not want to show any signs of sarcasm, or get his suspicious nature on alert. And the truth was she needed to be with her mom tonight. Not that she was going to avoid Nikko forever, she just needed to think of how she was going to handle that situation. And when. The man was definitely not off the hook for his actions, and he was going to get a piece of her mind.

She was going to switch over to read her mom's message, but before she could even look, Nikko texted back.

Nikko: What's up? :(

Your cock's up a brunette, fucker. That's what's up! Asshole.

Ronnie: My mom is sick. I'll ttyl.

Nikko: K. Sorry. Tomorrow then? <3

Tomorrow? Definitely. She wasn't slinking away like last summer. No way. She just had to get all the pieces together.

Ronnie: Sure. Definitely. I'll text you details later tonight. Need to take care of mom right now. She is not well at all.

Honesty. She'd give him a bit of the truth. She'd let the fireworks happen later. And not the kind of fireworks he would be expecting to get either.

Nikko: Anything I can do? I'll miss you tonight.

Sure you will. I bet.

Ronnie: No. Thanks. Ttyl.

Nikko: Sleep tight.

Shaking her head in disgust, she didn't bother to respond. She backed her texts up to see the one from her mom.

Lou: Hey hon. Don't want to rush you, but would like to talk to you tonight. Have some things to talk about, and your lawyer called. Can you come home before I go to bed around eleven?

She answered her mom right away.

Ronnie: I'm on my way now actually. See you soon. Love you.

Lou: Oh good. Got some news, good and bad, but don't rush. Nothing too serious.

Just like her mom, to worry about everyone but herself. Nothing too serious. Yeah right. At least her lawyer must have good news then, unlike what she thought earlier because she knew her mom's wasn't going to be. Even though her heart sank at the news her mom was about to tell her, she reminded herself she needed to be strong now. For her, and for Jay. There had to be some way to fight whatever she had. Determined to do whatever it took to help her mom, and beat this rap, she steeled herself for what was to come. She was ready to put up a good fight. Margaret returned and was curling a few pieces more of her hair, some final touch ups and a bit of hair spray to hold her new look all together.

"All done," Margaret announced, turning her around so Ronnie could finally see her reflection in the elegant mirrors Margaret recently purchased for the shop.

Ronnie gasped at the difference this new hair style, cut and color, made. "Fantastic," she announced, a slow smile spreading across her face. "I love it." Gone were the dirty blond waves, and pink streak. The platinum blond shaggy cut swung around her shoulders, the tips ending with a halo of red and orange. It looked like her hair was on fire. She loved it. It was Marilyn Monroe meets Katniss Everdeen. It was exactly what she needed. Something to remind her of her inner fire. Margaret was talented.

"It looks hot! The platinum suits you, and so does the fire."

Ronnie admired the look with a few more glances in the mirror tilting her head to see it at different angles. As it swung around her shoulders it looked like her hair was ablaze. But, she didn't have much time. She had plans to make, and her mom to see and console.

Ronnie hugged her friend good bye, tipped her generously even when Margaret tried to protest. She was ready to face her mom. Nikko could wait. Let him stew awhile, she mused. But he'd face his comeuppance soon. The prick. He'd realize the ice princess could burn too.

***

Ronnie pulled into her driveway. Jay was home; she braced herself and took several calming breaths before she got out of the car. Seeing her fall apart was the last thing her mom needed.

Turning the handle, she slowly pushed open the door. Her mom and Jay were in the kitchen putting away the dishes they apparently just washed. Jay was laughing about something. She found that odd. Just three hours ago, the bear of a man had been crying like a tortured animal. Her mom, still looked frail, but she was smiling from ear to ear. Ronnie cleared her throat to announce her arrival, and they both turned to her.

Lou's eyes widened at her daughter. Her hair! It looked magnificent. The steaks were gone; the blonde shimmered like the palest of gold, and was tipped with red, and orange. "Wow! I didn't know you were getting your hair done. It looks great. I love it."

"Thanks," Ronnie returned the smile. "I just felt like I needed to do something different, and then when the trial comes up, I can always just get the tips trimmed."

"Good idea," her mom nodded. "Although I really like the tips. My baby girl is on fire." Lou laughed and Jay added his own laughter after delivering a wolfish whistle.

Their good humor was beginning to really confuse Ronnie. So, she set her shopping bags down by the door, and approached them. But, she would let her mom take the lead, tell her in her own time. Her mind was trying to sort out this change in mood. Probably, putting on a happy face for her daughter. But she wanted the truth, all of it. Good and bad. She needed to know what they were dealing with so she could help her mom.

"Yeah, I like it too," she added. "Nikko wasn't in, so I got my hair done. Visited with Margaret."

"Oh, that's nice. I like her. She does good work. Really different, but stunning. I should go see her."

"You can't," Jay burst out. ""I heard the chemicals..."

Lou silenced him with a look.

Ronnie needed to know what was going on. "Why can't she?" she asked. She hoped it would encourage the two to reveal their secret.

Lou and Jay exchanged a look. Then a small smile. He patted and rubbed her back affectionately, and nodded.

Lou looked to Ronnie. "Sit down, baby. We've got some news."

"Yes, um . . . you mentioned some good news and bad news in your text," Ronnie prompted when her mom stalled. Jay and Louisa exchanged another secretive look.

Ronnie looked at them both curiously, and went into the kitchen and sat at the counter. "So, what's up?" She waited.

Lou looked to Jay one more time. "You tell her, Jay," she encouraged. Ronnie was so confused. The two were now grinning like the cat that caught the canary.

"You sure?" he asked. "You want me to tell her?"

"Yes, tell her." Lou laughed as he turned to face Ronnie.

Ronnie looked to him expectantly.

"Well," he started. "Your mom . . ."

"And you," Lou added when he stopped.

He gave her the biggest smile.

"Your mom and I," he emphasized, "well, we are going to have a baby."

A baby!!! Ronnie practically fell out of her chair. Her head snapped back and forth several times. Her eyes grew round. *Four months?* Her mother had said four months. She had assumed that it meant four months to live, but now it dawned on her. Her mother had meant she was four months pregnant.

"A . . . a . . . baby?" she croaked.

"Yep, I know. I was as shocked as you," Jay stated, seeing the worry on her face. "But, are you okay with this?"

She saw the worry there. *For her?* "Uh, yeah!" Relief swept through her. "A brother or sister. Holy hell! I'm more than okay with that. Holy hell!" She got off her seat and rushed around the counter pulling her mom into her arms, the mother she thought she might lose.

Her mom was mumbling something. She made herself focus on what she was saying. "Yeah, I'm already four months along. I have suspected it for a while, I took a test, and the doctor confirmed it today. But, I had no idea I was that far along."

"Oh my God!" Ronnie shrieked pulling her mom back and looking at her. "You're not even showing."

"I carried well with you too. I will be showing soon enough. My fifth month with you I gained like two pounds a week." She patted her belly which was only slightly rounded.

"Oh my God!" she repeated. "This is fantastic. This is great news. It's perfect and I couldn't be happier for you both," she cried into her mom's shoulder both relief and joy flooding her. She pulled back and gazed into her mom's eyes seeing the happiness there. Jay had lost his first child so tragically, and now he and her mom would have a child together. Her mom was thirty-eight, Jay thirty-two. They were still young and they deserved this.

"We are happy, too," Lou announced. The trio untangled themselves from each other. "That's why I have been so sick. But, I don't want you to worry about this. I'll love you always. No baby replaces my love for you."

"M-o-m," Ronnie shook her head. "That thought never crossed my mind."

She wasn't twelve. She was thrilled, this family needed good news right now more than anything. Her day had been so dark, and now this. She guessed it was true, every cloud did have its silver lining. But then another thought struck her. What was the bad news her mother alluded to? She didn't want to voice that concern just yet. She didn't want to ruin this moment. She wanted to embrace it and hang onto it for just a little bit. It was their time. But, the worry was there. The bad news must be from her lawyer then. She shook her head to clear her thoughts when her mom started to speak again.

"I know. The timing isn't great. We hadn't planned it. But, now that this baby is on the way, we have a lot to do. We just don't want you to think," she cleared her throat before she continued, "the baby will get in the way of us supporting you in this situation." When Ronnie was about to interrupt, Lou raised her voice and added, "Don't worry about this, you hear me. Focus on your case. Understand. I'll take good care of myself, too."

"I'll make sure of that," Jay added.

"Will do," she saluted the duo. She had thought she was walking into yet another nightmare. It was about time this family had some good news. "I'll focus on my case, but," she stressed, "I want to help with the baby stuff."

"We will have the baby in our room for the first few months, darling. By then, hopefully, you'll be cleared and then we'll worry about everything else. Jay is planning on adding a room onto the house," she beamed up at her very handy husband.

"Well, I can help with that," Ronnie nodded. "I'm pretty handy with a hammer, too."

They all laughed.

"It's about time we had some great news." Ronnie voiced her earlier thoughts. "Wait until you tell Ana and Monica. Monica is having twins, Jessica is three. You'll all be raising your babies together."

"Um," Jay interrupted. Lou looked at him, and her smile lessened.

"What?" Ronnie asked.

Lou looked to her. "We did get a bit of bad news today." And there it was. Gone in a moment. Ronnie waited, nodded at her mom for her to go ahead. "Mr. Stimson called."

"Okay," she encouraged her mom to go on.

"The tapes."

Oh god, they didn't show what they'd all hoped.

"Yeah, um, they show him walking away quickly, but he ducked into a rest room. So Mr. Stimson doesn't think they will help much. It just looks like he had to go to the bathroom. And, Mr. Stimson had someone go by to interview Gary in Maine. Get a feel for him, his character. Seems he has disappeared. Your graduation was supposed to be Wednesday. They are hoping he will show up for that. Mr. Stimson hired someone to be there and keep a look out for him. Hopefully, he will show. Even the police in Bangor have been called out to find him and talk to him. But, Mr. Stimson says his apartment has been cleaned out, his parents say they haven't seen him. That he went away with some friends for a few days."

"So they say," Ronnie interjected. The powerful Campbell's would surely not let the police question their son. They were super protective of their over indulged only son. The heir to the Campbell Timber Empire.

"Well, don't get too discouraged. Mr. Stimson said he would call back tomorrow and give us an update. Maybe they will track him down before the graduation," Lou added.

"Yeah maybe. And as for the graduation, that is a big if too," she mumbled under her breath.

If Ronnie didn't know him better, she felt in her heart he would hide out until her trial was over. Then another thought began to take hold. If he was hiding out, she did know a few places he would most likely go. What if she could get to him first? She knew all his hiding places. Yes, she most certainly did.

"Mr. Stimson and the police are looking for him, Ronnie. He'll show up," Jay added confidently when Ronnie had become quiet and contemplative.

And if he didn't. She could rot in jail for up to twenty years. There was no way in hell that was going to happen! Another plan was starting to form. But, she needed to act fast. She also wanted to deal with Nikko. There was no way in hell he was getting away with using her too.

***

Ronnie was ready by ten. She was just waiting for her mom and Jay to go to bed. They watched a movie together, and it was nearly over. She had gotten up to go to "the bathroom," and returned ten minutes later, and no one had been the wiser. In her room, which was right near the bathroom, she packed her bag, a backpack with what she needed. A couple of comfortable outfits, a jacket for when she got where she was going. Her money, wallet, some toiletries, and supplies, and her mother's ID, and credit card. She needed the ID, didn't plan on using the credit card. It was just back up. Getting out of the house would be the easy part. The rest, well, it would be tough, but manageable.

As the movie ran its course, she mentally composed the note she would leave her mom. Keep it simple, but reassure her. This was something she needed to do.

When the credits rolled, Jay got up pulling his wife to her feet as if she were already nine months along. It made Ronnie feel good knowing he would be here to keep an eye on her. She knew her mom would worry, of course, but she would be fine. She would be careful. This baby meant the world to them.

She was glad they were going to bed earlier than usual.

Before her mom left, Ronnie got up as well, and reached for her. Hugging her, she whispered, "Mom. I love you. I am so happy for you. Happy for you both. Everything is going to work out."

"Thank-you sweetie." Her mom returned the hug. Lou heard a note in her daughter's voice that made her worry temporarily. "Honey, for you too." She pulled back to look in her daughter's eyes. "We will get you through this. I don't have any doubts."

Ronnie squared her shoulders. She still had doubts, but she was now ready to do something about it.

They said their final goodnights, and as soon as Jay and Lou's bedroom door was closed, she went into action. In her room, she sat down on the foot of her bed to write Lou a note.

Mom,

Please don't worry. Sorry I had to do it this way. I think I know where Gary might be. I'm going after him. Take care of yourself and that sweet baby brother or sister of mine. I love you. If all works out as I have planned, I'll clear my name within the week. Please, don't tell anyone right away. I need a head start. Just a little one. Okay.

Love you,

Veronica

She folded the single sheet of paper in half, drew a heart on the outside, tented it, and placed it on the center of the beautiful quilt her mom had purchased for her.

Part one of her plan was done, and now it was time to start the second part of her plan. She hoped it would go off without a hitch.

She took her phone and texted Nikko.

Ronnie: Mom just went to bed. She's feeling better. Can you come get me? I can spend the night.

Ronnie played with the charm bracelet she always wore. A gift from Jay last Christmas. She was nervous. She needed Nikko to come get her. She needed his car. Luckily, she didn't have to wait long.

Nikko: ;) I'm on my way, babe. Be there in ten.

Perfect.

Picking up her backpack, she quietly slipped from her room stopping in the kitchen to grab a couple of things she needed. She would wait outside by the road. She didn't want Jay or Lou to see the lights of Nikko's car, and wonder, or come out. The lights were already out in their room, but Missy who was sleeping in her doggy bed in the center of the living room, lifted her head questioningly.

"Go back to sleep, Missy. Keep your eye on mom for me, will you," she whispered in the dark. Missy shook her head up and down as if she was answering her, and then snuggled back into her dog bed. Great dog, the best, she thought.

Heading to the sliding glass doors that led to the Florida room and outside, Ronnie quietly unlatched the locking mechanism to open the large panes of glass, and then slowly opened the heavy door. As soon as there was enough room for her and her bag to get through, she slipped past, and made her way outside. She slid the door back in place, and went by way of the back yard to the front.

Walking as quietly as she could, choosing sensible sneakers and comfortable jeans, she walked alongside of the driveway instead of on the gravel that might give her away.

Nikko would be here soon as the hotel wasn't far. Setting her bag down beside her once she reached the end of the driveway, she stooped over and unzipped the front pocket. Inside she retrieved the little plastic baggie, containing two capsules of an over-the-counter sleeping medication she swiped out of the medicine cabinet. They were Jay's. He took them when he was having a bad night. He had PTSD, and occasionally became very restless and agitated. These calmed him down pretty quick, and he was soon sleeping soundly. She just hoped they worked on Nikko. And although she was pretty upset with the bastard, she hoped there were no other side effects. Jay's dosage was two pills, so that was what she had taken. Her plan was to give Nikko one by slipping it into his drink, and if he failed to fall asleep quickly enough, she'd slip in another one.

She used her phone to research the drug while they were watching the movie, and felt confident it wouldn't kill him, but he, because he wasn't used to the drug, might have one hell of a headache afterwards.

She slipped the baggie into the front pocket of her jeans patting it down ensuring it didn't make a bulge. No sooner had she done that, she saw headlights approaching.

***

Nikko saw her right away. He found it odd to see her standing on the side of the road, a bulky bag beside her.

Pulling up next to her, she quickly got inside, and shut the door carefully.

"I'm glad you called, babe. But what's with the big bag?" he asked eyeing the black ruck sack she stuffed between her legs on the floorboard.

"Oh, well," she forced a smile, trying to blow off the question. "I thought I would spend the night."

"Um, okay." He sounded pleased, but from the squint of his eyes, she knew he was still suspicious. To distract him, she leaned into him to press a kiss to his cheek. He gave her his lips instead. Her stomach lurched at the contact, but she didn't turn away. The sparks that flew betrayed her heart and mind. She didn't want to feel the heat between them, but her body still responded to everything this man had to offer.

Nikko sensed there was something up with Ronnie. His instincts told him something was wrong even though her kiss was full of her usual vigor and passion. When they parted, he peered at her more closely in the now dark interior of the car. He noticed her hair then. "Wow, you got your hair done; it looks fantastic," he said, momentarily distracted.

"Thanks," she murmured not able to meet his gaze. She turned looking back towards her house one last time ensuring no lights flicked on, and her disappearing act had gone unnoticed for now. Turning back to him, she gave him a dazzling smile.

"Can we go baby, I don't want to wake up my mom. She was really sick, and Jay just got her to fall asleep. It was one heck of a day. I'll tell you all about it when we get to the hotel," Ronnie rushed to say, hoping her ramblings would distract him. But, he was still looking at her funny.

"Okay," he eased up slightly. After a moment of driving in silence he continued. "Bad day, huh?" He knew he was probing as he took the turns on the curvy road with ease, but his senses told him something was bothering Ronnie. When she remained silent, he picked up his speed a little.

Nikko gave her another sideways glance and feeling his eyes on her Ronnie knew she needed to respond. But her mind was racing as her plan was running through her head. Everything had to go just right. "Yeah, rough day," she murmured. She couldn't meet his eyes. She nervously checked one more time behind her, to ensure her departure was not noticed. She saw no lights, and let out a soft breath.

She's up to something, Nikko's mind was telling him. His every instinct said something was wrong. "Jay knows you came out with me then?" he asked, trying to get her to talk.

"Of course," her head snapped back to him. She needed to be more careful. He was picking up on her emotions. She needed to calm down and focus on him. She gave him a little laugh trying to make it sound casual. "You are not going to believe all that went down today, baby." She added the baby after a slight pause and hoped he hadn't noticed.

"Wow, it sounds like you did have one heck of a day," he threw in. "Sure you don't want to talk about it now?"

"Um, well, it sure was," she laughed, letting out her breath. She needed to keep him distracted and so continued. "It was crazy. And I'm sure yours was boring, just filing papers, and standing in line at the clerks and sheriff's office."

"Um, yeah, I got all that done today. Pretty routine stuff. Boring, I don't know," he added nonchalantly.

Boring my ass, she thought. She was sure Barbecue Bimbo had entertained him plenty. She hid the sarcasm from her voice when she spoke next. "My poor baby. It must have been a real snooze fest."

"Well," he laughed to ease the tension, "I was thinking about you the whole time, so that made it not so boring. I must say I was disappointed as hell when you texted you couldn't come. But, I guess you got busy with your mom and all. I hope she is feeling better. What was the matter with her anyhow?" he asked pointedly.

Ronnie wasn't going to be able to stall him much longer, so she threw him a bone. "When I tell you what was wrong with her, you are not going to believe it. But she was feeling much better tonight."

He could tell she was stalling. She wasn't answering his questions. It bothered him. She normally wasn't one to beat around the bush.

"Damn girl, you are really piquing my interest here. Did it have something to do with her nausea? Is she pregnant?" he teased smiling mischievously at Ronnie. "You gonna be a big sister?"

Startled that he guessed correctly, her head whipped to him and her eyes grew wide.

"Holy hell," he laughed. He couldn't contain it. Her reaction had given her away. "Oh my God! Your mom *IS* pregnant."

"Yeah," she laughed. "I can't believe you guessed it."

"I was teasing when I said it. But, holy hell." He let out a low whistle. It explained her concern over her mother. "How old is your mom anyway?" he asked out of curiosity.

His comment struck a nerve, and she couldn't' help but snap. "She's only thirty-eight. She had me when she was sixteen."

"Oh," Nikko said lamely. He heard the hint of annoyance in her voice. "Sorry, babe, no judgment. I knew she had you young. It happens."

"Yeah, it happens," she muttered.

Sensing her mood had soured, he tried to lighten the atmosphere. "So, is everyone happy about it?" he asked. He didn't think she would be the kind of daughter who would mind having another sibling. Her reactions were just so strange tonight.

Ronnie saw the hotel looming in the distance. She needed to save some of this conversation for later. She needed it to distract him. This is what she wanted to talk about when they got into his hotel room while she waited for the drug to take effect.

"Jay is thrilled. Me too. Just worried about mom, both of us." She didn't elaborate further. As they pulled into the parking lot, she enacted the next part of her plan. "I'm so thirsty. Got anything to drink in your hotel room?" She gave him a smile.

"Um, yeah, I got some juice, and ice tea. Or did you mean liquor?" he wondered.

"I actually could use a real drink tonight."

"Sounds like it," he responded. "I have some vodka, and rum, the little bottles. I could make you a screwdriver." He was pulling into the parking lot of the hotel.

"Perfect. I love those. I make them great," she offered. "How about if we both have one?" she gave him her most mischievous smile.

"Sounds good, and then you can tell me all about this crazy day of yours. Then maybe we can have a little fun," he winked, trying to lighten the mood.

"Absolutely," she purred. When he cut the engines, they both got out of the car quickly. He made his way over to her as they approached the lobby doors, and took her bag from her. It was surprisingly quite heavy. What did she have in there, rocks?

Ronnie noticed him mentally weighing her bag, so to distract him she reached for his hand and entwined her fingers with his.

He looked down at her and smiled. He loved the feel of her small hand in his, and her smile was nice to see. He quickly gave her a peck on the cheek. Being this close and with the light from the lamp posts in the parking lot, he really noticed her hair for the first time. Her hair was something. She had gone platinum, the tips astonishing, and it suited her. He couldn't wait to get her inside, and see it more clearly. He had liked it before, but this blonde was doing things to him. And even though, she was acting strangely it just might be due to her concern over her mom, and this new bit of news about a sibling had shocked her.

"I missed you," he murmured and bent down to capture her lips with his own.

Seeing him look down on her that way, Ronnie had to shake her head. He was saying all the right things. He sounded like he meant every word. It did strange things to her. It was a shame this was just a sham for him, a diversion while he worked. She felt the pang of disappointment anew. As his tongue sought entrance, she couldn't help but respond. It eased the ache in her heart if only for a moment.

Nikko gently dropped her bag down beside them and drew her closer, holding her close. Her body soon willingly conformed to his.

He held her like he cared. Soon Ronnie found she couldn't hold back. Her body responded to him immediately. She felt an ache in her loins, and surprisingly an ache in her heart. This would be the last time she ever kissed this man, and as he broke the kiss, and looked down into her eyes, a bit of her melted. He gave her a quick chaste kiss on the cheek, and lifted her bag from the ground. Winking mischievously, the gleam back in his eyes, they resumed their walk to the doors and the lobby. Ronnie wanted to cry. It was in that moment she realized she had fallen in love with the man. The fucker! What she was going to do in the next half an hour, well, it would shred her heart. But, she had to. Her life was on the line, and she needed this shadow to be gone so her mom and Jay, and new brother or sister could move on with their lives. She'd get over this. She hoped.

And as for Nikko, he had it coming. He couldn't keep toying with people like this. He couldn't take advantage of her while she was down on her luck. She wasn't going to let anyone use her ever again and steeled her heart for what was going to happen in the next thirty minutes. This was something she needed to do she kept repeating to herself as they entered the lobby and walked steadily to the elevators. Yes, something she needed to do, she told herself more resolutely even though she was still having her doubts.

Chapter Fourteen

Flight

Fifteen minutes later Nikko was snoring on the floor. Ronnie put a pillow under his head even though the cheating bastard didn't deserve it. Seeing him there, looking a complete and utter mess made her feel a pang of remorse. But just a pang. Her instincts told her last year this guy couldn't keep it in his pants. But she denied those instincts. It was her own fault. Again. Trusting the wrong guy. She shook her head in disgust. He was going to be pissed.

But she needed to focus now. Time was of the essence. There would be time later for regret. She rifled in his pants pocket until she found the keys to his car. He would be fuming when he woke up and realized she had taken his precious baby, his car. But she'd be careful with it. She wasn't that vengeful. She wanted him to know without a doubt not to mess with her feelings again.

She just needed his car for an hour anyway. To get to the airport. She closed her palm over the keys and looked down one more time at Nikko. It was a shame.

Getting her bag where Nikko set it on the dresser in the bedroom while she fixed the drinks, she opened up the top compartment and reached way down inside, past her clothes and felt for the plastic bottles she stuffed into them at the last minute. Revenge would be sweet. Sweet and tangy to be exact. She pulled out the two plastic bottles labeled Sweet Baby Ray's Barbecue Sauce. Both brand new. Jay's favorite. Another shame, she thought, as she screwed off the caps. Placing the lids on the bedside table, she peeled off the silver safety seals. Yes, she'd have to buy Jay more. But, this was worth it.

She put the little white caps back on, and walked quickly back to the living room area before she changed her mind and lost her nerve. Smiling down on Nikko, she put one bottle under her arm, and flipped the cap on the other. He was out cold. "So you like barbecue, you pig?" she said the words softly just in case he woke up. She was sure he wouldn't, but wanted to be careful just in case. She tipped the first bottle over, and began to squeeze. A shot of syrupy maroon liquid shot out of the bottle splashing all over his immaculately pressed shirt. It looked like blood. She hoped he would wake before the hotel cleaning staff arrived. But it was too late to worry about the consequences of that now.

She walked all around him continuously squirting the fragrant condiment down one leg and up the other until the bottle was empty. She set the bottle down next to Nikko's half-finished screw driver. She only sipped hers while she talked, knowing she would be driving. She didn't want to drink and drive. She needed her wits about her at the airport.

She uncapped the second bottle. She retraced her steps, squirting until Nikko was fully basted. "You'll never want barbecue again. Bastard. I guarantee it," she whispered over Nikko's body.

This bottle she kept in her hands though. A thought just occurred to her. Stooping, she placed it between his slippery muscled thighs. Again, she muttered her thoughts. "What a shame." And with one final look back, Ronnie retrieved her much lighter back pack, and walked out the door. She had places to go, and Gary to see.

***

Ronnie breathed a huge sigh of relief as she buckled her seatbelt. She was nearly ready for the trickiest part of her plan. She said a silent prayer this would work. Her mom and she looked so much alike. Except the hair color. She had taken care of that. She stopped at *The Todd*, a sex shop for couples in Tampa, knowing they were open late and bought a brunette wig. She stopped at a convenience station with an outside restroom, and despite the filth, took the time to put it on and felt it would pass muster. She mussed it up some, to go for the disarrayed look she wanted, and then headed to the airport. She got on a flight to Bangor leaving at one in the morning with a quick layover in Philly. All should be good, she just had to get past security in Tampa. Pinching her nose several times, she made it red and puffy, and rubbed at her eyes to leave some smudges from her mascara.

Her mom looked amazing for her age. She always took great care of her body and drank plenty of water. Her identification showed some fine lines, marks of her age Ronnie didn't have. But her plan was to be crying softly as she went through security. Going to her dad's funeral would be her excuse, thus the late flight. With the wig, the comfortable sweats she had on, the sloppy jacket, she figured no one would look too closely. She'd pass. She had before. She'd used her mom's ID to get into clubs when she was younger. It would work. It had to. Driving would be out of the question. She'd be caught before she got to the state line. She had to take this chance. Her name might not be on security's radar, but it might. She couldn't risk using her own.

And as she suspected, she was able to purchase the tickets at the self-serve kiosk using her mom's ID and credit card. She felt guilty about doing that and planned to pay her back every penny. She had originally planned on paying cash, but had thought it might seem too suspicious. Blowing her nose then wiping at it as she checked through security worked. They passed her through. When she went through the scanning machine, the female guard looked a bit longer than she would have liked. Ronnie mumbled, "Sorry, my dad died," and then more sympathetically the female guard waved her through. Relief and guilt coursed through her at the same time.

Retrieving her bag, she was allowed to put her ID away, and that was the last time she would need it. She let out a silent sigh of relief. Now she just needed her gate pass which she clutched close to her chest to get on the plane which was departing in less than thirty minutes. It should already be boarding now, she thought, as she picked up her pace to gate A17. She kept the tissue close, and head down solemnly as she handed her pass to the check in clerk who tore it in two and handed her portion back to her. She entered the tunnel to the plane and was ignored by the flight attendant as she passed by. Most of the people flying were already seated. She found her seat quickly and hunched down intending to sleep as much as she could for the four and a half hour trip that included the layover.

When the flight attendant announced for the passengers to put on their seatbelts, they would be taking off soon, she was able to relax somewhat and found she could breathe easier. She'd be in Bangor before six AM, out of the airport before anyone woke up, including her mother, an early riser. By six thirty she hoped she'd be in a taxi on her way to her grandparents. She needed her bike. It was the only way she could get to Gary, to where she thought he'd be anyway, undetected.

***

Ronnie slept during most of the flight. She was surprised, but glad she did. Exhaustion, emotional and physical, had overtaken her. The flight attendants had woken her to disembark in Philly, but when she informed them she was taking the same plane to her final destination they allowed her to remain. She had to do a lot this morning, then she would crash for the day, and take action tonight. She needed to have her wits about her when she saw Gary for the first time. He would most assuredly be suspicious of her surprising and sudden appearance, and she had to approach him just right.

As soon as the plane landed on the tarmac in Bangor, and began to pull slowly up to the gate, she unsnapped her seatbelt before the light turned off. She heard the travelers around her doing the same thing, and the flight attendant wasn't complaining. These late flights were never full, and most people slept. She had been lucky enough to have the row to herself, and thus avoided having to make small talk.

When the light finally clicked off, she was out of her seat in a flash and making her way up the aisle passing people who had put their luggage in the overhead compartment. She kept her bag under the seat before her. She hadn't wanted to waste time checking it. Also, she didn't know how many taxis would be waiting in arrivals, and she sure as heck didn't want to have to wait for one. Then there would be all the people arriving to take a flight. Bangor wasn't small, but she was sure her face had been plastered all over the news. She wanted to avoid being recognized by the newsmongers. The wig would help, but she didn't want to take any chances.

She hustled pass the flight attendant and cock pit crew who stood at the front of the plane wishing everyone well, and gave only a brief nod as she passed. Her small purse was already across her shoulder, but she shifted slightly to pull up her hoodie on her jacket before she walked out into the main terminal. She kept her head down, and began to walk around the slower people taking their time in the disembarkation tunnel. She had just a few of the first class passengers ahead of her, and she could see the door to the exit just up ahead. She would easily get a taxi, she thought, as she maneuvered past another couple.

***

In the terminal, she passed an older couple pulling luggage on wheels, and a younger man with a large ruck sack. She got a bit frustrated when a woman pushing a stroller stopped dead in her tracks in front of her to retrieve a dropped binky, but instead squeezed passed her ignoring the woman when she heard her curse at her retreating back. She needed to move. The large open area she emerged into was packed with people awaiting to board the plane she'd just gotten off of. She tucked in her chin, and again surged forward weaving around people blocking the aisle. She saw the escalator leading to the downstairs area and ticket counters, and quickly got on, walking down the moving steps until she was trapped by a man standing stock still unaware she was directly behind him. He was huge and carried a very large briefcase. There was no way she could get around him. Silently cursing, she waited impatiently. As soon as he stepped off the escalator she moved around him and began to walk by the ticket agents, and then the car rental booths towards the exit. Three taxis, waited outside. Glancing covertly at the drivers waiting to pick up a fare, she had to choose a driver and she wanted to be sure to choose the one that wouldn't be too nosy or talkative during the long drive. One was smoking a cigarette, and one was a woman. She picked the last one. He was older, and she hoped the least observant.

She made eye contact, and nodded towards his car. He nodded, and opened the door for her. She slid in.

The older man shuffled around the car, and took his sweet time and when he did get in, she noticed he turned on the meter before asking her where she wanted to go. When she told him, he smiled.

"No one to pick you up miss?' he asked curiously.

"No, sir," she answered. "I'm going to a funeral, and everyone's pretty busy," she offered giving him the story she was still going to use.

"Oh, sorry to hear that, sweetie. Someone close?" he asked looking at her in the rearview mirror.

"My dad," she mumbled, pulling out her balled up tissue and unraveling it, she brought it to her face.

"Oh darling, then I'm really sorry for your loss." He saw her swipe at her face in the rearview mirror, and felt guilty for asking.

The radio was on, and the music broke for a commercial. The DJ announced the six o'clock news would be on shortly and she felt a moment of panic. She hoped she hadn't been discovered missing yet.

"Hey mister," she asked. "I'm really beat, and since it is such a long drive, would you mind turning off the radio so I could sleep a bit," she asked. She didn't know if the news would report anything about her, but just in case she wanted the radio off, especially if they announced she had fled the state of Florida, and might possibly be in the area.

"Sure thing darling," he called over his shoulder. She watched as he reached towards the radio, and pushed it off. "I just gotta call my dispatcher and let her know where I'm going, then I'll even shut off the squawk box here."

His voice was full of concern and sympathy. Gotta love Maine. The people had heart. Well, most of them anyway.

She nodded, and thanked him, then slunk down in her seat. She used her back pack as a pillow, and pulled her hoodie tighter around her as the driver made his call to dispatch. She listened in, hoping the dispatcher didn't pass along any other news. When she didn't, Ronnie was relieved and comfortable enough to relax. She wouldn't sleep though just in case he turned the radio back on.

The car picked up speed shortly afterwards, and Ronnie knew they must be on the Interstate now. Soon, she thought. Once she got her bike, all would be good. She knew the trails around her grandpa's place like the back of her hand, she knew the woods. She knew all the trails in and around the Aroostook State Park. Knew the forests well. Gary's family owned an impressive cabin on Lake Echo at the foot of Quaggy Joe Mountain. The Campbell's controlled the timber rights in pretty much all of Aroostook County. Her bet was he was hiding there.

She peeked out from her hoodie, looking up at the trees whizzing by, the pine, the evergreen, the white oaks, and the fir trees. Yes, it was good to be home. She loved Maine. She loved these woods. It smelled like home, she thought as she got comfortable for the long ride ahead.

"Hey, Miss. We are almost there." Ronnie heard the strange voice deep inside her dream, and it took her a moment to realize where she was. Crap. She had fallen asleep after all, and to make matters worse, she had a crick in her neck. At least he'd been true to his word and the radio was still off.

Ronnie sat up, and looked around recognizing the area immediately. She was minutes from her grandfather's. Another brief panic hit her. She didn't know if there would be police there or not. She asked the driver if he could pull over here. He looked startled for a moment. Confused. "But the house is still a mile or two off."

"I'd like to walk and stretch my legs a bit. See the old place," she trailed off softly, adding," Before I have to go in and you know . . .," the tissue came out. She was trying to think of something logical to say. She couldn't tell him there might be police cars, and she didn't want her grandparents to see a taxi pulling up at eight o'clock in the morning.

"Oh, oh, I understand," he stated fatherly. "Before you have to face everyone and all the people trying to offer their condolences."

"Yes, exactly," she breathed a sigh of relief. Mainers were wise and always made astute assumptions. They were usually right too. But she had been lying to the cabbie anyway, and so she was perfectly happy to agree with his presumption. "I've got a lot of good memories of my dad walking me down this road to the school bus," she added to make the story more believable.

The car was stopped now, and she pulled out her wallet. Her ID slipped out, and she quickly made a grab for it on the floor of the cab. "How much, sir?" she asked as she fumbled to put it away her hands shaking suddenly.

"Um, it's 175.76 here on the meter, sweetie. Sorry." He gave her a sad smile.

She returned it. "It's okay. I expected it would be a lot. Here," she said handing him two one hundred dollar bills. "Keep the change."

"You don't have to do that, honey," he replied.

"No, you let me sleep, and were so kind. Really, it's no problem." She wanted him to have it. He was a kind soul. He reminded her of her granddad a lot.

"Well, thank you kindly. You're a beautiful sweet girl, and I'm sure your dad is looking down from heaven right proud of the girl he raised."

She nodded, hating the lie and the pretense, but she had no choice. Ronnie opened the door, swung her legs out. "Thanks Mister. It means a lot." Frankly, she had no clue where her dad was these days. She'd met the man once in her entire life. It had been in her first year of college, and she hadn't been impressed. But, this man thought she was coming to bury him, so she carried on with the façade.

The driver began to make a U-turn in the road, and she waved at him as he began to pick up speed. She began to walk towards her grandparents' house. It was about a mile and half away, and she wanted to get off the road soon in case other cars passed by, but made herself walk slowly, for one minute until she was sure the taxi was out of sight on this long straight stretch of road. She took one peek back, assured herself the taxi was gone, and then ducked into the woods along the side of the road. She walked in perhaps ten feet, before stopping. She was hidden from the road by a large pine, and dropped her bag. She unzipped it, and pulled out her hiking boots. These sneakers were no good for riding her motorcycle, and no good for this terrain. Lots of soft spots in the soil, and rocks could cause her to stumble and sprain an ankle. She couldn't afford to get injured now. She needed her hiking boots in order to get a good solid grip on gnarled tree roots, and branches too. She also knew going this way, around the back side of her granddad's property, there would be a stream she would need to cross.

Once her sneakers were in her bag, the wig was also removed, and she left it on the grass. She wouldn't be needing that again. Her helmet when she was driving would hide her features and her hair. She wouldn't be spending much time out and about anyway. Except for her trip to radio shack. Crap! She still needed the damn wig. Shaking out the dirt, she stuffed it into her bag and zipped it shut.

The only part of her plan that was going to be a problem was getting to her bike without her grandfather noticing her. He was an early riser, and he was always puttering around outside doing something. She would have to bide her time, stay hidden, and wait until he went indoors for lunch, then get into the shed. She knew where he hid the key. She'd make sure her tank had fuel. He always had gas canisters on hand this far out, so that shouldn't be an issue, and then walk the bike out hoping he wasn't looking out the back window until she was far enough away to get on and ride off. Simple right? Not really. Her granddad, Roland, was as sharp as they came. A former marine from Vietnam, he was crafty, and she learned from him. She knew how to be quiet, where to step, and where not to in these woods. But again, all those skills she had gotten at his heels.

Walking through these woods put her at ease. It was those special times as a child with her grandfather that made her decide to become a forest ranger in the first place. She breathed in the woodsy scents of pine and other fir trees. She listened to the birds and animals of the forest getting quieter at her approach, remaining silent until she passed. God, she loved it. The serenity. The peace. It was her true home.

Time was passing, and from the looks of the sun, nearing nine. She was getting close. She could see the end of the tree line that wound around her grandfather's property. And sure enough, she caught sight of his faded blue Red Sox cap through the branches. She stopped and popped a squat. Make yourself small, he told her many times. The smaller you are and the lower you are to the ground, the less likely you are to be seen. It's why the animals crouched to reduce their size and possibly their chances of detection. Her heart ached to run to him though, call out, "Pepere, I'm home."

But, he'd try to stop her. She needed to do this. Clear up this mess so they could all move on. Her grandpa was heading to the shed, but he stopped mid-stride, and just smiled. Turning around, he gazed at the woods. She ached to be held by the man she regarded as a father. He loved these woods as much as she. He stooped to pick up a rock, and tossed it into the air, catching it. He began to whistle and to move again. Slow measured steps until he reached the shed. He slipped the rock into his pocket, and approached the door to the shed. He unlocked it with the key he hunched down to retrieve from underneath the flower pot beside the wood pile. He went in, and Ronnie moved just a bit to relieve the strain in her hamstrings. She got comfortable. She may have to wait here awhile. As she stilled, the birds picked up their usual chatter, and she occasionally heard noises from the shed where her granddad was working. But, he didn't stay there long. Maybe twenty minutes and he began to approach the house.

Again, he stopped and surveyed his surroundings, smiling all the while. After a minute, he began to walk again. In another minute he was in the house.

Ronnie moved then. She didn't know how much time she would have. She went the fifteen paces to the edge of the trees, looked at the house, and watched the curtains for a moment before heading to the shed. Her grandpa left the door wide open. She saw her dirt bike right away. On it was a folded sheet of paper weighted down by a rock. Her helmet sat on the seat clean as whistle.

Hands trembling, she picked up the note. She opened it.

Chipmunk,

I've been all up morning sweets, and gave her a really good tune up for you. The gas tank is full. Your mom called me this morning and told me to be on the lookout for you, and to try and stop you if you showed up here. So, anyhow, my little chipmunk, you know how well I listen to your grandma and your mother, which is not very well. I love you girl. Be careful. I taught you everything I know so I am not too worried. But a little worried. I know you're innocent and if you need anything at all just call me.

Love, Gramps.

PS Give him hell. I never liked him for you anyway. And Grandma went shopping, so let me hear that engine roar.

Tears sprang to Ronnie's eyes. She loved that man. She grabbed the pen he left on his work table, and tore the bottom of the sheet of paper off. She wanted to keep his note and the rock. She slipped them into her pocket.

Gramps,

I love you. Soooo much. You are the best. Mom is pregnant by the way.

Love always, your chipmunk

PS I'll give him more than hell. I'll kick him in the arse.

Ronnie put the note on his table, picked up his small whittling knife, and stabbed it into the paper and into the wood.

Picking up her helmet, the one he lovingly cleaned for her that morning, she put it on over her head, and pulled her bike out of the shed. Her grandpa was in the window watching her. She waved. He waved back, and then gave her a thumbs up sign. Getting on her bike before she lost her nerve, she kicked started it, and the engine started right up. The man was a blessing. One more wave, tears in her eyes, she floored it, giving the bike a full three hundred and sixty degree spin in the yard before she headed to the trails just beyond the rear edge of her grandfather's property. She rode into the trees knowing her grandfather was watching her the entire time. Yes, that man always had her back. She had always been able to count on him.

***

Ronnie settled into the hotel room in Spragueville which wasn't far from Quaggy Joe Mountain and Echo Lake. Spragueville was a sleepy town for half the year, but come summer the lake and Aroostook State Park attracted many tourists, and during the winter the ski trails were quite popular for both cross country and downhill. Luckily the town was pretty busy right now with the campers and she could easily blend in and become lost in the crowd so to speak. She'd been here a couple of times before with Gary and some friends on small vacations, but she needed to be safe and keep her wits about her. She didn't want to be recognized by the locals, so she would steer clear of the most obvious places, and the local hangouts she had been In before.

For her hotel she chose one of the larger establishments figuring the workers would turn over more quickly and she wouldn't be recognized. She'd stay away from the quaint restaurants and the bars, places she went with Gary and their friends just in case. After arriving here, she hid her bike in a deer blind she and her grandfather used once in the Aroostook Forrest that would not be used since it was not hunting season.

She walked the three miles into town, and went to the local radio shack located in a strip mall. It was a small town, far enough from Bangor, but still when Maine people made news, it made the news. So she wore her disguise hoping it would be the last time. She picked up a throw away cell phone, one with voice and video recording capabilities. She also got an external microphone so she could put the phone in an isolated location, but record good quality voice without risk if she had to block the device or move away from it.

She also needed to call Gary on it, stroke his ego a little, and then maybe her mom too, so she didn't worry. Her grandfather had probably informed her mother she arrived safely and took her bike, but she felt confidant her mom wouldn't report her missing to anyone just yet. Her mom was probably worried, but would give her the time she asked for to try to get Gary to confess his role in this entire mess. The phone was necessary too because she couldn't use her own as it could easily be traced. Even the one she purchased could be traced if they figured out she was using it. She didn't want to think about the fact that the police might be tracing Gary's phone now that they were looking into his whereabouts. But she had to end this. She needed to move on from under this dark cloud. She needed to get on with her life without Gary, without these charges, and without Nikko too. The first two thoughts made her angry. The third made her sad.

After radio shack, she went to a convenience store to purchase a few food items. She was hungry, but didn't want to risk a restaurant or grocery store where people tended to be more watchful and observant. In and out was her plan. These stores, like the Seven-Eleven she chose, saw numerous tourists all day long, as people came in to purchase their gas and head back on the road.   The attendants and cashiers wouldn't be looking as closely, she hoped. She had to be careful. She couldn't afford a misstep now. She was so close.

She was back in her hotel by four PM. She made herself a peanut butter and jelly sandwich, watched the local news, and drank the milk she purchased. She was relieved to see no news reporting anything about her charges and or disappearance. She took that as a good sign.

Her motel room was pretty nice, but it wasn't equipped with a refrigerator. She finished her sandwich and tidied up. She was glad she hadn't purchased much, just some bags of nuts, granola bars packed with protein, and more water, all light and easy to carry. The loaf of bread, and small jars would stay here in the room. A local paper and a charger for her phone rounded out her shopping.

Exhausted, Ronnie decided to sleep until eight or nine that evening, and then make her first call to Gary. She hoped she could pull this off, and was counting on his overzealous ego to believe she was still in love with him, and needed him to keep her out of jail, and hidden. That was her plan. Throw up the offer of sex slave, in return for hiding her, and she would never tell anyone it was him who planted the drugs. But, and this was part of her plan, she needed to get him to confess his part in the drug smuggling, explaining why he had done it and how, get it on tape, and then present it to the authorities. She knew it wasn't going to be easy, but she had to try. She just hoped she didn't have to sleep with him before he spilled his guts because she really didn't think she could do it. Not now. After Nikko. The thought of how he used her stung anew. And as she tried to settle into her bed and get some rest, it didn't come easy. Nikko was on her mind, and how he would react to what she had done kept torturing her. And even though she knew she shouldn't care if he was all right, she did.

Chapter Fifteen

WTF?

Nikko's head was pounding. He couldn't even open his eyes. His temples felt like someone was trying to drill holes in his head with the cruelest of all power tools. He commanded his hand to massage them, ease the tension and had to concentrate on that action just to raise his hands. But instead of his temple, and hairline as he expected, he felt something sticky instead. His eyes flew open thinking the worst. He had been shot. But try as he might, he couldn't get off the ground. His head pounded and he briefly wondered where he was and what happened. He forced himself to breathe and think despite the pressure in his head. He focused. He was looking at a ceiling, and felt his temple again, and then put his hand in his line of vision, squinting to see what it was. When he saw the thick red paste, he nearly panicked again until the smell hit him. Barbecue. It was barbecue sauce. *What the hell?*

He then focused on pushing his upper body off the carpet with his hands still trying to recall the night's events. He had been having a drink with Ronnie. Sweet Ronnie. He had felt dizzy, and then that was it. He looked down at his body to see if he'd hurt anything in the fall, and his eyes flew open even wider. He was covered from head to toe in barbecue sauce. It just didn't make sense. And then another thought hit him. Where was Ronnie?

"What the fuck," he growled, as he pushed past the pain in his head to force himself into a standing position. He took two steps back gazing down at the mess on the carpet. It did look like a murder scene. He wobbled a bit until he regained his balance, and turned to go into the bathroom. Flicking on the light, he was met in the mirror by a horrible sticky mess. He was covered in the stuff. Not only did his appearance shock him, but there was a message scrawled on the mirror. His heart began to hammer in his chest. Ronnie. Where was she?

Because his head was still pounding he had to squint to read it. The letters squirmed like snakes. Soon his fear turned to shock, and then dismay, and then great disappointment. The message was from Ronnie. He had to read it twice. He couldn't believe this was her work.

N –

Thanks for your support and friendship. But you have enough friends at Jimbo's to keep you more than satisfied. Enjoy the barbecue.

Out, R

What the fuck? His head continued to pound as he tried to make sense of it all. Ronnie had done this to him.

Why? His mind screamed. Then it came to him slowly as he read the message a third time. The waitress from Big Jimbo's. He had run into her in the lobby yesterday. Ronnie must have seen them both leaving at the same time. It had been a coincidence. But obviously to Ronnie too many coincidences proved too much for her to believe.

Linda had been applying for a job here. And it had been just that, a coincidence, and nothing happened between them. The brunette had been polite, and they chatted a bit in the lobby, but there had not even been mild flirtation. He hadn't even felt the usual urge, which struck him as odd. He knew he was known for his flirtatious ways, but since being with Ronnie again, he never even noticed other woman around him. And as for Linda, she was on her best behavior with the manager looking on as the two walked out together. In the parking lot she even apologized for her behavior at the restaurant. He apologized as well and explained he had done it to make Ronnie jealous, but realized it had been wrong to toy with her that way. But, Ronnie, who may have just been driving by, wouldn't have heard their conversation. She would have seen two people leaving a hotel, talking, and he'd even given her a brief hug as he walked her to her car because he felt so guilty for his part in the flirtation and how it led to her actions.

Fuck! He couldn't believe his goddam luck. But Ronnie, ugh! She could have just asked him about it. The girl had some serious trust issues. He couldn't blame her after what she had gone through with Gary, the fucking scum bag. But with him, he thought they were learning to trust one another.

As he began to wash the barbecue off his face and neck, he realized last summer must have crossed her mind too. This did not bode well for them. And frankly, as mad as he was at her, and he wanted to put the girl over his knee, he was seriously worried she wouldn't give him a chance to explain. And that bothered him most of all. She still didn't trust him. And he could lose her over another stupid misunderstanding. Turning to the shower, he put the water on full blast, and began to strip. He needed to clean himself up and go see her. He had no choice, and neither did she. He was going to demand she listen to him, and then threaten to slap her little naked backside until she apologized and promised to talk things out before over reacting if something like this ever happened again.

Getting in the shower, and leaving his pile of ruined clothes on the floor, Nikko used the hotel soap and began to vigorously rub the sticky mess that penetrated through the fabric of his nice new cotton shirt. God, he still fumed. What had she been thinking? Apparently the ice princess, or so she seemed to him in the beginning, was hot blooded. And she had a vengeful streak. Not good, not good at all. An apology alone wouldn't do. He might have to return the favor, he smiled mischievously as the hot water did wonders for his pounding brain. But maybe something a little more flavorful than barbecue sauce, he thought. Mmm, chocolate syrup maybe? He imagined drizzling the stuff across her breasts and nipples. Now that was a mess worth cleaning up.

And then again, Nikko had another sudden thought. How had she done this to him unawares, and what was with the lingering headache? Had she drugged him? Holy shit! He needed an explanation. And she definitely deserved a spanking. He imagined it. And despite his anger, and the fact she basted him, and drugged him to do it, he had a raging hard on just thinking about her. Fuck man, he told himself, you need to get your act together when it comes to this girl. Nikko knew he was falling for her, and falling hard. The thought terrified him.

***

Two hours later, he was even more terrified. Arriving at Louisa and Jay's place by taxi, still fuming, he expected to find his car sitting in the driveway. After his shower, he realized with even more fury that she jacked his car. He was tempted to put her over his knee even if he had to do it with an audience. But his heart pounded thunderously, when he found only Louisa home.

***

With more morning sickness, Lou had taken another sick day. Even though it had eased up some, she also called in because she wanted to be near the phone in case Ronnie called. She was sick with worry for her daughter ever since she discovered her missing this morning. Ronnie usually joined her for breakfast and when she had not heard her stirring in the room, she peeked in on her only to discover her bed hadn't been slept in and a note tented in the center. After reading it she immediately called her father to let him know what was going on and to try to convince him to stop her. Then twenty minutes ago, she'd called again to ask if he had seen her. Her mother answered saying he was outside in the yard. She hadn't mentioned anything to her mom. She hadn't wanted to worry her. Her mom said he would be in soon for lunch, but he walked in at that moment and she was able to speak to him. He'd been pretty tight lipped with her mother in the room. He said he hadn't seen her.

She was just about to call her dad again when she heard the pounding on the door. It made her jump. Her first thought was that it must be the police. But then she heard Nikko's angry voice through the door. When she opened it, he flew inside brushing past her.

"Where is she?" he demanded to know.

When he asked where Ronnie was and Lou couldn't meet his eyes, his stomach sank. When he asked a second time, Lou looked furtively behind her, and stuttered when she finally answered.

"She . . . she went shopping."

"How? With what car?" he asked quickly putting her off guard, counting on her not telling her mother she dumped a vat of barbecue on him, or stole his car. "Jay went to work, and your car is here."

"Um, she went with a friend," she murmured, beginning to shut the door.

"What friend?" he put his arm against the door blocking her attempt.

"Nikko, please. The neighbors," Lou begged with her eyes.

He moved his arm guiltily, but as soon as the door was firmly shut behind him, he pounced again. He wanted answers. His eyes swept the room and Ronnie's open bedroom door. He saw her bed. She hadn't slept in it. His heart sank with his suspicions. "Lou, I know she took off," he announced. His eyes narrowed to look past her. "You have to talk to me and tell me everything. If the police find out she's gone, her bail will be revoked, you could lose your house, Jay his bike. But if I find her, bring her back, before they realize she is missing, then I can keep this between us. My brother's will be quite upset if they lose their bond," he warned her.

He saw Lou's shoulders visibly sag, and she stepped back. Shit. He was right. Again, he pushed past her further into the house, and stood tall in the middle of the living room.

"What happened Lou? Why did she run?" He was hoping it wasn't just their misunderstanding, and seeing Lou's fear, felt now more than ever it wasn't. When Lou didn't speak he went on.

"The more I know, the quicker I find her. I'll keep her safe. I love her, Lou."

He didn't mean to say that. But he knew it was true the moment the words left his lips. She could be in serious danger. He had to help her. Who knows what this whacko Gary is capable of or even if he was acting alone. A thousand scenarios were running through his head.

Lou's eyes went wide at his words. "You love my daughter?"

He hadn't meant to say it, it just slipped out. He nodded, and met her eyes.

"I haven't told her yet, and I'm not sure I will for a while after the stunt she pulled last night, but I do. I want her here and safe, just like you do," he added. "So please, tell me everything I need to know to find her."

Lou looked into the younger man's eyes. Could she trust him? She did want Ronnie home with her. God knew what she was getting herself into. She saw the fear in his eyes and made her decision.

"Um, let me get you the note." Lou turned towards the kitchen and went towards where her purse sat on the counter. "She went to Maine. I talked to my parents twice this morning. Once to tell my father I thought she would go there first, then again, just twenty minutes ago. I know he lied to me when I called the second time, said he hadn't seen her, but his voice sounded strange, but proud. So, I knew he was lying. She probably went to get her bike as I suspected she would."

"Maine? Her bike?" he questioned. "Already! How the hell . . ." he stopped as she placed the note in his hand. He scanned the few lines.

"Lou . . . this is not good. This guy, Gary, he could be dangerous if she tries to corner him. He could . . ."

He felt like he swallowed a lead ball. Fear for Ronnie, and the situation she was putting herself in, gutted him like a fish. He looked to Lou, and he saw his words were scaring her as well. He remembered Ronnie revealing she was pregnant, and immediately felt guilty.

"Lou, have a seat. If I can get there quickly, before she finds him, things will be okay. I also have to do this before my brothers find out, or they will send in the posse. Hell, they will be the posse. Will you tell me where to look, where she might go?" he asked following her to the sofa.

Lou saw the concern and love in his eyes, and nodded. Nikko took a pad of paper and pen he saw on the table and sat next to her on the sofa. Lou began to tell him all her thoughts about her wayward daughter's possible hideouts, and all she knew about Gary and the places he hung out in. Places they had gone together. Nikko had a good start when he left thirty minutes later. He was in a taxi, and headed to the Tampa airport. His ticket on the eleven thirty flight to Bangor, Maine was already booked thanks to his iPhone.

A little research on his cell told him she had a ten to twelve hour head start on him since there were only two other flights that had gone to Bangor. A little more digging and he was able to access the manifest. It wasn't legal by any means, but his brothers had some friends who knew how to get around the firewalls of many of the airlines, and if that failed they had friends who worked there who would give such information for a price. And his suspicion that she was on one of those flights was confirmed. He saw the name Louisa Russell on Flight Five-Sixteen. She had taken her mother's ID. Yes, twelve hours, but he knew she had to sleep, and he knew she had to travel much more surreptitiously than he did. He was already closing the gap. He'd find Ronnie, he vowed to himself. He would find her before the night was over. He just didn't know where he would put his hands on her first when he found her, her ass, or her throat.

Nikko's flight touched down at a little after three, and he was in his rental car soon afterwards. His instincts told him he needed his brother's resources in this neck of the woods, and he would call them tonight as they expected him at work in the morning. But if he couldn't find her by midnight, he might very well need them. He didn't think she would venture out in the day time. She had a motorbike for transportation, so she'd have to circumvent towns and foot it. His nice black sleek charger would eat up the miles and help him eliminate a few of the possible locations before night fall.

He would check her grandfather's camp in Presque Isle, the camp Gary's father owned on Lake Echo in Spragueville, and rule them out first. As both he and Lou discussed, she probably wouldn't go to those as the authorities would assume that was the first place she would go. The other three places on the list were much more likely locations, and he would check those closer to sundown—the bar her friends often hung out in, Gary's friend, Tom, had a cabin in the same vicinity as his parent's camp, or the small servants quarters on Gary's family's camp which was vacant unless the family was in residence. He had circled that one. It was a hunch. It just seemed like the place a weasel like Gary would hide, close to the money, and hiding in plain sight. He hoped his hunch paid off. He could check out the hotels too, but he didn't know what name she would use. He also didn't want to alert the authorities to the possibility she was missing.

Chapter Sixteen

Catch Her If You Can

As he suspected there were no signs of Ronnie or Gary being at the first two locations. His parent's camp was more like a chalet in the woods. The people were obviously loaded with a spread like that. The servants quarters were a half mile away, and he checked there as well since he was nearby. It looked to be a two bedroom cabin. Everything was locked up tight as a drum. But, that didn't mean Gary wasn't there. Tire tracks along the dirt road indicated someone had been their recently. Rain, and he had checked, would have washed the tracks away. It rained two days ago. Those tracks were fresh. The tire tracks were from a four wheeler, so it could just be a ranger or neighbor checking on the place. But it was definitely worth checking out again.

Nikko had gone in on foot, parking a quarter mile away on a side road. It was nearing seven, so he figured he should hunt down the bar, and wait outside for a few hours, then go check the apartment of Gary's friend and then come back here. His hunch was that Gary was here, and he suspected Ronnie would probably make a move tonight. He wanted to be nearby if she did.

He drove the thirty minutes back into the nearest town, and the local bar that catered to the residents and the seasonal renters, and those who had cabins in this part. He got some take out from a Chinese restaurant and ate it in the car while he watched the people coming and going. There was no sign of either one of them. He decided to go in and have a drink, maybe strike up a conversation with the barkeeper, and see what was going down in town that was newsworthy. He might drop Gary's name and see what the barkeep had to say. He'd be quick though. He wanted to be near the servant's cabin by nine thirty, ten at the latest.

Getting out of his rented Charger, he still wore the jeans he travelled in, and the t-shirt he bought at the airport. He picked up a UMaine sweatshirt at the one of the shops wanting to blend in. It would also be his ruse to get the barkeep to start talking.

The place was definitely a typical one-horse town bar. It had a couple of pool tables, some dartboards with games in progress, wooden tables and barrel chairs scattered about, and a long bar with plenty of stools. Only a few single men sat alone drinking at the bar. None of them were Gary, and none of the females were Ronnie. He'd recognize her anywhere.

Grabbing a seat at the end of the bar away from the other solitary drinkers, Nikko nodded at the old man who was filling a mug for someone else. When he dropped off the brew, the barkeep immediately approached him. "What'll it be?" he asked smiling and wiping the counter with his bar towel.

"A draft, Miller's if you've got it," Nikko nodded in the direction of the taps behind the bar.

"Sure do," the older man replied reaching for a mug, turning and filling his glass to the brim. When he set the mug before him, some of the foam on top spilled over and bartender who was on older gentlemen, was quick with the bar towel once more and began to clean up the mess.

Not wanting to lose him, Nikko plunged on with the story he planned to use to start up a conversation.

"Hey, I am supposed to meet some friends in town tomorrow. We rented a place, but I came up early to stock up. I just got here. We plan on doing some fishing while we are here. Can you recommend some great spots?"

"It's all good buddy. Just stay away from the state park. The rangers don't like it much if you are fishing there. They'll fine you for sure, no questions asked."

"Will do. Thanks for the tip," Nikko took a sip of his beer. "My friends will appreciate the advice but some of my buddies are from around here so I'm sure they'll be able to keep me away from the preserve."

"Some friends you say?" the barkeep added making conversation. Most bartenders liked to chat up the guests as it increased the possibility of a bigger tip. Nikko was counting on that. He put a twenty up on the counter just to be sure to keep the man's attention.

"Yeah, me and my buddies just graduated from UMaine and we wanted to have one last hurrah before reality sets in if you know what I mean," he laughed, picking up his drink taking another long swallow.

"Oh, I was young once too, son. I get you." He swiped the counter again. "I went to UMaine myself longtime ago," he added chuckling. "Do you play hockey, too?" The man was grinning from ear to ear. Must be a fan.

Nikko didn't know much about the game, but from the way the bartender asked, he was definitely an enthusiast.

"Nope, sorry, but I played baseball. A couple of my friends played hockey though, Gary Campbell and Tom Waldron," he looked down at his beer, when he noticed the man's eyes got wide. Gotcha, he thought. He knows them. Play it cool, he cautioned. Gary was obviously big news and his family's wealth meant everyone knew him.

"They coming up here, renting a cabin you say?" the man asked suspiciously. He obviously had to know of the Campbell's. They had the biggest place on the lake.

"Nah, Gary couldn't' make it. When I last talked to him, like three weeks ago, he was noncommittal. Said he might, but his folks have a place here, so if he does come out and hang with us, he'll probably stay by them." Nikko noticed the man's demeanor relaxed a bit.

"Yeah, I know the Campbell's. Who doesn't in these parts?" he added after a pause. He was judging Nikko. He wouldn't want to be caught gossiping about a local celebrity with a stranger.

Nikko knew he wouldn't get any more information out of the man. The barkeep was shuffling about, but had gotten quite tense when the name was first dropped. Nikko took another sip of his drink. He was nearly done with it.

He watched the barkeep continue to distance himself a bit at a time. He had to know Gary was in town, or in trouble. He was acting too strange. Either way, Nikko had a gut feeling Campbell was nearby, and this town would keep their mouths locked up as tight as a drum if they wanted business from the Campbells. He quickly polished off his beer, as the bartender moved down the line to refill other people's glasses. He left the twenty on the counter, nodded at the bartender on the way out, and left. It was time to go find Gary. And Ronnie. Where one was, the other would be as well.

***

Ronnie was nervous. She woke up and ate again, after a four hour nap. She ran out to get a cup of coffee, again in disguise, at the Dunkin Donuts down the block. She needed the caffeine to keep her alert. She also needed the courage. After finishing her life sustaining brew, she then worked up the nerve to call Gary. She dialed the number to his parent's servant's quarters. It rang twice, and he answered. It was Gary. Just as she assumed. She smiled to herself relief coursing through her.

"Gary, its Ronnie, please don't hang up, baby. I'm in town." She added the rest after his initial gasp of surprise.

"What the hell?" he growled into the receiver. "You shouldn't be calling me." Gary looked around the cabin nervously. He was standing in the kitchen. He peeked out the curtain windows, but with the light on he couldn't see a thing in the pitch blackness.

"Gary, I don't want to go to jail. Please baby. Hear me out. I am not asking for you to do anything you don't want to. I don't want to bring you down with me. In fact, I haven't even mentioned your name to the police," she lied. It was a big lie, but she hoped he would buy it.

"You . . . you haven't?" he stuttered. Maybe that's why no one was really bothering him. The police called his parents two days ago to ask to speak to him, but hadn't followed up after his parents put them off. His parents sent him here to lay low. They stalled the police by telling them he knew nothing.

"No, baby. I love you. I wouldn't want to ruin your future too. I know this is fucked up, but I really thought the police would just think someone else planted them. I didn't want them to think it was you. But, now they are really coming after me hard. I think I might go down for this. But never, never, would I implicate you." She got it all out like she planned. Focus on him, on keeping his name out. But drop the hint that she knew he was guilty. He reacted just as she thought he would.

"What? I don't know anything about those drugs Ronnie," he lied. He wasn't admitting to anything. She could be having the phone bugged.

"I didn't say you did, baby. Just . . . you know it wasn't me right . . . I mean you know how I feel about drugs . . ." she put in a little show of water works pretending to cry. "I can't go to jail . . . some customs guy must have done it, some drug dealer . . . I just don't know. But they covered their tracks so well." She was back pedaling, but wanted to ease his mind. She knew very well it was him, but she just couldn't prove it, and other than a confession, there was no other way to prove it.

"Well, what in the hell are you doing here? Why come to me?" he asked suspiciously.

She could tell he was nervous by the tone of his voice. "Gary, I love you. I thought you could hide me out for a bit until I can figure out what to do. Please, can I meet you somewhere, or come up to the servant's cabin?"

"You are here? Close? Um. I was just leaving," he lied. He had been keeping his head down and staying out of trouble since Ronnie's arrest like his parents suggested. They told him to come up here when they got wind from the university dean that reporters had called about the incident. His parents didn't want any more bad press. He had often come up here, on weekends to party with his friends, he even brought Ronnie a time or two. He never used his parents place, knowing there were security cameras in place when he'd come with his friends. The servant's quarters served him just as well for what he did there.

"Please baby," she begged. "I don't have anyone else to turn to. I thought you loved me."

"Um yeah, I did. But . . ." he was stalling. "My parents don't want me to have anything to do with you. They threatened to disown me, Ronnie," he whined.

Oh, the poor fucking baby, she thought. But, she couldn't say that. "Are they here?" she asked making herself sound concerned and praying they weren't so she could get to Gary and work her magic. Magic that would hopefully get a confession out of him.

Gary didn't know what to do. He couldn't have her show up here at his parents' compound. Even though his parents were out of town, it wasn't a good idea. He was about to tell her that when another thought occurred to him. What if someone recognized her while she was down town? Someone could report her, or worse. She could get picked up by authorities in the area. The locals were quick to gossip and they would assume he had something to do with it. Which he did of course, but he didn't want to add fuel to the fire. It would look really bad for him, and the Campbell name would be even more tarnished than it already was.

"No, they went to some conservation conference in Augusta." He needed to think this through. He needed to get her out of sight.

He sounded distracted, so Ronnie pounced. "My life is shit, Gary. I'm sorry to have bothered you, but I just thought maybe for just a few days, baby. You could help me come up with a way. Maybe I'll go to Canada. It's not too far. Remember the time we drove into New Brunswick via that small town. St. Leonard was it? When we went into that store to buy a drink and we were surprised when they gave us change in Canadian funds. I just don't know. I can't think right now. You were always so good at thinking through problems. You're the only chance I got," she sobbed, laying it on thick.

Gary felt a twinge of remorse. He hadn't thought he would get caught. Not with the stuff in her tank. He didn't think it would be picked up by the machines, or the dogs. Hell, the girl helped him get his fucking diploma and she was a pretty good lay. His cock stirring. He hadn't gotten any since the cruise. He had been holed up at his parents for the first few days, while they dealt with the media, and then sent him up here to keep his head low. They also planned on sending him to Canada as well, to work on their operation up in Aroostook, New Brunswick until after the trial. They didn't want the Campbell name to be tainted by his drug smuggling ex-girlfriend. If they only knew! They probably suspected he had tried drugs, and he wasn't going to admit it that's for fucking sure. But having Ronnie in town was definitely a big, big problem.

Could he trust her? That was the real issue. He could help her. Should help her. After all it was because of him she was in this mess.

"Not here," he muttered after what seemed like an eternity. "I can't have you driving up here, and people seeing you."

"I got my bike," she offered. "I can ride up on one of the trails, and then walk it in." She offered the solution quickly, the one she planned on all along.

He thought for a moment. "Yeah, that could work. Take Georgette Rush," he added. It was one of the lesser used trails by a narrow, rocky stream.

She knew that path. They had ridden out there before.

"I'll meet you, at the quarter mile mark, babe," he relented into the phone. He hoped he didn't regret this.

"Oh, thank you Gary. Thank-you. I didn't do this baby," she reiterated for good measure. "I just can't go to jail."

He ran his fingers through his shaggy blond hair. He needed to cut it, but hadn't gotten around to it yet. He was regretting it already when she kept whining about how grateful she was. She'd better be, he thought. "I'll think of something to get you out of the country babe," he grunted into the receiver.

"I'll be there in thirty minutes," she made herself sound relieved even though she was nervous as hell. She had to get him to admit he did it. It was the only way.

Chapter Seventeen

The Snare

Of all the fucking luck, Nikko cursed. He had been sitting outside behind a wood pile near the servant's quarters for thirty minutes. He left his car a half mile back on the same dirt road he'd parked on before. He'd pulled it off the road into what looked to be an old abandoned campsite. It was well hidden and he felt confidant no one would notice it. He walked on up to Gary's parent's place and stuck close to the tree line. Relief swept through him when he was a couple hundred yards off and saw a light in the servant's cabin up ahead. As he got closer, he could see someone moving about in what appeared to be the kitchen. He ducked behind the wood pile just in time when the front door opened and a really tall man walked out. He had nearly been caught. His heart pounded in his chest. He wondered if Ronnie was already here. He heard nothing but the guy. And the guy was Gary. He'd googled him, and saw pictures of him and his family at some local charity events.

He appeared unkempt now. Disheveled from the small glimpse he had before ducking behind the wood pile.

He was about to take another peek when he heard the sound of an engine roaring to life, and took the chance to peer around the side. Gary was at the wheel of a four wheeler, and he took off like a bat out of hell into the darkness. Fuck. Now what? Wait? Go look around? Where the hell was she? His blood was thundering in his ears. After the sound of the four wheeler could no longer be heard, he took the chance and got up stretching his legs. He made his way over to the cabin. Gary left the lights on, so he peered in the window. He was right about this being a kitchen in the front. When he peered in, he noticed no movement at all. He could see pretty much the entire cabin except for the bedrooms. No one was here. Fuck. The guy left the TV on, so he figured he'd be back soon. He'd give him a half hour and then head into town. He hoped he wasn't wasting his time.

He didn't have to wait long though. Thank goodness. After maybe ten minutes of crouching and getting eaten alive by mosquitos, with his patience wearing thin, Nikko thought he heard someone returning. The nocturnal sounds of the night creatures suddenly ceased. Someone was coming or the creatures wouldn't have gotten so quiet. After a minute of nothing but dead silence, his anger was up again at the thought that he had been wrong. Where in the hell was the guy, and where in the hell was Ronnie? His palm itched to really tan her hide. She deserved it for the danger she was putting herself into.

He shifted again, and then he definitely heard something, it sounded like voices approaching in the distance. Two voices, a guy and girl, but they were still too far off to make out what they were saying, or who they belonged to. His ears strained to hear something. Anything.

Fuck, he heard her. It was Ronnie. He couldn't see her yet, but it was her. He hadn't been able to carry his gun on the plane, but he was prepared to use whatever force was needed. He should have picked up something, and silently cursed himself for not thinking of it sooner.

"Thank-you Gary," she was saying. "I really can't thank you enough." Her voice was as sweet as syrup.

He heard Gary laugh in a way that sickened him. "I know a way you can thank me baby," he teased, breathing hard. They were just starting to come into view. Nikko's hands curled into fists. The hell she will, he thought.

"And thanks for leaving your four wheeler, and walking my bike in," she added. "It sucks that you'll have to go back out and get it later."

"I didn't want to risk leaving yours, someone finding it, and then running the plates. It'll be fine for tonight," he grunted again pushing her bike the last thirty yards. "Plus, you can thank me personally in about ten minutes." He laughed again.

He heard Ronnie's nervous laugh at Gary's innuendo and felt the acid in his stomach churn. This guy was going to have his dick cut off if he so much as touched her. She belonged to him now. The creepy fucking bastard had balls if he thought he would use his woman to satisfy his needs.

He fucking left her holding the proverbial bag, she was sucking up to him big time, and the dude was taking it all in. What fucking nerve. He slowly moved his position. As soon as the guy let go of the bike, Nikko planned to jump him. He moved slowly, but despite his best efforts and small twig snapped.

"Oh, baby. You know I will thank you, just the way you like. But first, I'd love some coffee, and maybe something to eat too. I haven't had much sleep either. But, I am famished and need to eat something. Got anything in that cabin of yours. I'll cook," she offered. She was using the cooking to buy some time. Hopefully get him to talk.

"I hope not too tired," he smirked at her in what was meant to be sexy, but only made her stomach roll. When she didn't answer, he added, "But we can eat first. I got some eggs, and stuff. And cold cuts. Hey, can you make me one of your omelets, baby? You know I am not much in the kitchen."

They were maybe ten yards away. Nikko's muscles prepared for the attack. Seconds now.

All was silent and that bothered Ronnie. "Who is there?" Ronnie called out. *Fuck!* She heard a slight snap by the wood pile. It could be an animal, but she doubted it.

"What the hell?" Gary yelped. "Someone out there?" He was looking around nervously.

"Shit," Ronnie murmured glaring in the darkness at the woodpile. The noise had come from over there.

Fuck! Nikko was pissed. She had marked him.

Gary looked like he was going to bolt and Nikko had no choice but to make his presence known. He stood. Ronnie spotted him right away.

"Nikko?" Ronnie winced. This was the very last thing she wanted. He was going to ruin everything. She'd just gotten here. He'd tracked her so quickly, and now he was going to fuck everything up. She needed to think fast.

"You know this guy?" Gary looked from one to the other. He held the bike in front of him like a shield.

"Yes, he is a fucking bounty hunter. He's here to take me back to Florida. Damn it," she cursed, and turned to Gary to lessen the blow. She whispered to him in the hopes he would think Nikko couldn't hear. "I don't want to involve you, baby. I never wanted that. I'll just go with him and hopefully he won't even concern himself with you." She winked at him hoping he would play along. For a moment he just looked confused, then Gary nodded.

A bit louder than was necessary, Gary spoke up. "Um, Ronnie baby, I had no idea you weren't supposed to leave the state." He lied so easily, Ronnie thought, even if it wasn't very well. Fucking coward, she thought. But she would play along. She needed to, especially if she hoped to convince Nikko to allow her to come back.

"Sorry babe, I didn't tell you that part. Just that I was out on bail. Fuck." She turned to face Nikko now who was watching them both warily. He had been silent up to this point, wondering what the fuck was going on. "What are you going to do?" she looked at Nikko pointedly praying he didn't fuck this up more than he already had. She kept her tone neutral. She didn't want Gary to pick on her and Nikko's relationship if you could even call it that.

"Well, well, well, Veronica Sears." He used her formal name. "I'm here to bring you back. So if you will just come along and play nice, we can let this guy go make his own omelet. There is a late flight, and we just might be able to make it back to Florida tonight." He gave her a malicious smirk.

Fuck! Fuck! Fuck! He was ruining everything. She narrowed her eyes, but kept quiet about the things she would really like to say to him. It wasn't the time. She turned her back to him. "Gary," she whispered. "I'm sorry. I'll go. I love you," she whispered and was about to reach in to hug him, but Gary pulled away from her distancing himself at the same time Nikko called out.

"Now." Nikko said the word forcefully. When she turned back to face him, he was leering at her. "If you will just come along," he stated more politely using his hands and very long fingers to beckon her to him.

What choice did she have? Fuck! Her mind screamed. She would have to convince him to let her go, give her one more chance to nail Gary. It was the only chance she had.

"Um," Gary started. "I think you better go, Ronnie." Gary wanted no fucking part of this.

Ronnie looked from one man to the other. She couldn't help but make the mental comparisons. Two men who had royally screwed her over. And despite Nikko's recent behavior, Gary was still the biggest loser in her mind. "I'll go," she stated, but didn't break eye contact with Gary. She chose to ignore Nikko for a moment more. "But can I have just a minute with my friend," she nodded towards Gary.

Nikko's eyes narrowed menacingly. "Just a moment, and no touching. I can't tell if either one of you is armed yet, and I am not taking any chances," he murmured gruffly. The guy wasn't getting his hands on his woman, he wasn't getting as much as a fucking peck on the cheek if he had his say.

Ronnie turned her back completely to him, and she stood on tiptoe. "Please keep my bike safe for me, Gary. It's got sentimental value." She then mouthed the words to him. She definitely didn't want Nikko to hear this. "I'll try to escape. I'll come back."

Gary just shook his head slightly and sharply in the negative. She used her eyes to plead with him. He nodded reluctantly even though that was the last thing he wanted. He just wanted her out of here now, and out of his hair. His parents would have a fit if this got out. He wanted them both off his property now. He needed to get the hell out of dodge and away from the trouble he knew he had started because he'd wanted to play the tough guy, and had gotten mixed up in things way over his head. "I'll take care of the bike. Have it shipped back to your granddads. Take care babe," he began to reach down to tug a strand of her hair the way he used to. A small part of him still felt bad for her.

"I said no touching," Nikko firmly restated, interrupting what looked like might turn into a tender moment. Again, the words, not with my woman ran through his mind.

Gary put his hands up in mock surrender, but backed up a step. "Gotcha!"

"Gary, one more thing, baby," Ronnie spoke softly as she began to turn. "What I said to you on the phone earlier. I meant. And I hope you keep your promise. I won't tell anyone I was here either. I love you so much. Thanks for trying." And with that Ronnie took a step back.

Her words confused the hell out Nikko, and when she turned he could see she had tears in her eyes. What the hell, he thought. Had she been fooling him all along? Playing him? Did she still have feelings for this jerk? Well, there was only one way to find out, and he would beat the answers out of her when he got her alone. And, he couldn't wait; damn he was pissed.

When she was by his side, he pulled out his handcuffs, and made her turn around.

"Is that really necessary?" she replied flipping her platinum blond hair over her shoulder and using every ounce of sarcasm she could muster.

Gary was already heading into his cabin not waiting around for the after show, so his answer was made softly for just her to hear. "I think it is, Ronnie. We don't want you going bat shit crazy, and dumping a gallon of barbecue sauce all over me again after drugging me, do we?"

"You might not want that," she murmured under her breath, when she heard the clasp of the door click into place. Gary was already safely inside. "But it sounds pretty good to me."

His icy blue eyes were at war with her soft brown eyes...she didn't budge. So, he tugged on the cuffs not so gently either in the guise of ensuring they were securely in place. "Walk," he commanded her and gave her a little push for good measure. He wanted nothing more than to beat that sassy attitude out of her.

The quarter mile to his car was done in complete silence. He was wondering what the heck Ronnie was up to, and what she'd been planning. She was wondering how she was going to convince him to let her go back and try to get a confession out of Gary.

She saw the dirt road in the distance. He must have parked his car there by the old Anderson place. She was running out of time. Then one of Jay's little euphemisms popped into her head. You catch more flies with honey, than you do with vinegar.

So, Ronnie began to cry.

Chapter Eighteen

A New plan

She was still crying when they reached the car, and he unsnapped her cuffs so she would be comfortable even though she didn't deserve it. He gently steered her inside the vehicle and quickly made his way to his side of the car. Getting in, he tried to ignore her for now. He wanted to get her out of here fast and get on the road. Away from here, and away from Gary.

After about a minute of driving, Nikko looked at Ronnie out of the corner of his eyes while he also tried to focus on the curvy dirt road. It was pitch black out, and there were no lights in this neck of the woods. He was so mad at her, had been so worried, it took him a full minute to react to those tears.

Once on the straight, he was able to turn to her slightly and still handle the vehicle. Her crying had only gotten louder, more hysterical in his mind, and he really felt her pain. He couldn't take the sobs any longer, and so did the only thing he could think to do in that moment. He tried to comfort her. "Ronnie," he murmured softly and tried to place a hand on her lap.

"Don't touch me," she snapped pushing his hand away. "You've ruined everything!"

Her reaction was so typically female. Exaggerated, emotional. It wasn't Ronnie either. It floored him.

"Me?" he sputtered, reacting. After what she had done, she accused him of ruining everything. What the fuck? Her tears weren't fooling him. "Ronnie! Don't dump this on me. You are the one who jumped bail. You are the one who drugged me. You are the one who dumped a gallon of barbecue sauce on me and stole my fucking car. And you sit there and cry, and blame me."

"Yes, I blame you." Her head whipped towards him as she backed into the corner of her seat. "You said you would help and support me, and the first chance you get you take Miss Barbecue Bimbo to bed because I was unavailable. You lied to me."

Her words stung. It's what he thought she had assumed. But, she had it all wrong. He prayed she would accept his explanation.

"Nothing happened with her, Ronnie. She was applying for a job at the hotel, and it was a coincidence. You really need to stop jumping to conclusions when it comes to us. I am so pissed right now, and those tears better dry the fuck up. You're not the innocent one here."

Yes, he felt bad. But, he wasn't putting up with these antics either.

His words gave her pause, shocked her, but she was so furious right now and unable to process it all.

"Yeah, likely story. I know your type, Nikko. Anything with legs and long eyelashes who bats her eyes your way. I fell for it once, I fell for you twice. Shame on me if I fall for that again," she spat then turned from him crossing her arms across her chest defensively.

"Ronnie," Nikko said, dropping his tone on octave. "You are pushing all the wrong buttons. When I get you back to the hotel, I have a real good notion to put you over my knee."

"Don't you fucking dare try," she threatened, looking at him. "I'll scream so bloody loud I'll burst your ear drums. And, I'm not going to your hotel either. I want my own room." She glared at him now. Of all the gall.

"Ah, hell to the no on that one, baby." He gave her a sideways glance. "I'm calling for a plane, getting us on the late flight, getting your ass back to Florida. But we need some place private to talk. If you scream then the police get called and your mom loses the house. So, think twice before you make that threat again." Her eyes remained narrowed. He let out a sigh of frustration, and softened his tone.

"Ronnie, there are some things we need to talk about." When she just continued to fume silently, he interjected. "Really Ronnie? What were you thinking drugging me? What the hell did you give me, anyway? My brothers are going to think I am a complete ass. Your mother could lose her house, my brothers a small fortune if the police catch wind of you being here," his tone was softer, but brokered no argument. She hadn't thought any of this through at all. Hell, she could have killed him.

His words stung. They cut deeply. "Is that all you think about? Your reputation with your brothers and the money. I gave you what you deserved. You made me feel like a fool. You never cared for me at all. I was just a job to you. And a way to pass the time. I was an idiot. I thought we were friends," she began to cry again somewhat in earnest hoping these tears would work.

Her words rained on him like ice. But her tears kept him from thinking clearly. He couldn't deal with the emotional aspect of it, and so reacted the only way he knew how. He snapped again.

"I told you to cut that shit out with the tears. I can't think straight right now. You fucked up, not me, whether you want to admit it or not. Don't blame me. Seriously, before our talk, you are going over my knee baby because you have been a bad, bad girl."

"Fuck you, Nikko!" she seethed, and wiped at her tears. They were real, but more out of frustration for her foiled plans than sadness, she tried to tell herself.

"Oh, we can do that too if you want." His eyes fixed on the road as he made a turn.

"Never again," she spit out.

"We'll see," he said more softly as he finished the maneuver, but his voice still had that same edge.

The car got quiet for a few minutes. When they pulled off the dirt road onto the highway, Nikko hit the gas a little and sped the rest of the way to town. Ronnie was in a whole heap of trouble, and his palm itched. No matter what she thought, drugging him and stealing his car, and putting herself into a whole fucking shit load of trouble was no excuse. The girl was going to get what she deserved. Then, he would work on the making up part. But first would come the lesson.

Ronnie sensed more than anything the seething anger below the surface. Nikko was really pissed. The things he said made sense, but she wouldn't, no couldn't deal with that right now. She needed to get her life back before she could think of anything else. She did feel a twinge of guilt for the drugging part. But there had been no other way. *Had there?* She shook away the doubts and risked a sideways glance at Nikko. His face was set in a grim line. She could see the pain and hurt below the surface. It confused her. As they got closer to Spragueville, Ronnie knew they were just two exits away, her doubts grew as did her fears. What in the hell could she do to convince him to let her go to Gary? The anger wasn't going to work. The crying either. She needed to try a different approach.

"Nikko?" she said softly. Perhaps some humble pie. And a little pleading.

He heard the difference in her tone right away, but he was still so mad at her it took a moment before he could respond.

She tried again. "Nikko?" Now her voice had a plaintive quality about it. It tore at him.

He sighed and finally asked, "What?" Not what he was expecting.

"Nikko, you can't send me back yet." His head snapped in her direction. They were at a light.

"What?" He repeated and looked at her like she was a moron.

"Please," she begged twisting her hands in her lap.

"Like hell. That is one of the first things I am gonna do!" The woman had obviously lost her mind.

She had to make him understand. "Nikko, listen. Please." She took a breath when he remained silent. "My lawyer is good, but he had bad news for me yesterday. His guys couldn't find Gary, and the tapes don't show much like he was hoping. I can't wait months while my whole life is in limbo. I think I can get him to confess. I really do."

"The hell you will," he again gave her that look that said she was being a complete dumbass. The light changed and he continued up the road to the hotel. It wasn't far now.

She knew he was pissed, but she just had to keep trying. Her time was running out. "But Nikko, I really think I can do this." Still, no response. "What if you help me, I'll let you help me? Then there won't be a trial, I can move on with my life. My mom is pregnant. She doesn't need this looming over her for months. Please, Nikko, if I ever meant anything to you, help me. You won't have to baby sit me anymore. Your brothers won't lose their money to the insurance company. I know if we put out heads together we can figure this out," she begged.

Nikko just shook his head. The silence passed until he pulled onto the exit ramp.

"Nikko?" she asked again in a near panic, her tone sharp. He looked at her. Her eyes shimmered. He saw the fear there of years of prison possibly looming in her future. His heart ached. He didn't want that for her. For them. "Please," she whispered. "Help me."

He was lost. It was in that moment he knew he was hopelessly in love with this crazy woman. A woman who drugged him, stole his car, and didn't trust him. Fuck his life! His hands gripped the steering wheel like iron. He looked back at the road and sighed. Fuck! Fuck! He knew it was stupid, but he would do it, if only to prove to her once and for all, how much he cared. But, he wasn't letting her off the hook for her actions. She needed to trust him and keep him in the loop. His eyes remained fixated straight ahead. Then his voice came out gruffly as he tried to mask the emotion there, after this revelation to himself, "We can talk about this more. Maybe. At the hotel," he finished.

Ronnie, let out her held breath. There was hope. Surely, he would help just to put this all behind them. She wanted this over too. For her, for her mom and Jay and the new baby. And, she wanted to move on and forget this whole horrid time in her life.

"Thank you," she whispered, as she settled back more comfortably into her seat. Yes, she wanted to forget about all of this. Put this hideous nightmare behind her. But a niggling little feeling, a little doubt persisted, and she knew, she wouldn't ever be able to forget Nikko.

Despite his infidelity, she had begun to really care for him. No, she had fallen for him. So that part of the nightmare would remain with her for a long time. It would take her a very, very long time to forget him, and an even longer time to ever be able to trust a man again. Her heart hurt. He said he might help, and that she took as a good sign. Her words had sunk in. Yes, it was just a maybe, but it was a start. She would continue to work on him in the hotel, tell him her plan. He could help her tweak it, and they all would be out from under this mess. His agreeing and his frustrated sighs, told her all she needed to know. He too wanted to move on, and put this and her behind him.

***

Inside his hotel room, Nikko flicked on the interior lights, and ushered Ronnie in before him. This room was not as nice as the one he had in Spring Hill. It was a simple, typical hotel room. She heard the door, shut behind her with a soft click. She turned to him, and was about to speak, but the fury she saw there stopped her cold.

"What?" she muttered. He remained mute. He just looked at her strangely for a moment more. She stared at him with her mouth open.

"Don't say anything," he cautioned. He was at the end of his proverbial rope.

She closed her mouth. It was suddenly dry.

He took two steps and stood beside her. She trembled at the anger she saw. She felt his hand at the button on her jeans. He pulled the material away and she felt the waistband release. She was too dumbfounded to speak. What was he thinking? She felt a downward tug and then heard the zipper.

"What?" she whispered clearly not expecting this.

"Say nothing," he repeated, eyes boring into hers, smoldering. He pulled her jeans down around her hips, and then she felt the cold air of the room on her exposed flesh. She stood silently, waiting. What was he thinking? He wanted to fuck? She was shocked into silence by her body's traitorous reaction to him.

He took a step back, and then looked her up and down, blue eyes on fire, molten. She swallowed several times. She felt the excitement begin to build.

He began to walk behind her, and she felt his hands at her waist, as he gently pulled her back towards the bed.

If she had to sleep with him one more time, she thought, she would do it. In the intensity of the moment her heart raced. She felt Nikko sink to the bed behind her, and then before her mind could make sense of what was happening, he hauled her to him. She was over his knees and he had panties down, and without warning, he struck. He was spanking her. Hard! *He had meant it.*

"Ow," she yelled.

"Don't scream," he threatened. "And, that was for drugging me," he breathed. She began to struggle.

"Oh, no you don't," she cried out after the initial shock from the first strike had passed. His arm lay over her back like iron pinning her to him.

Whack, came his hand again. "That was for the barbecue sauce."

"Ouch, Nikko, please," she begged as her other ass cheek flamed from the intensity of the slap he gave her. She continued to struggle, but kept her voice down despite the pain and humiliation.

Whack! "That was for stealing my car," he breathed as she cried out his name softly begging him to stop. The force of the blow took her air for a moment.

Again, his hand descended. "This was for making me worry." She gasped and cried and took it.

Whack! "This is because I care god dammit," and he hit her again with all the ferocity he thought she could handle. Her cheeks were on fire. She jumped each time he hit her, and by the sixth and final strike, she was crying and lay in a heap over his legs.

He slowly turned her over, and the tears he saw there were genuine. "Look at me, Ronnie," he whispered softly, brushing the hair out of her face. She looked at him sadly, the tears streaking down her beautiful face. His eyes lost their anger, she noticed even though she couldn't meet his gaze for long. His tone softened. "Ronnie. You deserved that." She sniffled and nodded.

She couldn't look at him still. She did. She knew it. His hand began to stroke her back, and still she could not meet his eyes. Guilt overwhelmed her. But when his lips brushed her shoulder, she turned and saw something strange and startling there in his eyes. She couldn't look away if she tried.

"And that was because I fucking love you, Ronnie. God help me, but I do. I came because of that, and I was scared to death you were going to get hurt. Not for my brothers, not for the money. I came because the woman I love was putting herself in danger." He saw her eyes go from pain to shock to surprise. He had one more thing to say. "Ronnie, baby, please believe me. I never slept with that woman."

She saw stark, bleak desperation in his eyes. Could it be? Ronnie ran the gamut of emotions. His words. She couldn't believe what she was hearing. She saw his eyes, and more than his words, she saw the honesty there. Suddenly, she didn't feel the pain his hand evoked, and she reached her hand up to touch his face, as a single tear formed in his eye. She swallowed. He watched her.

"I . . . believe you," she whispered. She did. But she couldn't find the words to express what she was feeling. Her shock was just that great.

His lips descended and the kiss they shared said it all. Ronnie grabbed the collar of his shirt and pulled him down with her to the bed. This time what they did wasn't fast, and even though it felt like their time was running out, he wanted to show her with more than words just how much he loved her. And she let him.

***

An hour later, Nikko was on the phone with one extremely pissed off angry Marino. Ronnie could hear Andreas pitching a huge ass fit through the receiver.

"You fucking bring her to Florida, now!" Andreas screamed into his phone.

"Andy," Nikko started trying to explain again what happened and what they wanted to do.

"Don't fucking Andy me," he yelled. "Don't screw this up."

"I'll bring her back. But there were no flights tonight. We couldn't make the last one. I just need twenty-four hours. This plan will work. I know it will."

His brother was lost, Andreas thought. Andreas raked his hands through his jet black hair trying to calm the fuck down. He was in complete shock. His brother woke him up to tell him he and Ronnie had gone to Maine. They wanted to set up this Gary, and get a confession out of him. *What the hell were they thinking?*

His baby brother then tells him, he loves the girl. *Holy fuck?* What a way to wake up! Blond hair, big boobs, and the kiddo thought he was in fucking love. He knew he wouldn't be able to talk his brother out of it. And here he was in Florida over a thousand miles away. He knew his screaming wasn't going to change Nikko's mind either. He was a man, and not the boy he once could boss around. And Andreas had to admit, his plan was okay, but hell, he didn't want his brother to get in over his head with no back up. But, still. He should have included him from the get go. *In love?* He shook his head to clear it. His brother was still rambling about the merits of the plan. He was going on about her possibly going to jail. He could hear it in the kid's voice. He did fucking love her. That was what shocked him the most. Yup, he knew there would be no talking him out of it.

He finally relented. "Okay. Okay!" He sighed into the phone glancing at the clock, and thinking of all that had to be done. "Just don't do anything till I get there, you hear me, you stupid ass," he threatened.

"What?" Nikko stammered unsure of what his brother meant.

"If you stupid morons who think you're in love after a few weeks are going to do this, then you are going to have back up." Andreas sighed.

"What?" Nikko was at a loss. "Back up?"

"I'm renting a plane first thing in the morning, and I'm bringing Blaze and Gio. I don't want you two going halfcocked on this thing. If it's gotta be done, it's getting done right," he exclaimed, rubbing his temple with his free hand. *His baby brother was in fucking love. Fuck this shit!*

"Hey, I can handle it," Nikko added defensively.

Yeah right. When love gets in the way you make mistakes, he thought to himself. But he kept those thoughts to himself. "Yeah, small potatoes. But I'd rather be there when this shit goes down. Just in case. We ought to be there by noon, hopefully earlier. Think you can sit on her for that long," he added sarcastically. He was sure the love birds wouldn't be doing much sitting.

"Yeah, but . . ." Nikko trailed, glancing back to Ronnie and shrugging his shoulders. She heard everything so he didn't have to repeat it.

She nodded her approval. Might as well have more help, she thought. It couldn't hurt.

"No God damn buts," Andreas interrupted. "You wait for me. Got it?"

"Yes, I got it," Nikko answered. He knew that tone from Andreas. He would wait for back up. He shut the phone and turned to Ronnie. His brother had already hung up. He knew he could have handled it, but the idea of using Ronnie as bait, well, it just made him more comfortable to know they'd have more back up . . . for her.

"Ronnie, you okay with waiting?" he asked sitting next to her.

One more day, she thought and this would all be over. Too emotional to speak, she nodded silently. At least they would have tonight, and he leaned down for a kiss. And again, they made love, him showing her and telling her again and again just how precious she was to him. But despite it all, she couldn't find the nerve, or the courage to say it back. *Not yet. Not now.*

Chapter Nineteen

Killing Time

Nikko winced sympathetically when he turned to face Ronnie. He'd just gotten off the phone with his brother. Andreas called back to let Nikko know their flight would be arriving at early in the morning. He also informed him they were renting a vehicle in Bangor, and then they would make a pit stop at a friend of a friend of Gio's who lived in the area to get some supplies, and would then proceed to their location. Andreas still hadn't sounded happy on the phone, but he was pleased they'd waited and hadn't gone off half-cocked on their own. He again reminded them to wait for his arrival.

"What did he say?" she asked. "I mean I'm sure I heard most of it, but is there anything I missed. Does this change anything?" she asked, suddenly nervous.

It was nearly midnight and he and Ronnie talked more about other things. Nikko admitted he loved her, repeating it often during their two love making sessions. He also reiterated his promise to help her. This would be over soon. They would all come up with a fool proof plan together. But, she didn't know if she could trust his brothers. What if it was just a ruse to make them wait and then they would nab her and bring her in. She was nervous, and didn't know who to trust anymore. Even Nikko.

Nikko watched the play of emotions across Ronnie's face. The woman he loved. The woman who had yet to admit her feelings to him. That worried him a little, but he did know she'd been through a great deal in the last twenty four to forty eight hours. He hated to admit to himself he'd like to hear the words, but he knew she cared, was definitely jealous, if he was reading the barbecue sauce incident correctly, and he was pretty sure it couldn't mean anything else. He just had to keep reassuring her.

He walked over to her as she dressed after making love. "Obviously, he still wants us to sit tight. They will be here early, so we have tonight to tweak this plan of ours." He saw the doubt. He pulled her to him, holding her, and looking down into her eyes, he spoke. "Ronnie, I told my brother I loved you. He will keep his word."

She licked her lips and he was sorely tempted to kiss her again, make love to her. "Are you sure? He won't just turn me in?"

He saw the fear wash over her. "No, baby, he won't. My brother is a man of his word if he is anything. He may be harsh, and gruff. He's got reason to be, but he is all about family. I love you and that means your family now too, Ronnie."

She lay her head against his chest and let out a small sigh of relief. He felt her relax, but still she didn't say the words back.

Time. Time, he told himself. She is afraid to trust right now. Her whole future, their future, depended on Gary confessing. When he and his brothers helped to clear her name, and she was truly free to make her own choices, then he would know for sure.

They stood for a moment, just holding each other. The silence in the room grew. But it wasn't awkward. It was comforting until he heard Ronnie's stomach growl. Amused, he looked down at her and they both laughed.

"Wow, that again," he teased, reminding her of the drive from the Courthouse. She blushed. Her stomach always betrayed her.

"The stomach wants what it wants. I didn't eat too much today," she admitted, "but I could wait for breakfast." Ronnie knew it was too late for room service in this hotel.

Nikko thought for a moment, then, "I can run and get something," he suggested. "But, I really don't want to leave you. How about we sneak out and grab some takeout." He didn't want to risk leaving Ronnie alone. If anyone reported seeing her the authorities would come. Being with her, he could show his credentials and say he would be bringing her in.

And he hated to admit it, but he also didn't want to leave her in case she bolted and tried something on her own again. She hadn't expressed her feelings for him, so he still had some doubts.

Ronnie sensed his misgivings, as he pulled back. She needed to trust him, but the thought to do this on her own crossed her mind. What if Gary sensed she wasn't alone any longer? What if he sensed there was something going on between her and Nikko? Waiting until tomorrow might be too late. What if Gary bolted? Would they be able to track him down again? She looked up at Nikko who was watching her, and gave him a smile. God, she did love him. But was his love real? And yes, she made love with him again, but she just didn't know if it was just a passing infatuation for him.

Well, she didn't really have a choice right now. He wouldn't leave her alone after her stunt in Florida. But she had to try. "But, what if someone sees us?" she sighed her response.

He gave her an odd look and puzzled it over. "I'll make it look good. I'll hold your arm in a controlling way, but I doubt someone will see us. It's pretty late," he added, glancing at his watch. "But, we will keep up pretenses just to be safe. You can even act like you don't like me." His eyes twinkled mischievously as he regarded her, waiting for her agreement. Her stomach growled again. "Shall we?" he teased, offering her his arm in a gallant fashion.

Although nervous, she laughed and took his arm. "Oh, can we get my things. I'm downstairs in room one twelve," she asked as they headed towards the door.

Nikko laughed, and she looked at him wondering why he was laughing at such a strange request. "All day I was worrying about you and you were right underneath me the whole time," he clarified.

"I prefer on top," she quipped. "But yes, I guess my room is below this one," she answered as she noticed his room number on the door when he shut it.

"Well, we can always eat later," he replied, "If you would like to show me. I do like that position," he joked. At that moment her stomach growled again, loudly.

She shrugged sheepishly and patted her stomach in response.

He shook his head sadly. "Ah, another time, then."

"Sorry," she apologized. "But that might be a bit distracting if we were . . . you know," she blushed.

"Probably," he grinned mischievously. "Okay, let's get you something to eat and try to keep the hungry horrors at bay."

***

They went down the stairs instead of taking the elevator since it was only the one floor, and she slipped her credit card like key into the electronic lock, and they both entered her room. She quickly filled her bag with the few things she purchased and her belongings.

They made their way outside past the lobby with only the night clerk to bypass. She briefly nodded in their direction, but said nothing and went back to perusing her magazine. They had already passed her when she glanced up a second time giving them one more look, but they didn't notice her more careful perusal. Nikko had taken ahold of Ronnie's arm in a possessive manner and they left the lobby to go to the parking area out front.

Cassie noticed the man was carrying a bag, and practically pushing a woman out the door. She shrugged and went back to her magazine. The girl was definitely Ronnie. Her hair was different, but it was her all right. The man, well, he was smoking hot, thus her second look. But obviously he was a little too controlling for her tastes. She liked her hockey players anyhow. Gary just missed her. He'd left only minutes earlier, and though she was tempted to call it in, she didn't. Gary would be angry, and she didn't want to make Gary angry. Especially if she had a shot with him as he'd suggested. But if he didn't show up, or call like he promised, she'd reconsider calling the police tomorrow. There might be a reward in it.

***

"Ow," Ronnie winced as they made their way out into the parking lot. He was steering her towards his car quickly. She gave him a dirty look, and then remembered their plan in case there were prying eyes, and was grateful he remembered.

"Sorry," he mumbled. "Just trying to make it look good." He threw her bag into the backseat, and shut the door making his way around to his side of the car.

The only place in town open twenty-four hours, was a Dunkin Donut's, and that would have to do. They had a few appetizing items, and it was where they were headed. Once in the car, Ronnie slunk down into the seat to be less visible. There were not many cars out on the road but she wanted to do her part as well. If they were going to try again for a confession with Gary tomorrow, they had to keep up the pretense that she was an unhappy, and unwilling passenger while out in public. There was no way he could find out they were working together.

***

But, it was already too late for that. Gary came to the hotel shortly after they left his cabin. He'd given them a ten minute head start. He figured the bounty hunter would be staying in town here. He'd wanted to be positive they were headed back to Florida, and he was in the clear again as Ronnie tried to lead him to believe. He needed to check out the situation for his own peace of mind. The stakeout was interminable and Gary grew more uneasy with each passing minute. He spotted the rental car right away. It hadn't budged for hours. When midnight came and went, he decided to go take a risk and go into the lobby. They were obviously not going to make the flight the bounty hunter mentioned.

Cassie worked at the hotel, and he hoped she was working tonight. He'd had a little fling with her last summer when he and Ronnie split up. She'd been creative, he remembered fondly. His cock stirred a bit. He needed to get laid, and soon. Maybe he'd take her out if Ronnie was out of the picture and he could breathe again. Then, he'd leave town. Go back to Bangor. Spragueville was getting on his last nerve.

Cassie caught his eye right away and gave him one of her typical come hither looks.

She was definitely a hockey whore. If you played, she was on you like white on rice.

He waved, and before he could ask anything, she was already speaking. "Gary, baby.

So nice to see you. What brings you by?" she asked, batting her heavily laden eyelashes.

"Hey doll, just in town for some R and R for a few weeks. Then off to Canada I go to work in my dad's company."

She pouted, but leaned over the counter giving him a bird's eye view of all she had to offer. It wasn't much, but he acted pleased anyhow. She was definitely no Ronnie in that department. A boob job would do wonders for her figure, and maybe some lessons on applying the right amount of make-up.

Gary pretended to be interested because he wanted some information. He hoped she had some. "Yeah, I'm in town until this Ronnie thing blows over." He went straight to the point. "I never should have gotten back with that trouble maker," he added for good measure.

He watched her reaction, knew she had been upset their little fling had been so brief. He also saw something like fear pass over her features, and his interest piqued.

"Yeah, I could have told you that," she laughed uneasily when he raised his eyebrows suspiciously. "In fact I think I did mention miss goody two shoes wasn't so innocent."

He nodded and leaned on the counter, getting closer. "Yeah, you were right." He gave her his infamous smile. "Can you believe the bitch tried to call me? Wanted me to be a character witness for her! I'm not going down with that ship. I don't care how big her tilts are," he joked. He purposefully glanced at Cassie's cleavage again faking interest.

When he glanced up to look at her again he saw that fear. He needed to see if she knew something. She was just acting too strangely. "Maybe you and I can hook up while I'm here Cassie," he threw her the bone first, wagged his eyebrows at her suggestively, then pounced. "My folks want me to keep my nose clean while I'm here, and they found me a place in the company up north until this shit blows over, but it doesn't mean we can't have a little fun as long as we are discreet."

She was still acting nervous, but was definitely interested. She licked her lips. "Oh, sure babe. Sounds great. I'd love to. I'm not working tomorrow night," she informed him, smiling and glancing over his shoulder briefly.

Fuck! Someone was coming. He should have asked to talk in the office. He began to sweat, but didn't turn around hoping whomever was getting off the elevator wasn't Ronnie and the bounty hunter.

"Mmm, sounds good. I'll call you." He said the words softly so as not be overheard, hoping it had come off sexily instead. When he saw her face relax, he looked behind and saw an older man stepping out of the elevator; he let out his breath. He needed to make this quick. He needed info. He turned back to Cassie. "You know, when I got that call from Ronnie, it kind of scared me. It looked like a local call."

Cassie again appeared suddenly nervous. "Well," she started. She didn't want to ruin her chances with hooking up with hometown hero, Gary Campbell, but she thought she had seen his ex. She hadn't been sure.

"What?" he asked, interrupting her thoughts.

"Um, I did see this girl, who kind of looked like Ronnie come in about two hours ago with some guy, but she was blonder so I wasn't sure."

Bingo, he thought. He smiled to encourage her to go on.

"Yeah, but she was holding the guys hand, and so, I didn't think nothing of it."

Holding his hand? What he fuck? Gary needed to think. *What did that mean? Was she holding it, or was he leading her in here?* His heart hammered in his chest. He needed to get out of here.

"You sure?" he asked.

"Well, um, yeah, that's what it looked like," she answered, but she seemed uneasy.

"Listen Cass, I'll call about tomorrow. I got your cell," he murmured, already turning before she could reply.

"Okay, call me," she cooed after him, but he was already through the sliding glass doors before she finished her sentence. Then a few minutes later, Cassie saw Ronnie again. And this time she was sure it was her. Her, but blonder. And this time, the dude hadn't been as nice. Strange. When Gary called, she'd tell him maybe she'd been wrong. Ronnie didn't look happy to be with him.

***

In his car, Gary sat thinking. He pulled out his cell, and checked flights from Bangor. The dude said he would get her on the next flight. But they'd missed that one. They'd have to leave soon, if they hoped to make the next one. He decided again to take a chance and wait to see if they left the hotel soon. He resumed his stake out on the rental car.

But, the hand holding had thrown him. *Did Cassie really see her or had she said that to make him doubt Ronnie more? Why the fuck would she be holding his hand if the guy was a bounty hunter bringing her in?* Yes, maybe Cassie just said it to make him worried, and make herself look better in his eyes. Women did shit like that. She hadn't even been sure it was Ronnie although he was. His nerves were at an all-time high. He didn't know how much longer he could take this shit. He had royally fucked up. *Why had he agreed to bring all those drugs from Jamaica?* God damned Brimeyers, his drug connections, they'd pressured him, said it would be an easy score. He pounded the steering wheel in frustration. Sweat began to accumulate on his brow, and under his arms. This situation was getting more and more fucked up by the minute. He was about to start the car and just head home, pack and get the fuck out, when he saw the lobby doors begin to open. His heart lurched in his chest.

He saw them right away, and breathed a bit easier when he saw how roughly the dude was holding, practically pushing Ronnie to his car. He saw her angry reaction and that made him feel better too. She didn't look happy at all. She wasn't with this dude. But when they left, he decided to follow them. Be sure they got on the highway. When they passed the exit to the interstate, his heart which was already hammering picked up even more speed. *Fuck! Where the hell were they going?* They continued on for two more blocks and pulled into the drive thru of the Dunkin

Donuts. Calm down he told his racing heart, as he passed by the store and made the U-turn. Just getting coffee for the road, he thought. But when he drove by again, and they were parked, his nerves picked up again. *WTF?* He pulled onto a side road, and shut the car's engine off. He'd wait and see how long they would be. Maybe just fixing the drinks.

Thirty minutes later, when they pulled out, he knew there was no way in hell they were making the second flight. *Fuck! Fuck!* His hands slammed the steering wheel of the car again as he continued to watch them. When they finally departed, he followed them right back to the hotel. He was fuming. The only good thing was he was manhandling her again. He wanted to leave, but there was no way in hell he could. Not until he knew what the fuck was going on. He wanted Ronnie out of Maine, and the fucking bounty hunter too. Glancing at the clock, he decided to go back to his cabin and get a few hours of sleep and resume his watch tomorrow morning. A quick check on flights told him there was a late morning flight. They'd better be making that one, he fumed as he headed back out onto the road. They'd better. That's all there was to it. There was no way he was going to be at peace until they were far the fuck away. The sooner the better.

***

Gary drove home slowly feeling pretty confident they were staying put for the night. He had a lot of thinking to do. Ronnie had no clue he was deeply involved in the drug world. She thought he merely had done drugs on occasion. She had no idea he had also been dealing on campus. His parents gave him plenty for school, but it wasn't the money that drew him in. He got a really nice allowance. It was because he despised living under the Campbell thumb, and his parent's constant scrutiny. His life was all mapped out for him, and it ate away at him. His father pushed him to study forestry. Life in the family business was not something he wanted to pursue, and when the hockey thing hadn't worked and his high school dreams faded when reality set in and his lack of real athletic talent had become apparent, he began to look elsewhere for the success that eluded him. He wanted excitement, and counting trees for the rest of his life wasn't going to cut it.

His life before Ronnie and college had been fun. He was the local hockey star. Girls had thrown themselves at him. He'd done pot in high school, tried other things in college, but he hadn't really been into the drug scene.

It was one night when he bought some coke for a party that it clicked for him. He paid a grand for the small vial he had gotten for a frat party. He stayed in the bar, and had a drink before heading to that party, and witnessed his dealer make ten more such transactions in the half an hour he had been there. Who knew Spragueville's local tavern keeper Johnny "Boy" Brimeyer had such a lucrative little side business. That was ten G, easy money in a tourist town. He could do that. He could do it in Bangor with the college kids easy.

The following weekend, he approached Johnny Boy, his dealer, offering his services on campus. Johnny hadn't thought he was serious at first and laughed him off. Why would the rich kid want to deal drugs? Gary practically had to beg the older man for the chance. He eventually wore him down, and the two struck a deal.

He earned very little at first, until Johnny and his brother, Freddy, who directly oversaw him, knew he could be trusted. In four months, he was earning five grand a month, and sometimes got bonuses. Yes, the Brimeyers had been pleased with him. He was helping to make them some pretty hefty profits.

But then, Johnny and Freddy soon came up with a new plan. They didn't have enough drugs to meet the needs of their new expanded market. His family and their travels were well known, and soon they began to expect him to smuggle shit in for them from out of the country. He balked at first. He didn't want to go that far, but the guys were really putting on the pressure. If he wanted to move up, he had to put in his part. He started small. Taking shit out from Canada, and bringing it state side. But for big scores you had to go further south. He brought some shit back for the Brimeyers from Mexico last summer, and over Christmas Break from Canada again. It was at their suggestion he go to Jamaica for them, and he came up with the cruise idea. A graduation gift from his parents to him and his friends turned into a shit load of dope, meth, coke, and pills for the Brimeyers. He researched on the net on how to smuggle it in inside the snorkeling and scuba gear. But, somehow the dog sniffers caught onto it.

Luckily, he put the shit in Ronnie's gear and not his own, and doubly lucky he managed to sneak away making it look like he was just going to the restroom. He had always been a fast thinker. He felt guilty passing it off onto Ronnie, but there was no way in hell he could do jail time. Poor Ronnie had no clue the shit he was into.

When her name and face were all over the news, his parents controlled and watched his every move. They'd yelled and screamed at him for getting involved with such a low life, and used their connections to keep his name out of the papers. If they only knew! But they didn't. They were just as clueless as Ronnie was.

Even the Brimeyers ordered him to lay low for a while. He knew enough to listen to them and that's why he followed his parents' orders. Last winter, another dealer of theirs just disappeared. He considered calling them now, but then thought better of it. If they thought trouble was brewing they might think it wise to get rid of him too.

He pulled into his parents' garage with the Toyota he was using. It was used by the servants and maid for shopping trips to town, and he closed the garage door. He then walked back to his cabin to think. Maybe they would make the next flight, he prayed. No need to panic and bring in the Brimeyers yet. A good night's sleep, and a drive into town in the morning to make sure the car was gone would mean the coast was clear. Nobody had anything on him. Not even Ronnie.

If he flew the coop now that would only make things worse and bring suspicion down on his head. He didn't want the Brimeyers to worry either or send someone looking for him. He still didn't know how far their reach went.

He opened the door to the servants two bedroom cabin and made his way inside. Yeah, a good night's sleep was what he needed. Maybe a smoke too, he thought, as he pulled out a little baggie he stashed in the butter compartment of the refrigerator. That would calm him and allow him to get a little sleep. He sat at the kitchen table to roll his joint, and to think.

Chapter Twenty

The Boys are Back in Town

Ronnie woke early. She was nervous, and as soon as she began to move, Nikko's eyes fluttered open. She didn't think she would ever get over the startling blueness of those penetrating eyes. His complexion dark, and his angular chiseled face broke out into a sexy smile. He was just too handsome. And, he'd told her he loved her again and again in the night. Each restless turn she had made resulted in him pulling her close to him and murmuring those words to her soothingly. And, she had yet to say it in return.

Despite their late night and their lovemaking, she was wide awake. His brothers would be here early to come up with a plan to get Gary to confess. It could all be over today, but she didn't feel relief. Because it still could all come crashing down upon her. There was the very real possibility this plan of hers wouldn't work.

"Good morning, beautiful," Nikko smiled down at her. "You okay?" he added when she just smiled sadly at him.

"Just nervous," she admitted.

"I understand," he murmured and nuzzled his face into the top of her head drawing her closer. "Whatever happens, babe, I am here. I'll be with you." He tried to instill as much courage into his words as he could muster, but he was afraid too. For her. Her idea to get Gary to talk with her, to record a confession, was rife with risk. Risks he didn't know if he wanted to take. But he, too, saw no other options at this time. She had no evidence, and no witnesses to testify she hadn't put drugs in her gear other than Gary. Him testifying on her behalf was beyond a longshot at best. His family probably feared it would tarnish their name. The guy had no record, no priors, and was from an upstanding family with lots of money and lots of pull.

Last night, after Nikko spoke to his brother and uttered those concerns, he encouraged Ronnie to call her mother so she wouldn't worry about her. Lou needed to keep their lawyer unaware of her daughter leaving the state for as long as she could. He also hoped to warn her the police may come looking around on occasion to ascertain Ronnie's whereabouts on behalf of the prosecution. No one could know she had skipped bail.

Ronnie had done that. Her mother was greatly relieved to know Nikko was with her, and his brothers were also on the way, and planning to set up some kind of sting. She also reluctantly informed Ronnie her attorney had called again to report that Gary's parents were successfully preventing the local PD from questioning their son. Her lawyer, Mr. Stimson, was working through the red tape, getting court orders to require him to testify and submit a deposition, but it took time to get the subpoenas signed by local Maine judges who were greatly influenced by the very generous Campbell family in their political campaigns.

Louisa also informed them that Mr. Stimson asked about Ronnie, and wanted her to call him the next day. Lou avoided two of his calls, or rather made excuses for her "out of town" daughter by saying she was spending the first night with Nikko, which technically had been true, but the night before that and last night when he called to update, she lied and said Ronnie had been out with friends and had left her cell phone at home. So, now Ronnie had to squeeze a call in to her attorney sometime today to ward off any suspicions he might have as to her whereabouts.

Luckily, Nikko was with her, and she would be able to use his cell phone to make the call. Hopefully the lawyer would be none the wiser that she'd skipped.

"Thanks," she murmured, shifting so he could fully embrace her, and nestled into his shoulder. He wrapped his arms around her tightly. She felt his strength and was glad for it. Again it reminded her that she knew she was in love with him, but she still couldn't fully trust herself to say the words. Her future was so uncertain. She still could very well end up in jail, and admitting her love to him would force him to wait, for some time, and then eventually he would move on. She couldn't expect him to wait out her prison sentence. It would be easier for him to go on with his life, if she didn't admit her feelings. She didn't want to ruin his life. It was bad enough her going to jail would destroy her mom, and her grandparents. She couldn't do that to Nikko too. That would break her.

And it wasn't about trusting him which is what he was probably thinking. She reacted strongly to seeing him with the barbecue bombshell because she hadn't been in a good frame of mind when she went to see him. Fears about her mom, the baby, her future, and her past mistakes in trusting Gary clouded her judgment. She did believe him now. His story made perfect sense. Still, she couldn't give that to him yet. It was all so complicated.

***

Holding her felt good. He didn't want to let her go, but knew his brothers would be here soon. Reluctantly he spoke and broke the moment of shared intimacy. "Let's take a shower," he suggested, beginning to move.

"Okay," she whispered.

Nikko could tell that she, too, didn't want the moment to end. He helped her out of bed and holding hands they walked quickly to the bathroom. He switched on the light, and then she let him pass as he made his way to the shower. Pushing aside the curtains, he began to fiddle with the water gauges to set the temperature. Both completely naked, he stood aside to let her step into the tub, and she immediately felt a bit of tension slip away as the hot water began to cascade down her body. He stepped in behind her and grabbed a washcloth and the bottle of shower gel. Squeezing a generous amount onto the cloth, he placed it under the spray for a moment then began to massage the wet cloth over her body working it into a lather.

Ronnie turned to face him when he announced her backside was spotless. He was leering at her with a goofy grin. She smiled at him and dropped her arms, an invitation to what she knew he wanted to do. He reached for her with the washcloth and began to massage the foamy lather across her torso and then delicately washed each of her breasts paying close attention to her areolas, and tugging her nipples with the cloth until they formed peaks and stood at erect attention to his ministrations. His eyes feasted on her beautiful body.

His ice princess. Last summer she had been untouchable, and now he wanted nothing but to touch her all the time. He hoped she felt the same way about him. He decided to put his bruised ego aside and give her the time she needed to express her feelings. He understood she would not trust so easily after all she had been through, and for the first time in his life he realized he could be patient for something he really wanted. She was worth it.

Her breathing was beginning to pick up as he stroked her breasts, and his cock already stood at attention. He took the soapy cloth and slipped it underneath one heavy breast, and then moved it downwards along her rib cage, then lower over her stomach.

Her breath came out in a hiss as he traveled lower and he cupped her core. She pushed into the cloth allowing him to have his way. But he wasn't ready yet. He wanted to finish what he started first. Easing the cloth down her legs, he felt her tremble. He slowly made his way up the other leg with the cloth to gently cup her again, and again she pushed into it.

Ronnie sighed her pleasure. And even though they didn't have much of it, he was taking his time. When he stood back up, he gently turned her and washed her back and arms again, making her lift them so he could glide the cloth all over her. When he finished, he then began to wash her rear with the cloth while gently massaging her curves.

"You have the sexiest body I've ever seen," he whispered, directly behind her. "I'd love to fuck your sweet ass." Those words were spoken with such an edge. His tone told her how much he wanted her this way, how much he desired her.

"Go ahead," she breathed. She had never done this before, but for him she would do anything. She just couldn't say that yet. This was the best she could do. "Fuck me, Nikko. I'm yours."

To Nikko, the invitation was too good to pass up.

She heard the cloth drop with a resounding wet flop.

He pulled her to him, and she felt his massively full erection pressed against her. He just held her for a moment, his arms like steel bands across her breasts. She felt his lips at her neck, and then his hands pinching her nipples, hard. She thrilled in the sensation of the hot water cascading down the front of her body, and the heat he emitted on her back. The steam from the hot shower misted around them. One hand dipped down to her honey drenched pussy, and he lightly caressed her, slipping one finger to her apex as he began to tease her.

Moving his hand and fingering her sensitive clit, he began to circle and stroke it gently, applying just the right amount of friction to heighten her arousal. Soon she was pushing her little ass against his cock. It got harder than he thought humanly possible as he probed her bottom gauging her resistance while he slowly inserted his index finger in and out of her already wet pussy.

"Baby, I'm gonna need you to bend down, and put your hands on the ledge."

Without hesitation she complied. She spread her legs instinctively, and she felt his cock pressed up against her ass a moment later. She was already slick and wet but not enough, and he reached for the baby oil she always used after showering. Popping the top, he poured a generous amount between her cheeks and coated his throbbing cock. He placed his hands on her hips and pushed against her gently even though he wanted to ram his cock into her depths. In this position he would be able to sink into her as deep as he could get. He carefully eased the tip of his shaft into her.

"Is that okay?" he murmured, breathing hard. A nod of her head told him it was. He pushed in a little deeper and she was so gloriously tight, he almost came.

"I'm okay," she whispered huskily. Determined to please him, she pushed herself onto him even more. Despite the slightly uncomfortable new experience, she was delighted with the new heights to which he took her.

Her body was stretching to accommodate him, and he took his time. "Relax, don't tighten up, baby," he cautioned. "I don't want to hurt you." He waited, took another inch of her, and then slowly pulled back but never broke their connection. He repeated this slow torture, entering and withdrawing several times until she moaned with pleasure. Only then did he thrust more deeply into her, and finally all the way. He felt his cock slide along her walls so slick and hot, and reveled in the angle that allowed him such depth. He felt the veins in his cock harden, and pulled out slowly, and then pushed back into her. Fuck, she was so sweet and so tight. That she agreed to this told him so much. The pure friction was his undoing, and he began to thrust in and out for all he was worth. She kept taking him, sucking him in, and providing just the right amount of resistance, clenching around his shaft as he pulled out.

"Finger yourself baby," he encouraged her. "I want you to find your pleasure with me." She complied circling her clit with her index finger while he penetrated her over and over again. The heat of the shower and his earlier foreplay found her soon ready to reach the precipice.

"Yes," she moaned. "Oh Nikko, it feels . . . so good."

"Damn," he couldn't even speak when his cock was fully impaled inside her. He began to move faster, in and out, and the sensation was so intense his balls tightened and he was about to explode.

"I . . . fucking . . . love . . . you," he grunted with each thrust until he couldn't hold back any more. He spilled his semen into her savoring each pulsating pump the tremors of his orgasm caused.

She hadn't come yet, so he slipped his hand around her to the apex of her pussy, his cock still fully embedded in her sweet treasure. He flicked her clit to exquisite extension, until her orgasm came. She tightened around him causing his pleasure to become intensified. Ronnie flung her head back, wet hair plastered against his chest, and cried out, screaming his name.

He held her for a moment longer, their bodies still joined until their ragged breathing returned to normal, but as the water began to cool, he reluctantly released her and turned her around.

Looking down at her, he saw her eyes were brimmed with unshed emotion.

"Baby, did I hurt you?" he asked.

She just shook her head and washed off quickly. She couldn't speak. He could see something was bothering her, but allowed her a moment to compose herself.

"I'm just going to go get dressed," she muttered, trying to pass him.

He tried to stop her, to find out why she looked so sad after the pleasure they just shared.

"Please Nikko. I just need a moment. You finish showering, and we will talk in a moment."

"Okay, baby." He reluctantly gave in. "I'll be out in five. My brothers will be here in less than an hour, tops. Order breakfast if you want," he suggested.

She nodded and he allowed her to pass.

***

When he emerged from the bathroom, she was dressed in a denim skirt, and tank top. The same one she wore when she was released into his custody from the jail in Tampa, and she was just getting off the phone.

"Breakfast ordered?" he asked as the towel he dried himself then wrapped around his torso slipped to the floor.

"Yes," she murmured. She sat on the edge of the bed while he began to dress selecting items from the clothes in his open suitcase.

"Good. Now you want to tell me what is bothering you?" he questioned as he pulled on his slacks.

"Um," she started. "I just feel bad because you keep saying . . ." She couldn't finish her sentence. The tears started to fall.

Nikko interrupted. "I love you."

She nodded.

"Baby, I'm sorry if it makes you feel uncomfortable. I'm new at this being in love thing. My first time and all," he tried to tease her, and she smiled slightly. He approached her with his t-shirt in one hand. "I know you have a lot on your mind, and saying those words back to me, yes, I'll admit I would love to hear them, but if you aren't ready to say it yet, I'm okay with that. I suspect you feel a lot for me, but with your situation, I completely understand."

Ronnie was dumbfounded. It was like he could read her mind, and the tears just came. The feelings and fears she had been trying to suppress for so long just came tumbling out. She nodded to let him know that was exactly what was bothering her, and he just pulled her into his arms, held her, and let her cry.

A few minutes later, her tears subsiding somewhat, he began to release her so they could finish their conversation. A loud thumping at the door interrupted their embrace.

"Honey, we're home!" Gio's voice boomed from outside the door while the incessant banging continued.

Giving Ronnie a chuck under the chin, he announced, "It seems the cavalry is here, babe. You ready for this?" he looked down into her puffy eyes.

"I'll just go in the bathroom, and splash some cold water on my face," she nodded as he hastily drew his t-shirt over his head.

He gave her a moment to get the door closed before he went to answer his brother's persistent rapping.

"About time you answered, baby brother. I was beginning to think you went out for breakfast." Nikko looked past Gio to see his other brothers were not with him.

"Where are Andreas, and Blaze?" he asked as Gio pushed his way into the room without an invite.

"Andreas is renting some rooms for us, and Blaze said he didn't want to interrupt if you were . . . you know, but I'm always game for walking in on some love birds. Where is busty?" he asked loudly, making the gesture with his hands while plopping down on the unmade bed.

"I heard that. And, in here," Ronnie announced, sarcasm dripping from behind the closed bathroom door.

"Oh shit," Gio murmured softly, pretending to be embarrassed. Then more loudly, "Sorry 'bout that."

"No you aren't," Ronnie called back, not giving him a second to think. Gio laughed heartily.

"I like her," he pronounced, giving Nikko his stamp of approval.

Then the bathroom door opened and Ronnie emerged. "Glad to hear it." She gave him a shifty smile.

"Nice tank top," he winked. Ronnie rolled her eyes. It was obvious Gio was the jokester in the family.

Nikko elbowed his brother not so affectionately, and Ronnie smirked at the duo. Gio just grabbed onto his brother and then wrestled his younger brother into an embarrassing headlock even though Nikko had a good four inches on him. Gio might not be as tall, but he was definitely more bulky in the muscle department, and Nikko had to struggle a bit to get out of it.

"Cut that shit out, now!" they all heard from the open door. It was Andreas who spoke in a voice that brokered no argument. He was flanked by Blaze who was smiling, but looked uncomfortable standing at the entrance to their room.

Gio and Nikko untangled themselves immediately at the eldest Marino's command. A moment of silence ensued until Andreas finally nodded at Ronnie, passed the threshold into the room, and only then did the sudden tension of the moment ease a bit. Andreas Marino was definitely a reckoning, and the undeniable patriarch of the family. Ronnie couldn't help but notice all the boys jumped when he told them to, and she witnessed it first hand with his next statement.

"Come," he ordered and turned. "Your breakfast is being sent to my rooms. I ordered more food." One after the other, the boys followed him down the hall, which left

Ronnie to shut the door and follow. They made two turns and stopped at the end of the last hall, where a set of double doors was open. Andreas had gotten himself a suite.

Chapter Twenty-One

To Catch a Crook

Ronnie entered Andreas' suite last trailing behind the others. Nikko waited until she passed before closing the door behind her. Andreas stood, hands on lean hips, waiting in front of a massive cherry wood conference table until they all stood around it. He didn't look pleased, and he was glaring at her.

He said nothing. His look said it all. He was pissed at her. Her stunt in leaving Florida.

"Andreas . . .," Nikko started from somewhere behind her.

"Say nothing," he stated menacingly between clenched teeth. "I heard your story last night. Now I want to hear hers." He indicated Ronnie with his chiseled chin.

Gio and Blaze got closer to the eldest Marino flanking him on either side. His sentinels. The three stood waiting for her to speak. Her mouth suddenly went dry being put on the spot. She felt Nikko's hands grasp her shoulders softly for support. She knew she needed to stand up to this man if she was going to pass muster with the head of this family. She was grateful for the show of support, but it was her mess, her bed, and she had to lie in it. She shrugged off his hands and squared her shoulders. She needed to show these men just what she was made of.

Nikko, behind her, felt nothing but pride for the woman he loved as she faced his brothers head on.

She wet her lips, and spoke firmly, with assurance. "I screwed up. I can admit that. I put my life in danger, I know that. I have heard it all from Nikko, believe me!" She rolled her eyes remembering the tongue lashing she got in the car, and the spanking later. "But I know I can get Gary to admit his part in this. I was close last night. If I can get another chance, I'm sure he will reveal something. I need to get him on tape." She pulled the recording device she purchased from Radio Shack out of her pocket.

Andreas just shook his head and smiled ruefully. *Amateur.* He nodded his head at Gio who automatically turned and snapped open a case on a side table behind him. He began taking out much more sophisticated equipment.

"Fine. Your equipment is better." Gio snickered and Andreas silenced him with a glance. She continued ignoring Gio's inappropriate comment. "Anyway, he's not very bright. Until Nikko showed up, I felt pretty confident I'd get him to talk, but now, I don't know. He's going to be suspicious. But, I've got to try. Before you take me back, I need to try one more time," she rushed out. "I'll do it your way. But, a trial is months away, and Gary will be in another country in just a few weeks. If I lose this chance, I lose my life. I am looking at years behind bars."

Through her whole speech, Andreas watched her eyes. The girl was tough, and determined. He had gotten that same impression the moment he met her. Nikko definitely found himself a feisty one. There would be no controlling her. He quickly glanced at his other brothers. They were grim faced too. He needed to know just one thing if they were going to risk their license, their business, on her.

And when he spoke, it was like a punch to the gut for Ronnie. "Do you love my brother?" His eyes didn't leave her face.

"I . . . I," her pause got her glares from all three. Gio looked over her shoulder at Nikko questioningly.

"Of course, she loves me," Nikko jumped in. He again reached for her and squeezed her shoulders taking a step closer to her. Her back was pressed against him.

Andreas made a face, his lips twisting into a curl. He grabbed the chair in front of him and pulled it out. "Sit," he ordered.

Nikko gave her a reassuring push, and held a chair out for her. She sat, and he followed sitting beside her. He took her hand from her lap and held it. And then his other brothers eventually did the same each taking their seats on either side of the chair Andreas pulled out.

"Hmm. Okay." He paused significantly before speaking again, but his expression showed his disappointment in his interrogation of her. "We'll do it, but this is how it is going to go down. You're going to call Gary and tell him you gave Nikko the slip late last night. You're going to tell him that he's going have to come get you because you don't have transportation. You're going to shack up in that abandoned warehouse we scoped out this morning."

Andreas stood and began to pace as he talked. "Gio, go move the cars. Nikko give him your keys." Gio got up and took Andreas' keys first, then held out his hand to Nikko who passed keys to him over the table. He was already leaving before, Andreas spoke again. When he saw the confusion on Ronnie's face, he clarified.

"In case your old lover boy decides to drive into town before you call him, we don't want him seeing two rentals parked out front. Gio knows what to do. He'll park one in the back by the employees parking area and one down the block."

Ronnie nodded. "Makes sense," she murmured. His look silenced her again, and he resumed his pacing.

"As I was saying, you're going to ask Gary to come get you at that warehouse down the block, tell him that's where you have been hiding. If he takes the bait, you are going to throw yourself at him. Kiss him, act your little heart out. Tell him you love him, and you'll do whatever it takes for him to take you to Canada with him. Make it look good. Real good."

"The hell she will!" Nikko jumped out of his seat, his chair flying backwards. He flew across the room to Andreas' side of the table.

"Listen," Andreas held up his hands to ward off his hot headed baby brother while taking a step forward as well. "We don't have time for games. If we are going to get this guy fast, we have to make it look good. We can't dick around." He placed a pointed index finger in the middle of Nikko's chest. "This girl, who loves you," the words dripped sarcasm, "is a fugitive. Her lawyer is probably getting suspicious. The police in Hernando County may decide to do a drive by, and what the hell happens if they announce it on the news that she's skipped. Gary boy, if he hasn't already, will disappear off the radar. He's fucking got the resources to do it too. We don't have time for bullshit."

"But," Nikko started, his face red, and grim. He looked at Ronnie.

"If she's got to stick her tongue down his throat, if she's got to grab his cock, and moan to get this shit done today, she's doing it." Andreas was holding nothing back. They didn't have the time, or the law on their side. They were aiding and abetting a fugitive.

Ronnie noticed Nikko's fists clenched at his sides. She knew this was tearing him apart. What man would agree to allow the woman he loved to do this? She wouldn't like it either if the tables were reversed. She had no choice but to take the decision out of his hands before this blew up.

"I'll do it," she jumped out of her seat. Nikko's head whipped in her direction. His anger was now turned in her direction.

"I don't want his fucking hands on you," Nikko started for her, and Blaze stepped into his path.

She hadn't even noticed the quietest of the four brothers getting up. She stepped between them.

"Nikko, please. If this can be over today, we can have a real chance. We won't have this dark cloud looming over us. Over my mother, the baby." Nikko's face still looked grim, angry, and he was still trying to get around her to face Blaze and Andreas. She was desperate to get his approval on this plan. She needed this over so she stated the one thing she thought would make him get on board.

"Nikko, please," she begged. "I know I haven't said the words, but I do. And I can't say them. Not until this is behind me. I won't say them until my name is cleared and I can offer you me, all of me, without another dark cloud looming on the horizon. I have nothing to offer you until I know we can have a life together. I can't say those words to you until I know for sure I can give you that. That's why I haven't told you I love you, because it wouldn't be fair to you. To give you false hope when I'd be going to jail. I couldn't do that to you."

Her eyes began to tear during her pleading, and when she finally saw a hint of approval in Andrea's eyes, she held back those tears with conviction. She squared her shoulders and waited for what would come next.

Nikko was finally able to twist out of Blaze's grasp, and he rushed to her. He held her, to him, this woman he loved with his heart and soul.

At that moment, there was a knock on the door. A strange voice called out that their order was being delivered. Their breakfast had arrived. Blaze went to the door, and Nikko turned Ronnie so she was hidden from any suspicious glances, but it hadn't been necessary as Blaze stepped into the hall to tip the hotel wait staff. He brought the heavily laden cart in himself.

Ronnie managed to get her emotions under control, and when Nikko felt she was ready to face them all again, he pulled away from her just enough to see her expression. "I love you baby, I do. I am just a man, and the thought of someone touching what's mine . . ." He couldn't finish. He just shook his head.

"Please, Nikko. It won't mean anything. I won't let him take it farther than that. I promise."

Pain flashed in his eyes, but he nodded bringing his hand up to his face to rub at the throbbing in his temples that started when Andreas described the new plan.

When they turned, Blaze and Andreas had the table all set and the platters of food all out within reach. They had given the two of them a little privacy for which they were both grateful.

Andreas gave her a nod, and a smile. "Let's eat. And finish discussing the plan. Okay?" He asked this time. Maybe she had finally made an impression. His tone was softer and had a hint of grudging respect in it.

She returned his smile. "Okay. I'm starved actually," she added as an afterthought. Then as if on cue, her stomach growled. Andreas's eyes widened. Nikko smiled for the first time, and Blaze after an initial look of surprise burst out laughing just as Gio came in the door.

"What did I miss?" he asked when he found them all laughing. Even Andreas was smiling. They filled him in as they ate. And they finalized the plan.

***

Ronnie was nervous. The men made her walk to the abandoned warehouse alone after they outfitted her. A little clip in her hair replaced her bulkier recording device. It had been one of many things Andreas had in his little bag of tricks. It was a simple unadorned barrette. She changed clothes, back in the ones she wore yesterday so Gary would assume she escaped sometime in the night and actually hid in the warehouse.

It was not quite ten, and cars were on the road. So she kept her face averted from the traffic just as she'd been told to in case she was recognized. Her cell phone in her pocket, and in her left boot, a small gun Andreas insisted she carry. She had been reluctant, but when Nikko chimed in saying he'd feel better if she had it, she agreed. It's not like she'd never used a gun. She'd been hunting with her grandfather more times than she could count, but the thought that she'd need it with Gary was just something she didn't think was necessary. But it made Nikko feel better, so she'd agreed. He and Gio had gone on ahead on point, twenty minutes earlier, to settle in and scout a good hiding place on the inside.

She stayed behind with Andreas and Blaze and they coached her on the call she would make as soon as she got to the abandoned warehouse a quarter mile from the hotel.

She heard a crackle in her ear. "Babe," Nikko said.

"Mmm-hmm," she responded to the question indicated by his tone. She didn't want people to see her talking to herself, although she passed the intersection and there was no one on the road at the moment. Still, she wanted to be careful. The massive structure with the words, Buddy's Inc. Storage in faded blue letters on the front was looming larger as she walked.

"We are in. The door on the left side is open. We're up in the rafters. Great view. There is an office, across the expanse. A desk, chair, filing cabinets, and an old sofa. Good spot. We have a bird's eye view." He wanted to reassure her she had plenty of back up. She wasn't in this alone.

"Okay," she murmured softly. She could say she slept there, Ronnie thought.

She was getting closer. Another hundred yards. The length of a football field. She knew Andreas and Blaze would be behind her in the rental. They told her they would park in the rear where there were some old large, storage containers, and dumpsters near the wooded area off the side that didn't face the road.

If Gary toured the parking lot first, he wouldn't see the car unless he pulled up to the dumpsters and actually got out of his vehicle to peer behind them. They wanted to watch Gary enter, be sure he was alone, and then would approach the building once Gary was inside. And once she had the information she needed they would storm in. Nikko and Gio would also make their presence known at the same time.

The plan was good as far as she could tell. She was grateful to all of them for getting on board and helping her out, for believing in her. She'd thanked them all before they split up. Nikko briefly pulled her in for a quick hug, whispering he loved her and to be careful before he had to leave.

"Anything for family," Blaze, expressionless, murmured. Gio smiled and patted Nikko on the back, while Andreas just curled his lip like he often did, and narrowed his eyes.

Once past the chain link fence that surrounded three-quarters of the property, she went to the left, and turned the corner. She saw the door Nikko mentioned and noticed it was slightly ajar. She quickly made her way to it, and slipped inside, shutting the door behind her. Then she was plunged into darkness. It was all up to her now.

Chapter Twenty-Two

Hooking the Bait

Ronnie took two steps and stopped. Total darkness overwhelmed her as the door behind her closed completely. Her heart raced indicating her fear.

"Stay calm," Nikko whispered. "You'll see soon, there are a few cracks in the sheeting in the roof. Just breathe."

She took his advice and took a few calming breaths. "Okay," she whispered, as the darkness turned to gray, and shapes began to take form.

"Once you're in the office, make the call," he encouraged. He, too, wanted to get this over with.

Ronnie took her first step now that her eyes had adjusted somewhat. A pile of empty crates to her right. Some barrels in the corner. Then she saw a glimmer across the large expanse. Glass. *The office?* She tentatively began to walk towards it hearing the rustle of paper and sand under her hiking boots. The framed room began to appear as she continued to walk cautiously so as not to stumble on any debris. She saw the door frame emerge from the gray, then the door handle. She grasped the cool metal, and turned. It opened easily.

Taking out her cell, she illuminated the interior. It was exactly as Nikko described. She dropped onto the sofa directly beside her, and then hesitated just a moment, before she pulled up Gary's number and hit dial.

"I love you," Nikko whispered before the little bug went silent.

***

Gary had been up early. He awoke from a deep slumber with a start; his first thoughts were of Ronnie and the shit she had almost gotten him in last night. He rubbed his hands over his face to wipe away the sleep that remained, and felt the bristles. He needed a shower and a shave. He also needed to clear his mind. He was still second guessing himself about calling in the Brimeyers. The last time he spoke to them, he reminded himself, they told him to lay low, and not to call them unless it was an emergency. They'd also told him they'd be watching, and to keep his mouth shut. He wondered if they knew about Ronnie. That she fled. That might make them change their minds.

If they didn't know, who would it hurt, he thought. First things first though, he needed that shower. He got up and made his way to the bathroom. Glancing at the clock he realized he slept through his alarm. It was nearly nine. He hustled. He wanted to get into town and be sure Ronnie and the Bounty Hunter were long gone. Once in the bathroom, he reached over to adjust the water temperature, and then he stripped.

He got in before the water warmed, enjoying the coolness of it. It woke him up.

He shook his head with a snap, and cold water from his shaggy mane went splashing across the walls and tile floor.

Once again he was thinking about the Brimeyers. If they did get wind that Ronnie was in town, they might get pissed he hadn't told them. What the hell should he do? The water began to warm, and he washed quickly. He could always say he hadn't called because that's what they'd told him to do. Play dumb.

Fuck, he just had to hope she was gone. That she'd taken the early flight. He wanted to get the fuck down town, and find out. He flung the shower curtain open and stepped out, not even bothering to dry off. Water pooled on the floor at his feet as he grabbed his razor, and shaving gel from the counter.

If she was still there, he'd have to call. That's it. Tell them and let them take care of her. Whack her, if they had to. Fuck! What a waste. He began to smooth the gel over his face working it into a lather.

He picked up his razor and made the first stroke.

But what if they whacked her and he was in town? That wouldn't look fucking good at all for him. He needed to get out of town. If anything went down, he didn't want to be here when it did. Goddammit it all. He didn't know what to do. Swish, another stroke, and he nicked himself.

"Fuck," he grunted at the sharp pain even though it passed quickly. He grabbed some tissue, tore off a tiny piece, and placed it on the cut to stop the bleeding.

Ugh! He was probably panicking for nothing, he thought, as he picked up his razor again and rinsed it before resuming his shave. She was probably in Florida. His paranoia from lying low so long was getting to him. He'd go to town, get some coffee, and then he'd fucking go home to Bangor. He was tired of this shit. Fuck his parents, the Brimeyers. He needed some companionship. He was going nuts. He'd keep his cool, he'd hang with some friends on the down low, put this crap behind him.

He finished shaving, and wiped his face. Buck naked, he crossed to the door, and went out to the room he was staying in and grabbed some fresh jeans and a UMaine t-shirt. He smirked at it. Ronnie had given it to him. Fucking shame. She'd been great in the sack.

***

Gary made the drive to Spragueville quickly and was nearing the hotel when something caught his eye. He did a double take driving to the Dunkin on Deerfield Drive. Fucking Ronnie was walking down the block. Alone.

What the hell? His heart pounded in his chest and he had to pull over. He watched her in the rear view mirror, saw her pass the intersection, and head to the abandoned Buddy's warehouse. She was acting shifty. She kept her head straight and slightly averted from the road. He might not have recognized her with her hood up, but she was twirling a platinum blonde curl with one finger as she walked, and she was wearing the same clothes as last night.

He watched her go around the side of the building, and then she disappeared from view. *What the fuck was she up to? Where was she going? Where was the bounty hunter? What and the hell was she doing walking down the block in broad daylight?*

His temples felt like they were going to explode. He didn't know what to do. Should he go after her? Should he wait here? After a minute, he decided he needed time to process this. Dunkin was just up ahead. He'd get coffee, and watch the place for a bit, maybe go check if no else showed up. He was through the drive thru quickly, and pulled back along the curb with a view of the warehouse.

His cell phone rang, when he was blowing on his coffee to cool it. Glancing at the passenger seat where he had thrown his phone, he saw Ronnie's number pop up, the same one that had shown up on the caller ID at the servant's cabin. *She was calling him? Again?*

"Fuck," he garbled as hot coffee spilled on his crotch. "Fuck god damn!" He slapped at his crotch, and moved in his seat as the searing pain took its sweet time to lessen.

On the fourth ring, when it went to voicemail, Ronnie's heart dropped. She tried the cabin first and hadn't gotten him. Now he wasn't answering his cell.

"Just try again, sweetheart, two times is a charm," Nikko's out of body voice whispered in her ear. He told her to try the cell when he hadn't picked up at the cabin and she'd panicked.

She hung up, and hit redial before she lost her nerve. On the second ring, Gary picked up. He wasn't in a good mood. "What?" he snapped.

"Gary, it's me Ronnie. Baby, you got to help me. I got away from that ass wipe bounty hunter late last night. Please, please, come help me. At least get me to my bike. I got to get out of town. I can't go to jail. I'll go to Canada, somewhere, and you'll never hear from me. Please," she begged. She got all the words out in a rush so he wouldn't hang up.

Gary was confused as hell. She sounded scared. "Where are you?" he winced still dabbing at his crotch although he knew very well where she was. He heard the fear in her voice, as he continued to shift in his seat to ease the throbbing in his dick. He was having trouble concentrating and he needed to.

"I got away last night. I hid in the old abandoned Buddy's for the night. I think I lost him. I checked around and haven't seen him," she pretended to sob softly.

"Why didn't you call earlier?" he snapped. The burn, plus paranoia, was making him crazy. If she was so afraid to get caught why was she walking right past him fifteen minutes ago?

"I didn't want to put you in jeopardy, baby, until I knew I lost him. I know we didn't get to talk much last night. I really don't want to bring you down with me. So I just hunkered down here until I thought the coast was clear. God, Gary. I am so sorry." Her stomach rolled having to apologize to him, but she went on anyway.

"The thought of you getting in trouble for helping me, kills me," she lied. "I am innocent, but I can't prove it, and I'd rather go down alone then bring you with me and tarnish your name. Your family's name."

Ugh, she wanted to puke. But she used all the words Andreas told her to use. 'Put him at ease. Let him know the most important thing to you is him, and his safety.' He had to feel at ease before he would even consider meeting her again. When he didn't respond, appeared to be thinking, she jumped right back in. Don't give him too much time to think, Andreas cautioned her.

"I love you Gary. I know we have had some rough times, but baby you're all I've got. I'm no good for you, I know." She cried harder. "But, to keep you safe, I'll leave the country, and you'll never have to worry about me again.

I just hope you can be happy. Just, please, please, get me to my bike. I can't risk going to your cabin in day light."

The thought of her walking to his place got his attention. The Brimeyers opened up the bar around eleven. He didn't want her walking right past them. "No, don't do that. Buddy's you, say?" he added even though he knew that's exactly where she was.

"Yes, please, please come," she begged.

"Fuck Ronnie," he murmured. He needed time. To think. He had to get this girl out of his hair. He fucking owed her that at least. His fucking drugs after all. "Give me . . . oh fuck! Give me about thirty minutes."

"Oh, thank you, thank you, thank you," she cried, "I love you so much. I promise, after this I'll leave you alone. Oh, baby." She was sobbing now with what she hoped sounded like relief.

"All right, Ronnie," he breathed heavily into the phone. "If I am going to get there, you'd better let me go."

"Okay, baby. Please hurry," she whispered as he clicked off. The sooner the better, she thought. And the sooner this nightmare would be over.

"He said . . .," she started.

"We got everything." It was Andreas' voice now. "You were holding the phone close to the barrette," he answered her unasked question.

"I'm going to ask for silence from everyone now though," he added. "In case hockey schmuck comes early. But, we are all in position. Blaze and I are in the little stand of trees. Hidden well. Once puck face gets here, and we're assured he is alone, we will get closer. Relax everyone, and sit tight."

"Okay," Ronnie whispered in the darkness to no one in particular. She felt suddenly very tired. Her fatigue motivated her to lie down, and curl up on the sofa to wait it out. The silence surrounded her, enveloped her like a glove. Even though she knew Nikko was watching, she'd never felt so alone in her life.

***

Nikko watched her through the infrared glasses he wore. His heart ached to touch her, to hold her. This would be the longest thirty minutes of his life. He felt his brother's hand squeeze his shoulder. They squatted on the cat walk, getting comfortable. Waiting. Soon, he told himself. Soon, it would be all over. Then, they could begin . . . To live.

***

Gary watched the old decrepit building and sipped on his coffee begrudgingly. He needed the caffeine, or what was left of it. No one approached the building. And no one left.

He had to make a decision. He felt like just stepping on the gas and getting the hell out of Spragueville, and was very tempted to do just that.

Thirty minutes later, he was nursing the last of his lukewarm coffee still trying to figure out what to do. He didn't have many options. He could go get her and bring her to her bike. Give her a bit of cash. But what if she got caught? What if he got caught helping her? Could he risk that? Fuck, fuck his life.

He slammed the steering wheel of the servant's Toyota, and then finished the last of the coffee in one swallow. He really didn't have much choice. He needed to finish this. He'd made up his mind. Opening the glove box, he took out the small derringer. His mother's. He'd taken it when he went into hiding just in case the Brimeyers showed up. He grabbed it at the last moment before leaving the cabin. He didn't know what possessed him, but he was glad to have it. Just in case.

Yes, he'd try to help her one last time, but that was it. He'd take her to her bike, and then she needed to split. But, he'd bring the gun just in case.

He started the car, and drove slowly away from the curb and around the empty building. He made a quick tour around the lot to make sure no one else was there. Seeing no cars, he swung around one more time. He saw the door on the back side by the wooded lot, and pulled up to it.

Taking one last look around, and again seeing nobody, he got out, slipped the gun in the back of his waistband, and stepped inside.

"We've got company. Gary is here, and he's alone. No talking. Let Ronnie do her thing." Andreas murmured to all those wearing the small earpiece.

The sound startled Ronnie out of her reverie and she was instantly alert.

"Love you," Nikko whispered one last time defying his brother's order. It was game time.

***

Andreas shook his head at Blaze, and said nothing. Fucking love, he thought, all it did was stab you in the back. Or in the heart. Then it usually walked right out the door.

Chapter Twenty-Three

All Good Plans Go Awry

Gary was inside. She heard him as soon as the door opened. A crack of light illuminated the floor also making his presence known. The yellow slash of light yawned across the massive concrete floor reaching the office.

"Ronnie," he called softly, taking a step into the massive warehouse.

"I'm here," she called out and got up from the sofa quickly. She opened the door, and he saw her standing there looking like she just lost her best friend. He looked around the darkness, and like Andreas told her, she gave him no time to think. She rushed him.

"Oh darling," she said as she ran to him. She thought she saw a look of panic cross his face. But, she paid it no mind. He was planted in front of the door, and she ran the last few yards throwing herself into his arms. "You do love me. You still care," she breathed and planted her lips on his.

Gary was shocked by her suddenly affectionate attack. Ronnie had never been that type before, but he supposed her situation and fear was causing her to act out of the norm. It took him a moment to respond.

Her arms were wrapped around him, her body pressed tight. He was a man and his body reacted to her ample breasts pressed up against him. What the hell, he thought. One last time for good measure. He leaned down to take more from her. He found the side of her face and then her lips. He urged them open and stuck his tongue inside, tangling it with hers. She was grasping at his back, and he thought of the gun he tucked inside of his waistband and realized this wasn't such a good idea. Not yet, anyhow. He broke the kiss and forced her a step back out of the light.

Ronnie grabbed his arms for support or she would have toppled over. "Gary," she questioned, wondering why he'd pushed her away.

"I just wanted to get out of sight," he murmured, trying to nuzzle her again. But he held her arms at her sides this time to keep her straying hands away from his concealed weapon.

"Mmm," she groaned as he tilted her head back and nipped her cheek and then trailed his tongue down the side of her face. "I've missed you," she mumbled, faking her desire for him.

"Ronnie," he whispered, "Is there someplace back there we can . . ." he indicated with his chin behind her.

"A small sofa," she broke away and took his hand to lead him there. Just before reaching the door, she called back over her shoulder, "But can we talk first. I need to get out of town, and I don't know if the bounty hunter who was chasing me left or not. I tried to make him think I would hide out in Bangor next. Graduation and all. I'm so scared." Ronnie was just rambling trying to distract him from wanting to take things further than she was prepared to go. She knew Nikko was watching and hated having to do even that much with Gary.

"I don't think he will be looking here. Good spot, actually," he murmured. "I looked around and didn't see anything suspicious before I came in."

"Oh, that is good. Thanks Gary. I feel safer knowing you're here and you're going to help me. I love you, Gary. You don't know how much this means to me," she said, turning to face him once inside the small office. Not giving him a chance to try to change his mind, she just continued on like Andreas told her. "I just need to know you'll bring me to my bike. I was thinking you could look over the maps of the trails with me. Remember last summer, when we went camping, and we went riding. We got through to Canada into that little town. What was it, St. Leonard? I was thinking I could go there. Then once there, I could maybe find a place to hide out for a week or two, rent a cabin from some old timer in the woods, or just squat in some abandoned place. I've got some money, but . . ."

"I can give you a bit more," he leaned against the desk. He needed to get the gun out of his pants. He definitely was interested in a little more of what Ronnie had to offer. He'd talk to her for a while then try to stash it out of sight after distracting her. They could have a little fun, and then after eleven when the Brimeyers were safely ensconced in the bar, risk getting her out and driving her up to his cabin. He'd drop her off a ways back and then get her bike. Drive it to her, then foot it home. It seemed like a good plan to him.

"Oh, you'd do that for me," she leaned against him, and he was forced to hold her, but he kept his hands on her forearms just in case. "You still care," she murmured and laid her head against his chest.

"Babe, I feel bad, I do," he admitted. "I don't know what the fuck to do. But, I'll help you as much as I can. It's the least I can do," he nuzzled her hair inhaling the fresh scent. Hmm, he thought, he hadn't expected that. It smelled like aloe. He pulled back and looked at her curiously. "You slept in this dump all night?"

He was looking at her strangely. "Yes," she saw his eyes narrowing and he was looking at her hair. His nostrils were flared, inhaling. She smelled the air, and noticed the scent of the hotel shampoo. "But it was really late by the time I got away," she added quickly. The bounty hunter, Nikko, was pissed that the flight was booked, and then he made me go with him to get something to eat at midnight. All the while, I was trying to think of a way to get away."

Some of the truth, she thought making this up on the fly as she went. He looked so wary of her, but she hoped he would buy the story. She continued to weave her tale giving him no time to think and see the holes in it.

"He then hand cuffed me to the bed when we got back, but I asked to use the bathroom and take a shower. I just couldn't fathom being chained up like that all night. After bitching about it for an hour while he tried to sleep on the floor, he finally relented. He let me into the bathroom. I was trying to scramble for an idea. There was nothing in the bathroom that would work, so to delay I took a shower, and then when I got out an idea came to me. I got dressed back in these clothes, but let the shower keep running. I yelped and yelled out trying to make him think I slipped. I was standing on the counter with the top of the toilet tank in my hand, and when he came bursting in, I smashed it on his head." God, it was ludicrous, but she thought it could have happened.

"What the hell, did you . . .?" His look was one of shock, and he instinctively reached up to rub his head as if she smashed it on him.

Gary seemed to buying it so she continued to weave her tail.

"No, he was still breathing. There wasn't even any blood, just a big old goose egg where I got him. I checked to be sure he was breathing and then I split. I didn't even stop to grab my bag, just my cell and my wallet which he left on top of his suitcase. What a moron. Must be a lousy bounty hunter."

She hoped Nikko wouldn't be too upset with this part of the story. But felt it was necessary to make her escape sound more plausible.

"He'd locked up the rest of my things in his car. But with my cell, thank goodness, I was able to call you. It's one of those throwaways too, so I don't think it can be traced. But like I said, I didn't want to call you until I knew the coast was clear. I did venture out this morning and I didn't see his car, and then I came back here. Again, baby, I don't want to bring you down with me. I love you too much. I can't do that to the man I love. I know I can't ask you to flee with me and that breaks my heart. Maybe someday. But I just can't go to jail," she was crying again. She was getting loud too.

"Okay, babe. Fuck, though, I can't believe the dude didn't call the police out on this though." Her story sounded crazy. He was still unsure although her timeline fit with what he had seen. She'd definitely taken a big risk looking about this morning, but if what she said was true, that she risked getting caught again to not put him in jeopardy, she must really love him. He thought she was getting bored with him this past semester, but maybe he'd been wrong. He did have a lot to offer to a girl like her. And although he hadn't seen much of the bounty hunter, he doubted the guy would not call for back up after getting smashed over the head. "I'm sure he has to have woken up from his little nap now," he added. "Why hasn't he called in the police?" he wondered aloud.

She had an explanation ready. Andreas thought he might ask this and prepped her for it.

"He is a bounty hunter. His brothers own a bail bonds business in Tampa, I think. They posted my bond. If he goes to the cops, they lose the bond."

"Shit," he thought "I hadn't thought of that." He was scratching his head.

"Yeah, so I think I'll be okay if I can just get to my bike before he thinks of that."

Chills went up Gary's spine. "Fuck, Ronnie! What if he is staking out my place again?"

"Oh shit!" She acted surprised, but it was exactly what Andreas wanted him to say. She pushed back and with the sofa at her calves she took a seat.

"Well," she started. "I didn't think of that, but maybe I could just walk," she murmured softly.

"It's like sixty miles to the border. Longer if you are taking the trails. It'll take you three or four days, maybe longer." He pushed the hair out of his face. He did feel bad, real bad about her dilemma. Taking her back to his cabin to get her bike was out of the question though now. He wasn't going to be caught with her again. No one, absolutely no one, could see them together.

Ronnie pounced. "It's not your fault baby. I've been on hikes almost that long before. I know how to survive in the woods. I'll be okay."

Damn it. The guilt was ripping him up. He fucked up this girl's life. He even loved her once. Thought he had. After their first break up, he treated her less affectionately. He liked his variety too, and had no plans to settle down with her. His parents would have never stood for it anyhow. She wasn't blue blood enough for them.

"I guess that's the only way," he said softly, trying to think of something he could do to make this a bit easier on her, but nothing was coming to him. "Okay, well, I'll run out and get you some supplies. But, I'll have to use cash so nothing suspicious can be traced back to me," he murmured callously and shifted on the desk. He felt the gun press up against his spine.

She felt confidant she had Gary on her side. But, she needed to go for the kill now. It was time to press for more. "Gary, I can't believe you are doing this all for me. I just wish . . ." she trailed off and sniffled into her shoulder.

Crap, Gary thought, she was going to start crying again. "Wish what?" he asked slowly reaching for the gun behind him. He needed to hide it out sight if he was going to have a little fun with Ronnie before he ran out to get her some things for her trek. He definitely wanted one more piece of her. It was the least she could do for all his help.

"I just wish this all never happened, the drugs. My life is fucked and we can never be together. But," she looked up at him and smiled.

"What?" he asked distractedly, still trying to figure out a way to dump the gun without her seeing. He'd almost pulled it out to place behind him, but stopped at her expression.

Go for the kill, Ronnie thought. "Maybe in a year or so, I can call, we can be together somehow," she put on her most hopeful face. "You'll never be happy working for your father anyway."

As she suspected, his face turned sour. He was looking at her like she was nuts. Maybe she had gone nuts, he thought. And he had driven her to it.

"No baby, that ain't gonna happen. After today . . ." He got up from the desk and stood before her, legs spread out. How was he going to say this? Today had to be the end. He didn't need her bugging him for years. Best to be blunt. "I care for you and all, but this was never going to be permanent. I think you knew that. I can't have you ruining my life."

"But Gary," she stood and faced him feigning shock and anger. "Don't you love me?"

"Sweetheart, we had fun, and yes, I thought I did at one time, but now with this shit, there's no fucking way. My parents weren't ever going to support this thing we had.

Even if it was fun while it lasted." He tried to reach for her to soften the blow.

Her face turned bitter in the blink of an eye, just like Andreas told her. 'Act like the woman betrayed which you are,' Andreas had said. 'Attack.'

"You fucking bastard!" She hit his chest with her fists, and he grabbed her wrists forcefully preventing her from doing too much damage. "I thought you loved me. I gave you my heart. I know those drugs were yours, you bastard. I was willing to not tell anyone, I was willing to hide for you. I was even willing to let you believe I didn't realize they were yours." She kept trying to hit him, but her hands were clasped at the wrists and he held them firmly, painfully. Ronnie let out the fury she'd been holding back for these last two weeks. But she also watched his reaction to her words. First there was shock, then anger, and then his eyes narrowed into menacing slits. He looked like a caged animal. It's exactly the effect Andreas had wanted her to achieve so he would slip up.

"Whoa, whoa," he kept repeating trying to control her thrashing. "Cut this shit out, Ronnie, or I'll leave right now, and walk out. Then you'll be on your own."

"Don't you fucking dare walk out on me again, holding the bag, you fucking asshole. I loved you. Gary, you know those drugs were yours. And I know those drugs were yours. You did drugs before. And, I have pictures. You smoking pot," she lied. "Passed out. I was going to go to trial, thinking there couldn't possibly be enough evidence to put me away. But just in case, I had those pictures stashed if it didn't go my way. I was going to use them last minute only if I had to. But just maybe I need to get them to the press. You have ruined me. And god dammit, I won't stand for it." She continued to twist and try to get her wrists free.

"You fucking cunt," Gary hissed. "This was your plan all along. You have been playing me all along. Now you are trying to blame me. Bitch," he released her pushing her away from him, and then his hand came out like a snake. He slapped her hard, and she fell to the sofa behind her. It stung, and shocked her, and she reached for her flaming face.

Gio had to hold Nikko down to stop him from jumping and going to her rescue. He nodded no, forcing Nikko to see him and stay put. Gio knew Ronnie had to be close to getting him to slip. The guy was angry now and that's when they made mistakes. Nikko knew this too, but he wasn't thinking with his head right now, he was only thinking with his heart. Gio saw the fury in his little brother's eyes, and couldn't blame him. No man should ever hit a woman. It was one of his biggest taboos from when he had been on the force. He'd seen too many woman brutalized and it sickened him. For Nikko, who loved Ronnie, this moment had to be so incredibly enraging. In his mind, Gary was no man. He was a coward; he used and hit women. Gio wanted to throttle him too. But in just two minutes it could all be over. Keeping his arms around his brother, he let him know with his eyes to just hang on a bit longer.

"You slut," Gary continued standing over her. He was unsnapping his jeans. You do want me to go down with you, and well, that ain't happening baby. "I'm going to fuck you one last time, for old times' sake, and then I'm . . ."

"Going to what?" Ronnie snapped, still holding her bruised cheek too dizzy to get up.

Gary just laughed as he pulled the gun out of his pants before he let them drop to the floor.

"You've got a gun," Ronnie whispered, suddenly terrified. Nikko almost leapt down upon them, but again Gio held him like iron.

"One more minute," he mouthed to Nikko.

"Yes, so no more fucking smart talk from you. But, I'm not going to use it on you Ronnie. Not yet, anyway. Although I should because of your little attempt to blackmail me here. But, that's not going to happen. So what, I've smoked pot. I'm not worried about any fucking pictures. But you on the other hand, with that mouth of yours. Well, that worries me. So, I'm going to tell you the truth now, have my way with you, and then I'm afraid it's gotta be lights out, Ronnie. I can't have you fucking shit up for me. Such a shame," he muttered, looking down at her cleavage. "I always loved your tits."

Nikko nodded at Gio who again held up one finger. They were going to get the information they needed. They watched as Gary put the gun on the filing cabinet out of Ronnie's reach.

Gary grabbed Ronnie's hands with one of his and held them like steel above her head. He fondled her breasts roughly with the other. She was still too weak to fight back, but she felt her strength returning in her fear. She winced in pain as he pinched her nipple hard, and he laughed.

"You were just a great piece of ass from the wrong side of the tracks to me after our break up," he sneered while he kicked off his shoes. He still stood before her, and then smacked her one more time across the face with the back of his hand. While she was stunned, he quickly slipped down his jeans and pulled out his cock. "A piece of ass I liked to fuck, but you ruined it with that break up, and then when you came back, well, it wasn't the same. You acted all holier than thou, and you watched my every move like you were my god damned watchdog or my parents. I stuck with you to get through school. You thought you were so god damn smart, but . . ." He got closer, put his face right in front of hers and laughed. "But I'll tell you this bitch, cause I am going to kill you when I am through fucking you. You were right. Those were my drugs. I have been dealing for a long time, and I got myself my own nice little stash. I don't need you bitch, and I don't need my parents. I didn't mean for you to get caught, but shit happens. And it couldn't happen to a sweeter bitch than you." Gary reached for her shirt. He was going to tear it off of her, but instead all hell broke loose.

That's when Ronnie heard Nikko roar, and she felt a cool rush of air descend from the rafters. "Fucking bastard!" he screamed. "Get your god damned hands off my woman!"

Gary was stunned; he whipped around and reached for the gun he left on the old filing cabinet. He got his hands on it just as Nikko, who landed like a cat, jumped up and smashed his fist into Gary's face sending him flying through the plate glass window of the office. Nikko quickly recovered from the fall and gave chase bursting through what remained of the door frame to go after him.

Gio was there too, and Ronnie tried to get to her feet. Gio helped her, pulling her up as she saw Nikko round the corner into the massive expanse of the warehouse after Gary who was lying in a pile of broken glass attempting to rise from the concrete floor while also pulling up his pants. But it was too late. He was cornered. The door to the outside flew open.

Turning her head, which still ached from the head spinning slaps Gary had delivered, she saw the other two Marinos running in, guns aimed. She looked back to where Gary had been, where Nikko had gone, and noticed that he too had been distracted by the opening of the door for just a moment. Like a wild animal Gary lifted his gun. Her heart almost burst out of her chest, when she saw he had the gun pointed at Nikko.

"No!" she yelled for all she was worth. Ronnie tried to tear herself out of Gio's grasp, and yelled again to warn Nikko at the same time. "Nikko!" she screamed and the gun fired.

Nikko fell to the side and hit the cement. He wasn't moving. She saw something that looked like oil seep out from the side of his body and she knew it was blood. She continued to scream until her world went black.

Chapter Twenty-Four

Back to Reality

Ronnie woke up in an ambulance on the way to the hospital. Gio was with her sitting beside the gurney. His face looked grim and he didn't even notice when her eyes fluttered open. He was watching the road ahead.

She cleared her throat. He looked at her strangely as she tried to sit up in her panic. "Where is he? Nikko?" He pushed her back down firmly, eyes revealing her worst fear.

"He's in the other ambulance on the way to the hospital. He lost a lot of blood, baby girl, but it was a clean shot through the shoulder. No vital organs," he told her.

He'd been shot. She hadn't dreamt it all. Her stomach churned. Despite Gio's assurances, his face revealed he was just as fearful and worried as she.

"Is he going to be okay?" she asked again needing more.

"Ronnie," he started and faltered.

She could tell from his tone he was trying to be patient with her. He'd probably rather be in the other ambulance with his brother, but someone had to ride with her.

"I'm not going to lie. He lost a lot of blood, but the paramedics are with him now, and they are giving him IV fluids to increase the blood volume. We'll know more. . ." he stopped short and glanced towards the front of the ambulance. "We're almost there," he patted her hand. He looked tired and twice his age of thirty-one.

She knew he must be incredibly worried about his brother, but she was too. Yes, this was his brother, but she loved him. Sudden guilt overwhelmed her and the tears came, silent but they came.

"I should have told him I loved him," she choked out, feeling like her whole world dropped out from under her.

"Yes, you should have," he agreed and dropped her hand suddenly.

Ronnie felt lost. If something happened to Nikko she didn't think she could take it.

The ambulance continued on for another interminable minute. The siren, the only sound, blaring above them as it sped towards the hospital, and Nikko.

She couldn't keep quiet any longer. "Andreas? Blaze?" she asked wanting to know if they were okay.

"Andreas is in the other ambulance with Nikko. They left a minute or so before we did. And Blaze was with the cops who were picking up Gary. He'll drive to the hospital with the rental when they are done questioning him. There will be cops at the hospital Ronnie, for you. They'll probably take you in until we get this all cleared up."

"Take me in? But I want to be with Nikko," she winced as she tried to sit up again. He pushed her back done once more. Tears started to form in her eyes. She couldn't go to jail, not without knowing Nikko would pull through. "Please, can you convince the police to let me stay until we know something?" she begged, grasping for his hand.

He sighed, but gave her hand a reassuring squeeze. "I'll try, but I can't make any promises." He was looking toward the front of the ambulance again and he let her hand drop. "We're here," he announced. Her stomach felt like she swallowed lead.

"Gio let me sit up, please, just to see if I can see him being wheeled in. Please!" He looked at her more kindly this time, but she couldn't blame his earlier looks of disapproval. He, hell, all the brothers, probably blamed her for this. Nikko would never have been in this situation if it hadn't been for her.

He shrugged and relented. She sat up quickly and her head swam with the sudden movement, but she was just able to get a glimpse of Nikko being wheeled into the double bay doors. She noticed his arm, the one with the IV tubes in it giving him precious fluids to keep his heart pumping, and that was her last sight of him. Again, she felt woozy and had to lie back down. Her opportunity to have it all seemed lost, and this time it was her fault. Her biggest regret was not telling Nikko she loved him too.

***

It felt like he had cotton in his mouth, and his head pounded like someone hit it with a sledge hammer. He winced and slowly opened his eyes, quickly shutting them at the glare of overhead lights, bright. Too bright. He winced and let out a groan.

"Nicky?" He heard Andreas and felt something on his right shoulder, and opened his eyes just a crack, revealing his brother blocking out the painful light.

"Yeah," he muttered past the cotton.

"So glad you're awake little brother." He heard Andreas, and his voice sounded thick.

"What happened?" he muttered trying to get up, and felt a shooting pain in his left shoulder.

"Don't move, Nikko," Andreas cautioned. "That bastard, Gary, shot you. You got out of surgery an hour ago. You lost a lot of blood, so you don't want to open that up."

Andreas had been beside himself with worry. He couldn't take losing another family member. He'd lost his parents, the woman he was going to marry, and now this. He had been relieved as hell when the doctors came out of surgery and announced what the paramedics reported. A clean shot. The orthopedic surgeon on call put in a few pins to help the healing process, but with some therapy he would regain use of his arm and shoulder. Then, finally they'd let him come into the recovery room to see for himself.

"Ronnie?" Nikko asked through parched lips. His first thoughts were of her. He hoped nothing else had gone wrong after he passed out.

"She's okay, upstairs I think. She fainted and passed out after you were shot. A nasty concussion where she hit her head. So they are keeping her overnight. But they got a guard on her."

"A guard. Why? I want to see her," he winced again and tried to move.

"They still got to hear the tapes and get in touch with the Florida prosecutors. And, don't move," Andreas's tone commanded, reminding him not to open up his stitches. "I'll try to arrange it," he promised as Nikko continued to struggle.

"Please," Nikko looked up at him feeling suddenly tired and groggy.

Andreas saw his brother's eyes fading. "Rest," he told him softly brushing the hair out of his eyes. "I'll make it happen." But, Nikko hadn't heard that. He had passed out once more.

***

Ronnie was in a room. A police man stood outside. She had been told by a nurse they would be keeping her overnight, and was relieved. She had to see Nikko, tell him she loved him before she was carted off to jail. She saw Gio pass by her room. He was talking to a man in a black suit. The detective maybe. She watched the door, hoping he would turn and she could catch his eye, maybe get some news about Nikko. It had been hours since he'd been wheeled into surgery.

Then she saw Blaze appear, and then both men tore out of her line of vision. Fear penetrated her soul. She got up quickly, and the IV the nurse fastened to her hand tore at her. "Fuck," she winced at the pain, and stopped a moment to regain her composure. She turned her legs to the other side of the bed grabbing the IV pole as she stood more carefully this time.

"Not so fast, Miss Sears. Get right back into bed," a voice bellowed from the door way. She turned to see the man who had been talking to Gio earlier.

"I have to see Nikko. And who are you?" she asked, refusing to sit at his command.

"I'm Detective Alexander. I have a few questions for you. So, let me repeat myself which is something I don't like to do. Sit," he commanded.

She didn't move. She glared at him eyes narrowing. "I'll sit," she said, "And I'll answer your questions, if you'll answer mine first." She needed to find out why the brothers had taken off like that. She needed some news about Nikko.

The detective glared at this little blonde hellion. Nikko sure had his hands full with this one, and he wasn't just talking about the chicks breasts. Shit, and those were a handful. "What's your question, Miss Sears?" he asked crossing his hands over his chest blocking her view of the hallway. It didn't mean he would answer it, but he was curious.

"Where did Gio and Blaze go? They rushed away so quickly. Is Nikko okay?" she spit out in a rush.

"That's two questions," he looked at her with a wry, amused expression.

"So what!" she stomped. "Just tell me, where did they go and is Nikko okay?" She began to round the bed determined to find out for herself if this detective was going to be a dickhead. She'd get past him somehow even though his massive frame blocked the exit.

He wasn't going to budge and she obviously couldn't move him. Could she? She glanced at his feet in police issue shoes. She wished she wasn't barefoot, and had her hiking boots on. She'd get him out of her way in a hurry. He noticed the direction of her eyes, and knew what she was thinking. Oh yes, Nikko would have fun with this one. "Okay little lady, back in bed and no funny business. Your boyfriend was out of surgery an hour ago, just woke up, and is headed to recovery. He'll be in a room down the hall in about an hour. Now, get into bed." He began to move toward her forcing her to back up or be pushed.

The tension she had been feeling for the last three hours began to slip away. He was in recovery. He was going to be in a room down the hall. Her heart began to beat.

Her shoulders slumped in relief, and she turned and headed back to her bed, being extra careful to hold her hospital gown shut. She didn't want this beast of a man getting his thrills by feasting his eyes on her backside.

The cop had to chuckle at her feeble attempts to maneuver the bulky awkward IV pole while clutching her gown closed. "I'll turn around."

"Good!" she barked.

"Just for a second though," he laughed. "So make it quick."

Frigging idiot ass cop, Ronnie grumbled to herself. But she moved quickly and got into bed, pulling the covers over her legs discreetly as he turned back around.

"Okay Miss Sears," he approached the bed and pulled out a little black notepad from his inside breast pocket. "Now, it's my turn for some questions."

"Shoot," she said, looking away from the beast of a man. He looked like he lifted trucks instead of weights. Why in the hell did men think women found juice heads attractive? The man was built like a Mac truck.

He snickered at her attempts to avoid his gaze.

"I usually like suspects and witnesses to look at me when I'm questioning them. It kind of helps me to determine if they are being honest with me," he added patiently.

"For crying out loud," she turned her head. "Just ask your dumb questions." The sooner she got this out of the way, the sooner she could see Nikko. She crossed her arms. Cooperate, she reminded herself. She was still in some serious trouble, but her worries over Nikko made her push everything else to the way side. The sooner she cooperated, the sooner the bear would get the hell out of there. Then, she wouldn't have to see him until he picked her up tomorrow to cart her to jail.

"So, first question. Gary Campbell admitted putting the drugs in your equipment in Tampa?" he asked.

"Yes! We have it on tape." He just nodded and took his time writing it down in his little notebook. He even licked the tip of his pencil. She rolled her eyes. Obviously this guy was going to torture her with his methodical interrogation.

"Okay. Thank you." He turned and began to exit the room.

"Wait?" she called after him totally confused. Was this a joke?

"What?" he turned, hand on the door.

"That's it?" she asked eyes widening in surprise.

"Yep, we got the tape, and it is being sent to analysis now in Bangor, and we've recorded Gary's voice. I've got statements from both Gio, and Blaze. I've got to talk to Andreas, and Nikko. If the tapes are good. We will know in a couple of hours, then it's a wrap."

"What do you mean it's a wrap?"

"We've been on to this Gary fellow for a while now. Suspected him in this Tampa thing, but wanted to keep it under wraps until we could bring down the bigger fish. You really didn't need to come down here. We have been keeping an eye on him and the Brimeyer Gang who he works for. You would have been cleared anyhow. The tape makes it nice and tidy with Gary though, so thanks for that."

"The Brimeyers?" she asked in confusion.

"Yes, the Brimeyers," he told her as she laid there mute with shock. "There a local drug scum outfit. We were just a few weeks away from busting them, but with Gary in custody, we might be making a little *dealio* with the little rich kid, and get them sooner rather than later. Give him fifteen instead of twenty for turning them in. They were Gary's main supplier, and they have been dealing locally for nearly a decade. They have been working with Gary to extend their reach into Bangor, and they have been using him to bring more product into the state." He shrugged like this was not news to her.

Gary had been up to a whole hell of a lot more than she thought. She was flabbergasted. But cutting Gary a deal was out of the question. "You're going to cut Gary a deal!" she scoffed, appalled at the thought of him getting off lightly.

"I think you'll be fine with the Marinos for fifteen years, Miss Sears. Plus, I don't think prison is too kind to pretty boy rich kids. We'll be on him when he gets out." Detective Alexander stood there for a moment waiting to see if this little package had any other questions. It seemed she was still too stunned to speak. He had things to do. "Have a good day," he said and gave her a mock salute as he exited.

Holy hell, she thought. "Wait?" she yelled again.

"What is it now, Miss Sears?" he asked with an exaggerated sigh popping his head in the door again. It was his turn to roll his eyes at her.

"I'm not going to jail tomorrow?" she asked, a warm feeling beginning to course through her.

He shook his head and smiled again. "Maine cops aren't idiots. We have been investigating this drug ring for quite some time. We have been watching this group in the hopes of also getting their suppliers. We know you're squeaky clean. Florida will get all our reports." He nodded again, and this time she let him go.

She was free. Free to be with Nikko. That is if he still wanted her. Her mind ran rampant with doubts. Would he? Want her? Would his brother's accept her? After all they'd been through, they might . . . her fears were back. They'd said she was family, but that was before she'd nearly gotten their brother killed. Hell, she'd be reluctant to have her new baby sister, or brother involved with someone who'd put their life in danger, and she or he hadn't even been born yet. What the hell was she going to do? What the hell could she say?

There was nothing to do, but wait and see. And it seemed like hours before anyone came to her room even though it wasn't. She was watching the clock. The next person to open her door though made her smile genuinely for the first time in a long time.

"Gramps," she burst out.

He rushed to the bed, her grandmother at his heels. "Nana," she added when she saw her grandmother was there too.

"We came as soon as we saw it on the news," her grandmother choked through her tears.

Although he wanted nothing more than to crush his little granddaughter to his chest, Roland stepped back to let his wife in first. It was the right thing to do after all.

As soon as his wife moved to go to the other side of the bed, he was there holding her close. His little sidekick. "Glad you're safe chipmunk," he whispered in her ear. "We love you."

"Love you too Gramps, Nana." The tears were coursing down her face. It felt so good to have someone there who loved her.

"I could have killed that old man," her grandma said, indicating her husband, "when I found out he helped you. Don't you ever do something so stupid again!" she admonished, shaking an old finger, gnarled from years of baking, sewing, and gardening, at her granddaughter and husband of nearly fifty years.

Ronnie nodded. Her nana was known for her lectures. What could she do? She took it, noticing her grandpa winking at her over her nana's shoulder.

Ronnie was so relieved to have them there, but yet her thoughts kept straying back to Nikko and the Marinos. She quickly filled them in on her talk with Detective Alexander, and both her grandparents were thrilled to hear the news that her name had been cleared. Her grandmother fanned herself when she talked about the Brimeyers, scared for her granddaughter who had gotten so close to a real live drug ring. Ronnie wanted to be honest with them and tell them everything herself as it would be all over the news anyhow. It would be better coming from her. But, she knew what her grandmother must be thinking as she saw a myriad of emotions cross her face. She had been in far more danger than even she thought.

The nurse interrupted them deep in conversation when she came in with a tray for dinner. And even at the smell of the hospital food, her stomach betrayed her.

"Eat something, bebe," her grandfather encouraged pushing the hospital food tray towards her, revealing a slice of turkey and mashed potatoes with gravy. And though it was hospital food, Ronnie wasn't about to turn it away.

"I'm calling your mother. She'll be so relieved," Bertie announced, pulling her cell phone out of her oversized purse. "What with the new baby and all," she grinned from ear to ear, "this will make her day."

"You told her," Ronnie laughed, taking her first bite of cold, dry turkey, dipping it into the potatoes to make it more palatable. This meal reminded her so much of another meal, very similar, but in a different location when she'd thought her life was over. Now, it seemed it was just beginning, but she needed to talk to Nikko first to know for sure. She needed to see him.

"Of course," her grandfather laughed at her accusatory comment. "She needed some good news to get me off the hook for helping you," he winked.

"I love you Gramps," she reached for his gnarled hand and squeezed it as her grandmother chattered away in the corner.

After her nana filled her mother in, she passed the phone to Ronnie who had eaten nearly everything by then.

"Hi Mom," she answered perkily.

"Oh you . . ." her mom let out a shaky breath of relief through the receiver.

They talked for a few minutes, and Jay popped on to tell her he was happy, too, that things seemed to be working out all right for everyone. They'd even had a call from Tampa saying the charges should be dropped as soon as they got word from Detective Alexander. He'd contacted the prosecution and called Lou personally, not twenty minutes ago, to say Ronnie turned herself in, so the bounty was secure. That bit of news flabbergasted Ronnie. Why would Detective Alexander say she had done that? She expressed those thoughts to her mom.

Her mom laughed and then awkwardly admitted, "Oh, well, I actually know him. He dated Ana."

"Oh my God! Small f . . ." she caught herself before she cursed in front of her grandparents. ". . . world."

"Yes, it is. It didn't last, but they had some fun, let's say." After a few more minutes of chatting with her mom, her mother finally broke off. "Okay, baby. I'm going to let you get some rest. I'm glad your grandparents are there with you. Grandma said they will stay in a hotel tonight and you can go home with them. Is that okay?" her mom asked.

"Um," her mind flew back to Nikko. "I guess. But Nikko. I need to talk to him. I'd like to stay here locally for a while at least while he recovers," she looked at her grandparents her eyes pleading for them to understand. Her grandmother scowled. Her grandfather winked.

"Okay, well don't upset Grams. You know how she gets. Break it to her easily. Maybe ask them to stay in the hotel with you until Nikko gets out?" she whispered softly.

"Good idea," she breathed. "Love you Mom," she said before hanging up.

"Love you too, sweet heart. Call me every day and keep me posted."

"I will." And with that they both hung up.

***

Lou sat by Jay on the sofa. Relief swept through her for her daughter. She was glad this nightmare was behind her, behind all of them, yet she felt guilty not being there even though her doctor advised her not to fly right now.

Jay sensed her disappointment. "She'll come home." He pulled his wife onto his lap and patted her stomach, his baby inside this remarkable woman.

"But where is home?" she asked sadly, thinking of what the future might hold for her head strong daughter.

"She's sweet on Nikko. More than sweet. She'll come here," he stated with confidence and gently kissed his wife's lips. He needed to distract her. Soon she was only thinking about those lips.

Chapter Twenty-Five

Love's Bounty

There was a soft knock on Ronnie's hospital room door, and her eyes fluttered open. Despite her nerves, she managed to doze off. Her grandparents left to get two rooms together at the hotel for when she was released tomorrow. They also wanted to freshen up and grab a quick bite to eat before coming back for evening visiting hours. Her grandfather also promised to bring her something back that was better than the hospital food.

She glanced at the clock. It was only six-thirty.

"Come in," she called out groggily sitting up a bit, but stopped short when the door began to open and she heard a male voice in the hall.

"Get out of the way, Nurse Daniels," she heard Gio announce. "I've got Dr. White's permission right here."

"But orderlies should be doing this," she heard the nervous nurse announce.

"My brother was going to get out of bed and do this himself. He wasn't waiting two hours for the orderlies."

Ronnie saw the foot of a bed being pushed through the door.

"Well, let me help you then," the Nurse sighed loudly, knowing she wasn't getting this large man to stop what he was doing. "Give me that pole."

She heard Gio's rumble of laughter at the nurse's command. She'd already picked up on the fact that everything turned into a sexual innuendo with this man.

"Yes ma'am. I mean Nurse Daniels," he teased, answering her with just the right amount of sexual undertones. "Nice uniform by the way," he added at the pretty lady with the mop of sandy hair framing her oval face. She blushed.

The bed was almost entirely through the doorway and Ronnie could make out a form upon it. Her heart beat faster.

"What's going on?" she asked sitting up straighter in her bed.

"Ask him," the nurse announced, revealing her name plate that stated she was Lacy Daniels. It was the same nurse who had come in earlier to give her some medication.

Gio peered around the corner, face tight with concentration. He finally answered her question. "Baby brother didn't want the private room. He wanted a roomie, but he passed out cold again on the way here."

"That's Nikko?" Ronnie sat up straight.

"Stay in bed," the nurse ordered when it looked like this patient, too, was going to get tangled up in this mess.

Ronnie sat back down. Her heart raced. Nikko asked to be here. In this room with her. She had been so worried, but his first thoughts when waking had been to be with her.

With one more push, Gio had the bed all the way in. He bumped it against the door frame, and jostled Nikko who groaned in his sleep.

"Be careful with him," Ronnie cautioned, wincing for Nikko. She examined him more closely as Gio moved his brother's bed over to position it next to hers.

"Geesh, that's the thanks I get for all this trouble," he teased.

"Oh, sorry," Ronnie giggled softly. Obviously Gio letting him come here, meant he didn't hate her. "Where are your brothers?" she asked. "Did they know you were moving him?"

The nurse hastily plugged all the equipment back in. When Gio looked back up from watching the cute nurse's derriere, he saw the fear in Ronnie's eyes. He decided to put her mind at ease. His brothers had been too anxious about Nikko to pop in on her. They had also been answering questions from Detective Alexander and other officials while he had been running around doing all the drudge work. He may have to reward himself, he thought wryly, checking out the cute nurse one more time.

"No, but they'll be fine with it. They ran out to get something to eat. They're bringing me back something." When he still saw her doubtful expression, he gave her more words of encouragement. "They know you love him, I told him what you said in the ambulance. He loves you. You're family now and to us that means a lot. No one is mad at you, Ronnie." He winked at the nurse, and she blushed again as the door swung shut on her.

"Oh, thank you," Ronnie cried, a small gasp escaping her lips. She had been really worried about what Nikko's brothers thought of her. Her worries dissipated when Nikko murmured in the bed next to her. It sounded like her name.

"I'll leave you two alone for a bit," Gio offered as he looked at her and then back towards the door. "I'll keep my brothers away too. For a bit. You've got an hour," he winked conspiratorially. Without waiting for her answer, he began to leave.

"Thank you," she mouthed the word as he left.

"Oh Nurse Daniels, honey," she heard him call out in the hall way. She couldn't help but laugh. He was such a tease, that one.

Nikko was waking to her left, and she reached over to take his hand. It was wonderfully warm.

"R-ronnie," he murmured, coming to wakefulness.

"I'm here," she whispered and squeezed his hand reassuringly.

He tried to sit up and groaned from the effort and pain. "You okay?" he asked and winced at the same time peering at her under heavy eyelids.

"I'm fine," she hastily moved, swinging her legs onto his bed careful to avoid jostling him. She slid into bed next to him.

"Oh good," he let out a breath and cracked one startling blue eye fully open. "I love you, Ronnie."

She propped herself up on one elbow, lying on her side, careful not to move him too much for fear of causing his injured shoulder any pain. When both of his eyes were on hers and he moved his right arm, the one nearest her, and luckily the one that wasn't injured, she was able to snuggle into the crook of his arm. She gazed at him one more second before finally saying the words he longed to hear.

"I love you too, Nikko Marino. I love you!" She kissed his lips, and pulled back. "I love you," she kissed him again. "I love you." And again.

"Thank God!" he whispered. And despite his injury, he was kissing her back. This bounty was worth it.

The End

(Keep reading for a sneak peek at Blaze's story

Beautiful Chase – The Marino Bros.)

Sneak Peek From:
Beautiful Chase – The Marino Bros.

Prologue

The Nightmare

... three years earlier

His heart pounded in his chest beating a furious tattoo. It was much later than normal for him to head to his fiancée Nicole's apartment. She wasn't expecting him tonight. He had a paper due tomorrow for his Constitutional Amendment Rights course and he told her he'd be working late. It was his last class that he needed to ace in order to graduate with his law degree, and he was also cramming for his BAR exam next month as well.

Nicole had been patient with him. For the last two years, their relationship was strained because of all the time he needed to put into his studies. But they had been together for four, and he knew she was the one. Once he found a job with the Prosecutor's office in Manhattan, he was planning to propose. It was just after one o'clock and he had been packing up to head to his apartment in the city when he had gotten the strange text. It had been a picture of Nicole dancing with someone. The picture revealed her kissing that someone, someone he recognized. And it floored him. It must be some kind of mistake. He had to ask her about this, and see what it all meant.

Nicole was finishing her undergraduate degree and shared a small apartment with two other girls. They were both out of town this weekend, and so he let himself into her apartment with the key she had given him.

He was immediately struck by the sounds of passion. It shocked him. He really hadn't expected that. But the sounds he heard could not be denied. Those were the sounds she made with him. He knew that murmur of satisfaction very well.

"Oh God, yes," she purred. "Yes, baby, fuck me."

His heart that had been beating so fast, now began to slow, but he could feel the blood pumping in his brain. What the hell? It couldn't be. Nicole, sweet and innocent when he met her as a freshman, and he a senior. He had fallen for her innocence Immediately. Her southern charm, and wavy brown hair reminded him of photos of his mother when she was just married. His mom died six years earlier. He still felt the pang of her loss, and his father's. They died together in the end.

But Nicole. It just seemed so unreal as he crept down the hallway. He had been her first. Well, he thought that, but this picture told a different tale. A tale he hadn't even suspected her capable of.

Yes, she had expressed loneliness these past two years at times, but he thought she understood. He was working hard for their future together. But from this picture, it was him, who didn't understand her at all.

"Oh, Alex, baby, that feels so . . . so . . ." her voice trailed off.

He couldn't believe it. She was with Alex. Alex, a friend to both of them. He liked Alex right away when they met. They had become great friends. A serious student, here on scholarship, playing ball for the university. They had met Alex at a party two years ago, and quickly developed a friendship over their shared love of the game, and the similar professors and classes they had taken. Alex was studying law too.

He could hear his heart pounding as it tore into shreds. Not only was Nicole betraying him, but Alex as well. It was too much. He almost chose to turn and leave, but some sick perverseness overtook him, and he had to see it for himself. Had to see the woman he loved fucking their friend. He had to witness this betrayal.

He walked down the hallway, and saw Nicole's bedroom door slightly ajar.

"Oh, Alex, so good. Yes . . ." she murmured. He couldn't hear Alex at all, didn't want to, but he still walked forward, as if in slow motion, towards that door that loomed larger as he got closer. His tunnel vision made it appear like it was miles away, yet he was just steps away from seeing her, seeing them together.

"Oh-oh," her cries of pleasure were coming faster and getting louder. He could hear her thrashing about on the bed. He could envision her there, gripping the twisted sheets like she did when he pleasured her, and it sickened him. How could they destroy them all with this act?

Just one more foot to go and he took that final step as Nicole cried out her final release. "Oh fuck me. Yesssss!" He was standing in the door, and now there could be no denying it. There she was, Alexandra Martin, at the foot of the bed on her knees, licking Nicole's pussy, sucking her clit, while she climaxed and reached her pinnacle. Nicole's brown waves were splayed across the sheets just like he imagined, as she gasped for breath, and Alex crawled up her body taking her nipple into her mouth and suckled at the rosy peaks. Breaking free of her nipple, Alex whispered to Nicole, "I love you Nicky. Always."

Nicole reached a hand upward to take hold of Alex's auburn hair, and in her dainty fist grasped it pulling him closer. They began to kiss, and soon Nicole used her body to turn Alex onto the bed.

He took a step back in that moment, back into the shadows of the hallway, but not before Alexandra saw him. He took a breath, he hadn't realized he'd been holding, and turned without saying a word. He walked down the hallway, and out the door, closing it softly behind him. He took the stairs two at a time, not wanting to wait for the elevator. He just had to get out. Out of the building, and out of the city. At twenty-five when he thought his life was just about to really begin with a family of his own, he realized that it simply wasn't. His faith had been tested before, but now he had lost it. This betrayal and the image of the two of them together would be burned into his mind's eye forever, into his soul it seemed in that moment. Happily ever after wouldn't happen for him. Not now. Not ever, he thought bitterly as he made it to the bus stop just in time to catch the city transport.

And four years later, when he woke up from that nightmare it was like he had lived it all over again. It was the reason he had agreed to move from New York. It was the reason he didn't trust woman. It was the reason he took what he needed, and walked away. That was how Blaze felt, and there wasn't anything, or anyone, who could ever change his mind again.

More Books by MJ Nightingale!!!

Her erotic romance series, Secrets & Seduction, is the tale of three different couples with secrets that may destroy their chances of finding their happily ever after. These books are definitely books you will NOT want to read in public.   Check them out. They are available on Amazon for your kindle and Barnes & Noble for your nook.

Fire In His Eyes

Ex-army buck, Victor, teaches innocent sexy school teacher, Monica, all about sex, and not the old-fashioned variety your grandmother was used to either. Filled with gut wrenching emotional turmoil due to Victor's secrets, you can be sure one of them will melt and the other will burn.

Fire In His Eyes http://www.amazon.com/Fire-His-Eyes-MJ-Nightingale-ebook/dp/B00HFVMWOO/ref=sr_1_1?ie=UTF8&qid=14030 52999&sr=8-1&keywords=fire+in+his+eyes

Afraid to Love

Teddy is not your average bartender by any means. A cop on the mend from 9/11, he wants nothing but good times and to live each day to the fullest. When it comes to the bedroom, well, hmm, let's just say he is not your average Joe. Then, he meets a fiery red-head named Ana, and she can teach him a thing or two in the bedroom. He falls for her, but she pushes him away. Why? Because she has so many secrets, and they make her Afraid to Love.

Afraid to Love http://www.amazon.com/Afraid-Love-Secrets-Seduction-Book-ebook/dp/B00JA0ZGQY/ref=sr_1_2?ie=UTF8&qid=1403053047&sr=8-2&keywords=afraid+to+love

Afraid to Hope

Jay and Louisa are both battle scarred, but ready to start anew. His scars are not just from the war in Iraq, and hers are not just from a teenage pregnancy that resulted in raising a child alone. The scars in them run deep, and they both have secrets. Can two people so deeply wounded learn to trust each other enough to share those secrets? And if they do, will those secrets make or break them?

All three of MJ's books in the Secrets & Seduction Series will have you turning pages, reading in the dark, and wanting more. Will her characters find their happily ever after? You'll have to read to find that out. But one thing, I can tell you is that they are hot, hot, hot!

Coming Soon from MJ Nightingale!!!

More of

The Bounty Hunters series – The Marino Bros.

Beautiful Bounty by MJ Nightingale

(Book 1 in The Bounty Hunters – The Marino Bros.)

Ronnie Sears has a college degree, a promising future, a boyfriend, and a plan. But, her perfect life comes crashing down around her in the blink of an eye. Arrested, framed for drug smuggling, and facing years behind bars, Ronnie sees no choice but to run. Only she can prove her innocence.

Nikko Marino is a sexy, devastatingly charming bounty hunter. His job, as told to him by his older brothers, is to keep an eye on the curvaceous blonde. Make sure she doesn't run. But what his brothers don't know is that he and Ronnie have a past. He and the Ice Princess are more than mere passing acquaintances. She makes his blood burn, and he knows how to warm up this woman.

Nikko wants to prove himself, but this beauty might just take him down. With his reputation on the line, will Nikko, the hot-blooded youngest Marino, fall for this temptress? Will he be able to protect this beautiful bounty from herself, from the man who framed her, but most importantly can he protect his heart?

Beautiful Bounty is the first book in *The Bounty Hunters - The Marino Bros.*

Suspenseful, erotic, and romantic, these books are packed with passion, sex and characters you will love. What more could you want?

Beautiful Chase by MJ Nightingale

(Book 2 in The Bounty Hunters – The Marino Bros.)

Bella Chase led a simple life. She was a good girl who worked hard at a job she loved, had good friends, and enjoyed her life. She just fell for the wrong guy. A bad boy with a bad reputation. When he maliciously involves her in a crime that goes awry, and someone is killed, it is her life on the line. She has no choice, but to flee. She not only faces life in prison, she faces a death sentence if she talks.

Blaze Marino is done with women. They can't be trusted. Period. Not even the good girls. When his next case lures him to the hills of Tennessee, hunting down another "good girl", Blaze is torn between taking down this natural beauty, and losing himself inside of her. He, who has vowed to never love, or need again, is drawn to Bella and he just can't help himself.

Terrified, Bella doesn't know which way to turn. She doesn't know who to trust.

Jaded, Blaze can't fight the pull of attraction. He doesn't know if he can trust her.

He has to chase her for his job. Or so he keeps trying to tell himself that.

Beautiful Chase is the second book in *The Bounty Hunters - The Marino Bros.*

Suspenseful, erotic, and romantic, these books are packed with passion, sex and characters you will love. What more could you want?

Beautiful Regret by MJ Nightingale

(Book 3 in The Bounty Hunters – The Marino Bros.)

Lisa Rasmussen, formerly Lisa Raphael, has had enough of her manipulative abusive husband. He has forced her to his will, tortured her both physically and psychologically, and she wants out. Her sham of a marriage to Albert, son of the blue blooded Rasmussen's of Manhattan, has to end. But, Albert has vowed to never give Lisa her freedom. He owns her. Body and soul. Her plans to blackmail him to get out, will not go unpunished. Albert will strike first.

Gio Marino knows Lisa. He knows of Albert. After all, Lisa left him to marry the son of the luxury classic car dynasty. So when Lisa calls him begging for help, he is floored. Not only because she called him, but because of what she has been accused of. Attempted murder! She had meant everything to him, but after what she did nearly a decade ago, he knows not to trust her, but the temptation to see her in an orange jumpsuit is just too hard to resist.

Lisa is full of regret. She has a lot to feel guilty about. But, she doesn't have any one else to turn to. She needs Gio. He is the only one she can trust even though he might never be able to trust her again.

The minute he walks into Riker's and sees her, he knows he has made a big mistake. The emerald eyes, the flawless skin, the fiery hair, bring it all back. Especially the regret. Can he help her? Does he want to? And why, after all these years, does he find her beauty so hard to resist?

Beautiful Regret is the third book in *The Bounty Hunters - The Marino Bros.*

Suspenseful, erotic, and romantic, these books are packed with passion, sex and characters you will love. What more could you want?

Beautiful No More by MJ Nightingale

(Book 4 in The Bounty Hunters – The Marino Bros.)

Catarina Stone is a woman of mystery, and she likes to keep it that way. But she is thrust into the limelight when two of her "girls" are slain by a serial killer. The Tampa Madame, as she has been dubbed by the press, is being hounded by the media who want to find a connection between the killer and her. She reaches out to Andreas Marino of The Marino Bros.

Cat has done her research, and knows she needs a professional, a person experienced in catching psychopaths. She needs Andreas. The police are baffled, and the killer must be caught before another one of her girls is mutilated, then murdered.

Andreas Marino, the striking eldest Marino, does know serial killers. It used to be his job. But not anymore. Not since one of those sick bastards claimed his parent's lives, and destroyed his own. He doesn't want this case, not at all. Not until he sees her.

The strikingly elegant Madame intrigues him. She is an enigma. And, Andreas can't get her out of his head . . . and the need to have her in his bed. When she shows him copies of the note left by the killer, signed "Beautiful No More," the thought of her exquisiteness destroyed reignite a flame in him he thought long dead. He must catch a killer. He must save the girl. If he doesn't, Andreas will be lost this time . . . forever.

Beautiful No More is the final book in *The Bounty Hunters - The Marino Bros.*

Suspenseful, erotic, and romantic, these books are packed with passion, sex and characters you will love. What more could you want?

Acknowledgements

This writing journey is not an easy one. I have had many loyal supporters who have been with me since I published my very first book. Lacy Daniel, Shannon White, Ronda Brimeyer, and Dina Alexander, you have been with me from the get go, believed in me, and have always been there for me. Thank you so much. I don't know where I would be without you.

MaryAnn Jordan, what can I say? You are an amazingly talented lady and you epitomize class. You keep me grounded and afloat. You are my life preserver. Seeing your positive posts and encouragement keeps me going. Your friendship means so much. You'll never know.

IEZ ladies on Facebook; A.d. Ellis, Victoria Brock, ML Steinbrunn, Andrea Michelle, Jen Andrews, Sandra Love, EJ Shortall, and Andrea Long, you ladies give me so much encouragement and support. I am glad we found each other. You each bring so much joy to my life. I know I can count on you for anything. Your books, your words, your stories; both fictional and real, have broken and mended my heart countless times. I wish you all much success as we take this journey together. I am thankful we all found each other.

Melissa Gill, thank you, for creating such a beautiful cover for me. I look forward to working with you on the rest of this series. Your talent, creativity and professionalism are outstanding. Thank you for coming to my rescue when I needed you.

Keriann, love and hugs, lady. Thank you for taking my book and making it better. Your eagle eye and sensitivity is greatly appreciated. Thank you for being critical when I needed it.

The bloggers that have supported me also deserve my debt of gratitude. Without your support and help this journey would me much more daunting than it already it is. Thank you for bringing my books to your reader's attention.

I also want to thank my family who supports me, and helps me find the time to write in my crazy, hectic life, knowing that I need this outlet. I love you all, and appreciate you letting me go on this journey.

And lastly, for all my readers who found me when I published my first series of books, and have continued on this journey with me with The Bounty Hunters, thank you for those amazing reviews, and those notes, and just for being the best darn fans ever. I do this for you.

About the Author

MJ Nightingale has been a teacher for over two decades. Writing is her new career, and something she has wanted to do for a very long time. But reading has been a part of her life since she was a child. She has been an avid lover of romance novels, and they have always held a special place in her heart. When not working, or writing, or spending time with her children, she devours books all summer long, and any type of fiction; thrillers, crime, suspense, contemporary, and drama.

She has published four novels, all contemporary romance, and her new series, The Bounty Hunters, will add an element of suspense to her already complicated character portrayals. Fans of MJ will not be disappointed.

She currently lives in Florida with her wonderful husband, and sons. And, she loves to hear from her readers.

You can contact her on Facebook, twitter, and Instagram, or visit her website.

Facebook: https://www.facebook.com/pages/MJ-Nightingale/185806224943537?ref=hl

Website: http://mjnightingale.weebly.com/contact.html

63946925R00213

Made in the USA
Charleston, SC
14 November 2016